THE
GHOST
CHRONICLES

MARLO BERLINER

To Susann,
Hope you
enjoy
the book!

Marlo Berliner
Christmas
2016

THE GHOST CHRONICLES
Copyright © 2015 by Marlo Berliner

Published by Teddy Blue Books

Print ISBN: 978-0-9969724-1-3

Cover Copyright © 2015 Marlo Berliner
Cover artist: S. P. McConnell
Interior formatting: Author E.M.S.

For my children, Michael and Andrew.

Thank you for believing in me.

I love you.

CONTENTS

May you be in Heaven half an hour before the devil
knows you're dead.

– Old Irish blessing

CHAPTER ONE

DEATH

Saturday
2:37 PM

MICHAEL COULD FEEL the warm blood running down his face. Fully regaining consciousness, he had no idea where he was, or what had happened. He tried to lift his eyelids, but they wouldn't budge. Moving any part of his body failed, so he just lay there, with an overwhelming feeling of having been pressed inside a small box. His head felt very heavy, as if doubled in size, and a rushing sound in his ears stifled his hearing. Indistinct voices warbled nearby, but he couldn't quite figure out whom they belonged to, or what they were saying.

As he opened his eyes, his vision blurred. After a few seconds, the inside of his car came into focus and his mind flashed through the last scenes in his memory. *I was driving...there was a bend in the road...and sunlight reflecting off the grill of a truck...*

His stomach lurched as he stared straight ahead. *Oh, my God.*

The tractor-trailer and his car sat inter-twisted at the front, a pair of grotesquely conjoined twins. The jagged edges of his exploded windshield framed his view of the crumpled wreckage and an acrid smoke drifted in searing his nose.

With great effort, he moved his head an inch and glanced downward. The car's steering wheel and dashboard lay crushed against his chest. He couldn't even see his legs, let alone move them.

Tilting his head upright again, a thick, warm liquid rose up the back of his throat and a rusty, unpleasant taste crept into his mouth. He'd been elbowed on the basketball court enough times to know—*it's blood.* At that moment, a very strange question popped into his head. *Shouldn't I be in tremendous pain? Why don't I feel any pain?* Oddly enough, he didn't feel any sort of fear or panic, either.

A peaceful, detached calm settled inside him and his mind slowly drifted back to the beginning of this beautiful spring day. He remembered his plans and how excited he'd been. *Well...I guess my day's not gonna go as planned.*

One breath later, his body shuddered, his sight faded and his heart stopped.

CHAPTER TWO

DAD

Saturday
9:33 AM

MICHAEL SHIELDED HIS eyes as the late morning sun struck his face. *Five minutes...just five more minutes.* He cracked open one eye and squinted at the clock. *Shit. It's that late already?* Scooting over toward the window, he reached for the cord and jerked the mini-blinds up. A surge of warmth and energy shot through him as he surveyed his backyard. The grass needed cutting but other than that it was a perfect day. Not a cloud in the sky. *Today's gonna kick some serious ass.*

Like a man on fire, he sprang from bed, completed a few quick stretches and headed for the bathroom. He brushed his teeth and ran a comb through his unruly hair. Good enough. He couldn't be bothered wasting time in front of a mirror. Quickly tossing on an old t-shirt and a pair of gym shorts, he headed downstairs for breakfast.

The rich scent of coffee wafted up from below. His mother must've been up for a while already. As he entered the kitchen she smiled and said, "Good morning."

He instinctively bent down so his mother could stretch up on her toes and give him a tender kiss on the cheek. She then set about making him some eggs and toast, while he took a seat at the table across from his brother.

Chris played with his breakfast and didn't acknowledge him.

How freakin' annoying. So he's gonna pretend like nothing's wrong. Deciding the best way to approach the subject, Michael thumbed through the newspaper. Unfolding it with a snap, he gave his brother a long, hard glare. "Mom told me you got in another fight at school yesterday."

Near the stove his mother sucked in a deep breath, but didn't turn around.

Chris grumbled something inaudible and slouched in the chair. "Yeah...I did," he barely mumbled.

Michael tensed, bracing for the inevitable battle. He slapped the paper down. His nervous habit kicked in and his knee began to bounce under the table. With some effort, he willed it to stop. As calmly as he could, he said, "So...why the hell did you pick a fight *this* time?"

Chris rolled his eyes. "I *didn't* pick a fight," he said, getting defensive. "The guy just got all...in my face."

"Yeah, it's always the *other* guy." He struggled to not raise his voice. "You sure you didn't get all in *his* face?"

His brother glowered at him. "Don't start..."

Heat rushed from his neck to his cheeks. "Oh, I'll *start* alright." He leaned across the table until he was only inches from his brother's nose. With his gaze boring a tunnel through Chris' skull, he said, "*Look*, I told you before to cut out this crap. Mom shouldn't have to deal with your *bullshit*.

This is the *last* time I'm gonna warn you."

"*Alright*...I know," Chris muttered, twisting away from his stare. "I'm *sorry*. It won't happen again."

Michael searched his brother's face for sincerity. No way to tell if Chris really meant it this time or not. Finally, he plopped back in the chair with an exasperated sigh. Picking up the paper again, he said sternly, "You better make *damned* sure it doesn't."

"It won't...sorry," Chris repeated, sounding more repentant this time.

Michael processed the tone of his brother's voice and relaxed. It was impossible to stay irritated with him. He scowled for another second and then tackled the next issue. "How was the algebra test yesterday?"

Chris glanced up from his bowl of Rice Krispies. "Easy, I think I aced it."

"Good." He reached for the mug of coffee his mother had put on the table. "Did you get your biology project back yet?"

Chris shook his head. "Nah, you know MacGuire. She's the slowest at grading *anything*."

"Yeah, I remember," Michael said with a nod. "One time she took a whole marking period to grade a project of mine." He sipped at his steaming coffee. "Let me know when you finally get it back, though...I'm curious."

"Sure, but I think I did fine on it. Thanks for your help."

"No problem, man," he said with a tiny smile, "anytime."

Chris pushed the sports page across the table. "Yankees won last night."

"It's about time they broke the losing streak. It was getting depressing."

His mother put his breakfast in front of him. "How was your date with Melissa?"

"Fine…we hung out over Craig's house. He had Lauren over." He took a bite of his eggs and then added, "We watched a movie."

"You guys have *got* to get those girls interested in sports," Chris said with a chuckle.

Michael gave a lop-sided grimace. "Tell me about it, man."

At that, his mother laughed. "It took me twenty-five years and two sons before I was ever interested in sports."

Michael flashed his mother an affectionate grin. "Yeah, we know and we love you anyway, Ma."

Chris finished his cereal, got up from the table and placed his bowl on the counter. "Here, I got about three-quarters of the way through," he said to Michael, referring to the crossword puzzle that he now tossed at him.

The crossword competition was a long-standing tradition. Each morning Chris would see how far he could get with the puzzle and then Michael would finish the rest. His little brother would undoubtedly check later on to see if he got all of the answers. Usually he did. His father, the king of crossword, had taught him well.

Chris took his Yankees cap off a hook by the back door and put it on. "I'm going to meet the guys at Central's field, Mom. I've got my cell phone if you need me."

Michael exchanged a quick, meaningful look with his mother. *Come on, Mom. Say something.*

6

"Make sure it's *on* this time or you won't *make* it to sixteen," she replied, giving his brother the evil eye before kissing him on the cheek.

"I will, Mom. See ya, Michael," Chris said quickly.

He nodded as his brother darted out the back door. A few minutes later, he finished his breakfast and put his dishes in the sink. He hugged his mother lightly. "I'm taking Sam for a run."

His mother hugged him harder and gently patted him on the back. It was her way of telling him it was okay to be himself. Only when he was running or playing basketball did he ever feel truly normal. His mother was the only one who really understood how hard he struggled everyday with his ADHD. Never allowing the doctors to push Ritalin on him, she had treated him in her own way—with more love and more patience. And he loved her for that.

He turned to leave but she gently touched his arm. "Thanks for talking to your brother. He looks up to you…and he listens to you."

"No problem, Mom. He's a good kid." He could still see the worry on her face though, so he added, "He's gonna be okay."

A tiny smile played at the corners of her mouth and then dissolved into uncertainty again. She turned away and began to rinse his plate. "I think I saw your iPod on the dining room table if you want it," she said.

"Thanks Mom, I'll grab it."

He found his iPod, stuffed it in his pocket and went to the living room to find Samantha. The five-year-old lady of leisure lay curled up on a cushion by the hearth. As soon as

Michael walked into the room, his canine friend sprang up, tail wagging furiously as she bounded over to him. Kneeling down, he gave the dog an affectionate squeeze and rub on the head. He got the usual return of affection, a bunch of big wet licks to the face. Then, he grabbed her leash from the end table in the hall, made her obediently sit while he put it on, and opened the front door.

They stepped onto the porch, enveloped by a fragrant spring breeze, the hint of summer's approach heavy in the air. *Senior summer.* The laughter of some children playing in a backyard drifted gently down his tree-draped street and suddenly, he was as excited as a little kid with a golden ticket to the chocolate factory. *This is gonna be the best summer ever.*

He turned on his iPod, strapped it to his arm and put in his ear buds. A few clicks later and Led Zeppelin belted out *Black Dog.* Today's music was okay, but he had gotten his taste for classic rock from his dad and thousands of hours playing Rockband.

Across the street, his neighbor was washing her father's SUV in the driveway. *Maybe she's trying to butter up her old man for a car?* Michael grinned. *Nah, I bet she got caught sneaking out again.*

Sweet sixteen just last month, Jamie was cute, perky and wearing a dangerously skimpy pair of shorts this morning. As she stretched to reach the windows, her body curved over the hood in a way that naturally grabbed his full attention. His lecherous musings only lasted a second though. He brushed them aside, mostly because of her age, but also because thinking about her like that was *way* too bizarre. He and Jamie had grown up together; she was practically a little sister. Besides, she wasn't the hottie on his mind today. Seeing Melissa later consumed his thoughts entirely.

Michael started his morning run with Sam as he had almost every Saturday for the last two years. *Now, where should I take Melissa tonight? Rosedale Lake? Nah. Grandma's beach house.* The drive to Seaside Park would be a little longer but totally worth it. Ever since his grandmother passed away, his family took turns with his Aunt in using the old bungalow. No one would be down there this weekend. It was the perfect place.

So preoccupied with the music and his own happy thoughts, he scarcely noticed that he and Sam had run three miles already and reached their usual destination. Entering the wrought iron gates of Saint Ann's cemetery, Michael yanked out his earbuds and turned off his iPod. As always, his whole mood swung one hundred and eighty degrees.

Careful not to tread on the green grass, he walked the familiar path to his father's grave. He made Sam lie down at the foot of his father's plot and put the leash on the ground beside the dog. Then he went close to the headstone and knelt down. *Damn it.*

An animal had uprooted the flowers he and Chris had planted earlier in the spring for his father's birthday. As best he could, Michael arranged the flowers and fixed the loose soil with his bare hands. The pest had tossed some of it up onto the headstone. With his fingers trembling slightly, he brushed the dirt out of the carved epitaph,

'Eric William Andrews'

'Beloved Husband and Father'

The cold granite seemed to seep into him, freezing his heart. More than two years had passed, but the awful ache at the pit of his stomach was still there. A little less severe, but definitely still there. All the time.

As he rubbed the dirt off his hands, he glanced around. No one else was close by, only Sam, and a few lifeless statues bearing witness to his visit. So he rolled off his knees and sat on the soft grass, leaning against the side of the headstone. Even with the rays of the warm June sun beating down, the hard stone still felt cool against his back.

"A beautiful day, huh, Dad." He paused, almost as if anticipating a reply. "Chris is doing fine. He's out playing baseball, of course. It's better than playing video games or watching the old hypno-box, right Dad? Mom's okay, too…I think she was going out shopping or something."

He drew a long breath. "I'm taking Melissa out later today. We might meet up with everybody down at Seaside…" he hesitated, pondering the best way to approach the subject, "and…um…then I'm thinking I might have Melissa stay over at the beach house with me. I'm really into her, Dad. She's a great girl. I know you always thought so, too."

A gentle breeze rustled through the trees above like a whisper. Michael paused, wishing his dad were really there to talk to. *No doubt, Dad would've understood.* A hollowness filled his chest and he didn't know how to make it go away. So he just continued.

"Don't worry, Dad. You know I wouldn't push her into anything. Lately…well…she's been sending off these vibes. I dunno…I think she might finally be ready. So, I think I'm gonna ask her if she wants to stay over tonight. If she says yes, great and if she says no…I guess I'll just have to wait a little longer," he said, slightly shrugging his shoulders. *I've waited this long and she's worth waiting for.*

A cardinal swooped low from the tree overhead and Michael watched it join a friend in flight. He hated these one-sided conversations, but they were all he had. Who knows? Maybe his dad could actually hear him.

"By the way, Chris got in another fight at school this week. I told him to knock it off and not make trouble for Mom. I don't know what his problem is sometimes. It's like he's…angry all the time. I try to talk to him about it, but I don't know if I'm doing any good or not." He fell silent again, listening to the birds chattering in the trees. "Well, I better get going," he said finally. "I've got to help Mom with some things around the house today. I love you, Dad…be well."

Before he stood up again, he folded his hands loosely in his lap and thought about saying a quick prayer. A few moments passed in silence while he debated. Soon, his muscles stiffened and he clenched his teeth, fighting the usual spike of anger and bitterness. He'd tried this time. He really had. It seemed pointless though. *What's the use in talking to the man upstairs when you know he doesn't listen?*

Standing up, he forced back a single rogue tear that threatened to escape. He'd learned out of necessity to control the waterworks. His dad had taught him at a very young age, real men never cry. *Besides, if you cry they gawk at you with that god-awful pity in their eyes.*

As he left the cemetery, he turned his iPod on again and

scrolled through the music. *Let's see...something to numb the pain.*

One tap and the screaming of Slipknot filled his head. *Perfect*

CHAPTER THREE

CRASH

11:15 AM

NEARING HIS HOUSE, Michael spotted Melissa's car parked in his driveway. She stood on the porch waiting.

That's weird. What's she doing here?

As he bounded up the steps two at a time he said, "Hey, my favorite brunette, what's up?" He reached out to embrace her, but she crossed her arms over her ample chest and twisted her face into a pout.

"Your *favorite*?" She said, evidently pretending to be jealous. "You mean you have more than one?"

"Oh, yeah," he teased, "at least twenty." Smiling warmly, he quickly closed the gap between them and folded her in his arms. At five-seven, Melissa was by no means short, but he still towered over her. He had to hunch over a little as he planted his lips on hers and kissed her deeply. She slipped her arms around his neck and they enjoyed a minute or two of tongue-hockey before he pulled back.

"I thought you had to work today," he said, his hands still on her waist.

"I do," she replied. "In fact I only have a few minutes. I tried calling, but you didn't answer, so I figured I'd just come over. I had to run an errand for my mom anyway."

"Well then, I guess I got lucky." He bent down and kissed her again. "What time are you done with work?"

"Phil only needs me from eleven to three."

"Great, that'll give me time to get some things done around here for my mom."

"Where are we going anyway?"

"It's a secret," he said, toying with her. "Just make sure you bring a bathing suit."

With a naughty look in her eyes, she asked, "Should I bring something to sleep in?"

His heart slammed into overdrive. *Is she asking what I think she's asking?*

He'd been dating her for two years. Yet, out of respect for her, he'd been really patient with the physical aspect of their relationship. Extremely patient. Each time they'd come close to doing the deed before, he could tell she'd been scared and unsure. Lately, he sensed she might be changing her mind.

Only one way to find out. "And if I say, no…and that I want you naked all night, what would you say?"

"Sounds good," she answered softly, her mouth slowly curving into a smile.

His right knee started to wiggle nervously and his eyes went wide.

"Really?" he asked, leaning back to get a good look at her face. He wanted to make sure she wasn't joking.

"Yesss," she purred seductively, pressing herself against him. Her firm breasts were practically poking through her thin shirt and her soft belly came up to about the height of his groin.

Instantly, he went rock hard. It took him a second to think straight. Gently, he cupped her chin in his hand and repeated the question, "Really?"

She answered by grinding her hips into him and rubbing her breasts teasingly against his chest.

"Oh my god, I love you," he said with a moan, as he pulled her up on her toes, slightly bending her over and thrusting himself against her body. His mouth met hers, his kiss hot and fierce as her body arched into him.

A minute later, Melissa forced herself to pull away. "I'd better get going," she said, breathless, "or I'll be late for work."

"I'll pick you up at three," he called out as she ran down the steps.

She opened the door to her car and yelled back, "Okay then, I'll have my mom drop me off at work. Love you."

"Right back at ya," he said with a wave.

• • •

Caught up with the sweet vision of Melissa in his head, Michael had all but forgotten about Sam, who was lying on the porch next to him waiting patiently. He took the dog inside and then went out the back door to cut the lawn. As he unlocked the shed, a familiar voice called his name. Turning around, he saw his next-door neighbor, Mr. Jasinski, wave to him from his yard.

Michael walked over to the fence. "Hey there, Mr. J. How are ya?"

"I'm good, I'm good," Mr. Jasinski replied, shaking his

15

hand and giving him a friendly slap on the back. "No basketball today?"

"Nah, the Shore League doesn't start until the weekend after graduation. I'm not even sure if I'm gonna be able to play this summer 'cause I'll have to leave early for Pitt. Our coach wants all the freshmen to tour the athletic facilities and attend a special four week training."

Mr. Jasinski slowly shook his head. "I can't believe you're going to college already. It seems like only yesterday you couldn't even see over this fence." He gestured at his height. "*Now* look at you."

Michael laughed a little. "You're right, time sure has flown."

"You know, I still remember the day your dad put up that basketball hoop," his old neighbor said, reminiscing. "You couldn't have been much more than five."

"I think I was in first grade," he clarified, "so I must've been six."

"That's right. All I know is you were *so* excited. Do you remember dribbling around your father in circles, saying you wanted to be like Mike?"

"Yeah, I remember that," he said, with a lighthearted laugh. "Dad taught me my first pump fake that day."

After that day, he'd spent countless hours in his driveway, mastering the pump fake, executing figure-eight drills, and shooting baskets by moonlight. By the time he was in high school, he'd transformed into what his coach described as, "a talented power forward". A four-year letter-winner and captain of the basketball team, in the past year he'd lead Branchburg High to a 24-3 record, averaging twelve points a game. Now all his hard work was about to pay off. In the fall, he looked forward to playing for University of Pittsburgh, an NCAA Division I school.

"Your father would be so proud of you," Mr. Jasinski said. "You know that."

"Yeah," he answered in a hollow voice, "I know."

An awkward moment of silence passed between them as they remembered the man missing from both of their lives. Over the years, Mr. Jasinski had become one of his dad's closest friends. They fished together, played cards, and of course, had a mutual obsession for watching college basketball.

"Sometimes I can't get over how much you look like your dad," Mr. Jasinski said. "You've grown into an outstanding young man."

"Thanks," he responded, glancing at the ground in embarrassment. "Let's just hope I've got game."

"Oh, I know you do," Mr. Jasinski assured him. "I bet you can't wait."

"I am *stoked*, that's for sure," he answered with enthusiasm, "but I may have to bide my time a little. As a freshman, I might not play in that many games right away." Impatiently he added, "I just wanna get my *chance*, ya know."

"Don't worry, your time is coming," Mr. Jasinski encouraged. "You'll get your shot. Personally, I think you'll be playing in the NBA someday."

He smiled broadly. "I sure hope you're right, Mr. J."

"Me too." Mr. Jasinski chuckled as he clapped him on the back once more. "I'll be able to say I knew you when."

. . .

11:40 AM

For now, hoop dreams would have to wait. Michael still had the lawn to do, and he wanted to finish quickly so he could enjoy this gorgeous day. Getting his dad's old riding tractor out of the shed, he tried not to feel the usual sense of melancholy that so often accompanied this task. For it was at quiet moments like this, when he did the things his dad used to do, that he missed him the most.

As he began the first few passes at the backyard, memories rushed forward like they were from only yesterday. In his mind's eye, he could still see his dad sitting on this same tractor, with his earphones on, listening to the Yankees game on the radio. He vividly recalled sitting on his big-wheel when he was little and pretending to cut the grass. His dad would flash him a great big proud smile and wave to him from the tractor. When he was old enough, his dad let him sit on the tractor and would ride him around. It really didn't seem like all that long ago.

Damn it, I hate cutting the frickin' grass.

No matter how much he resented his responsibilities, though, he worked his butt off all afternoon. He mowed the lawn, put the tractor away, wrapped up the newspapers and fixed a loose board on the back porch stairs. By the time he finished, the temperature had spiked to ninety degrees. *God, it's getting humid out.* With sweat pouring off his body, he decided a shower might be a good idea. *Especially, if I want Melissa to come anywhere near me.*

He went inside, grabbed a quick sandwich and sat down in the living room to watch the news while he inhaled his lunch. The large grandfather clock in the adjacent foyer chimed, reminding him of the time. *Two o'clock, I better get my ass in gear.* As he started up the stairs, his brother came in the front door.

Turning around, he asked him, "How'd ya do?"

"They still can't hit my curveball," Chris replied, as he stuck his nose up with a confident air.

Michael gave him a friendly fist bump. "Never have, never will, bro."

If fast pitchers could be described as "bringin' the heat" then his brother could be considered a flame-thrower. Chris had a raw, natural talent that Michael hoped would one-day lead his brother to a seven-figure salary, a Nike endorsement, and a trip to Cooperstown. He also hoped his encouragement would help, so he doled it out in heaps.

A big smile lit Chris' face. "Yankees are gonna pay me millions someday," his brother boasted.

"Don't you know it, man," Michael replied with a beaming smile of his own as he went up the stairs.

Once in his bedroom, he stripped off his sweaty clothes. Stepping into the shower, he hummed along to a Beatles tune stuck in his head. In record time, he showered and hung up his wet towel. He threw his dirty clothes in the hamper and put on a pair of comfy, beach shorts. Spraying on some Fierce, his favorite Abercrombie cologne, he went to his closet to find his dark blue Hollister shirt, Melissa's favorite.

Standing in front of the long mirror on his closet door, he quickly checked his appearance. Half the girls in school would give up their Uggs, or anything else for that matter, to go out with him. They followed him around like a pack of lovesick, crazoid puppies. *It's so incredibly freakin' annoying and it's only because I'm captain of the basketball team.* Any one of them would probably sleep with him in a heartbeat, but so what? The only one he really wanted was Melissa.

Before he left, he penned his mother a note. She always gave him plenty of freedom, because he never gave her any reason to worry. All he wrote was not to include him for dinner, and that he'd call later to say what he was doing. He never lied to his mom, ever. With everything his mom had been through, she deserved a son she could trust. Secretly, he hoped his good example might rub off on his brother, who wasn't always so truthful.

He finished the note with his usual salutation—Love ya, Ma and poked his cell phone, *two-thirty. I better hurry if I'm gonna pick Melissa up by three.*

As he slid behind the wheel of his beautifully restored '67 Mustang, he realized *his* car could stand a good wash too. A bit of guilt nagged at him. *I should've woken up earlier and cleaned the car.*

The Mustang was his baby and he treated her like it. His father had acquired the car four years ago from an uncle who had passed away. In rough shape and badly in need of some attention, the car had been sitting in a garage, gathering rust and cobwebs. A four speed with a 440 six pack under the hood, it definitely would've been a crime to let it rot. So together, Michael, Chris and his dad had worked countless hours restoring the Mustang. They raked their knuckles, swore like inmates, and got oil stains on the driveway, but they had the best time ever. The restoration even came out pretty damn sweet, too.

Michael latched his seatbelt and turned on the radio to his favorite station. A song called "Melissa" by the Allman Brothers, his father's favorite band, was just coming on. *It's a good omen, right Dad?* He almost felt like he had his father's approval. *Melissa will definitely give me the green light tonight.* His stomach quivered in happy anticipation and his leg bounced lightly on the pedal. As he pealed out of his driveway, he couldn't have been in a better mood.

A rural two-lane highway, Route 206 over time had become a major thoroughfare in New Jersey. Today, traffic was unusually light as he traveled south toward Montgomery. Tapping his thumbs on the steering wheel to the beat of "Sweet Child of Mine", he approached a bend in the road.

At that moment, traveling in the northbound lane was a tractor-trailer. Behind the wheel, a very weary and exhausted Bill Higgins was doing his best to crank up the same song on his radio. This had been a long haul and he was running behind schedule. He'd run out of ephedrine hours ago, but would buy some at a truck stop further along his route. *No time to stop for a nap now, I have to keep going.* Bill sped up as he turned into the curve. *The radio... will... wake.... me..... up......*

Rounding the bend, Michael saw the truck swerve left and cross into his lane. He caught barely a glimpse of the driver slumped across the wheel. With the rig barreling towards him, his mind had little time to register the impending disaster and absolutely no time to avoid it. Sunlight bounced surreally off the shiny grill, blinding him as he slammed on the brakes.

The crash was tremendous. In an instant, the world turned from bright white to murky black and the last sound in his ears was the deafening roar of metal eating metal, glass fracturing and tires screaming.

CHAPTER FOUR

WAITING

MELISSA LEANED DOWN and sniffed her shirt. *Ugh! Fries.* She hated smelling like greasy food but working at the TGIFriday's on Route 206 put money in her bank account. The extra party funds would come in handy at Pitt in the fall. Eagerly, she waited for her shift to be over. Michael would be there soon, and she needed a few minutes to change clothes and primp a little. Not that he made her feel like it was all about her looks. She knew he liked *her,* maybe even loved her. He was the whole reason she'd chosen Pitt over all the other schools.

Melissa waited on her last table and headed for the ladies room. Taking off her apron, she released her long hair from the loose ponytail that had confined it. Cascades of wavy, chestnut hair fell about her shoulders. She grabbed a handful and sniffed. *Freesia, good.* At least the stink hadn't permeated her hair. Twisting strands of it around her finger, she remembered her conversation with Michael earlier. Naughty thoughts danced through her head and her stomach did a pleasant little roll. She had decided last night that with college only months away, she didn't want to make Michael wait any longer. What if he met some other cute co-ed?

In a few minutes, she was dressed and walking out of the

bathroom. At that moment, she started to hear the wail of sirens in the distance. The sound grew louder and she looked through the large front windows of the restaurant in time to see two police cars speed past. A half a minute later, two ambulances zoomed by, obviously in a huge hurry and headed in the direction Michael was coming from.

Probably another accident on 206. *Oh, damn...I hope this won't make him late.*

• • •

A few miles away, Melissa's mother, Karen, was in the middle of her shift at Princeton Hospital's Emergency room. The day had been unusually slow, only a few stitch ups, bee stings and a broken bone from a fall off a swing. Nothing even remotely interesting. All in all, a very boring day in the ER. Just the way she liked it.

Karen glanced at the television on the wall while she tidied the magazines in the waiting room. The local news was panning in on a horrific accident between a big rig and a car. At the bottom of the screen, they gave the location—Route 206, Montgomery Township. *That's not too far from here. So much for a peaceful morning, we're bound to get them.*

She almost turned away from the television, but then she noticed something about the crushed car. It looked like Michael's—same color, same make, same year. And then she saw it—the University of Pittsburgh sticker in the back window. Her pulse nearly doubled and her heart raced with adrenaline. *Oh my God, it* is *Michael's car.* She was almost sure of it.

Karen tried desperately to scrutinize the scene, to see if she could recognize the exact stretch of Route 206 where the accident had occurred. She quickly grabbed the remote control and turned up the volume so she could listen to the broadcast.

Nancy, the admitting nurse, called out from behind the front desk, "That's kinda loud."

"Quiet down," Karen responded sharply, motioning for Nancy to shut up.

Was Melissa in the car? Had Michael already picked her up? Frustrated at the lack of details the station was giving about the accident, Karen threw her hands up in the air. Instead of the wreck, the camera went back and forth showing the traffic backup along Route 206.

The face of a serious, young reporter popped up on the screen. "As we speak, rescue personnel are attempting to extract one of the passengers using the Jaws of Life."

Karen almost screamed out loud, *"Who?"*

Who? The driver? The passenger? That was it. She had to know, right now, so she yelled at Nancy to get her cell phone from her purse.

"What's the matter?" Nancy scrunched her face up in confusion, as she shoved the phone into her hand. Then she glanced at the TV, and back at Karen with a look of concern. "What's wrong?"

Unable to answer her, Karen stood there frozen.

Melissa's cell phone was ringing, and ringing, and ringing.

She's not picking up. Why isn't she picking up? Franticly, Karen tried again, hoping maybe she'd made a mistake. *My*

God, she prayed, *let her answer. Please dear God, let her answer the phone.*

•   •   •

Melissa sat at a booth near the kitchen. Growing bored, she began doodling hearts on a napkin. A friend startled her out of her daydream.

"I think you left your cell phone in your apron, 'cause it's ringing."

Melissa jumped to her feet and said, "Thanks," as she took the phone from the girl. Quickly sliding her thumb across the touch screen without looking, she expected to hear Michael's voice. Instead, her mother barked in her ear, "MELISSA?"

"Yes," she responded, confused by the high, panicky tone of her mother's voice. "Mom, why are you yelling?"

"Oh, nothing...nothing." Her mother's breath rattled in her cell like she'd been running up a flight of stairs and was gasping for air. A few seconds later, her mother asked her more calmly, "How was work today?"

"Uhhh...just fine, Mom."

"Okay, well...call me later, alright?"

"Sure...Mom," Melissa replied, somewhat perplexed by her mother's abruptness.

Talking much faster than usual, her mother said, "Great, talk to you later honey."

Melissa ended the call and shook her head. *That was strange. Mom sure seemed a bit off.* She sat there wondering for a moment or two, but then let it go.

Where the hell is Michael? He's always on time. A minute later, her curiosity got the best of her. Picking her phone back up, she tapped the screen to dial his number and waited for him to answer.

CHAPTER FIVE

BEGINNING

SOMEWHERE, AMONG THE twisted metal of what used to be the Mustang, Michael's cell phone rang. Hearing the sound, he opened his eyes...or so he thought. Believing that he must've blacked out, he instinctively tried to sit up. As he did, he raised a hand to his head, and at that moment, reality struck like a sledgehammer.

My body stayed behind! He could see through his arm and his torso, right back at his body still lying slumped on the seat.

Holy crap! I'm moving free of my body! Maybe I'm in shock, his mind tried to comprehend. *Am I just hallucinating? This can't be happening.* Then, swift and painful, the truth hit him. *I want to go back, I have to go back. I don't want to die! God help me, I don't want to die!*

In an act of pure desperation, Michael did the only thing he could think of, and quickly slid back down into his body. Trouble was he knew right away this wasn't going to work. He couldn't physically feel anything, not his body, the leather seat, the shards of glass, pain, nothing. Nothing. The dreaded question bubbled up like a corpse rising to the surface. *Am I really dead?*

One thing he knew for sure, he was conscious. Surprisingly, he wasn't floating over his body as he might've imagined. Out of habit, he reached for the handle to open the door of the car. To his utter astonishment, his whole arm went right through it. For lack of a better idea, he cautiously let the rest of himself follow.

Now standing outside of the car, he didn't immediately move from the spot, nor did he turn to look back at his body. Dread pulsing through every inch of him, he stood rooted to the pavement. Completely freaked out, the truth of his situation was overwhelming. Leaving his body behind was not an action taken lightly—that was for sure.

He looked around and surveyed the chaos unfolding before him. The wreckage was unbelievable, a mangled mass of smoking metal. The tractor-trailer had crossed the center line and hit his car head on. The heavy truck had completely smashed in the front of the Mustang and pushed the car onto the narrow shoulder of the road, almost into the tree line beyond. The front cab of the tractor-trailer was charred and had obviously burst into flames upon impact, but the fire was now out.

Firefighters and paramedics were running and shouting instructions at one another, as they tried to get into the driver's side of his car.

He stepped out of their way, though he didn't exactly know why. They had begun to cut away at the doorframe with a large lobster-claw-like saw, the Jaws of Life. He'd seen it before on television.

Feebly, his lips whispered what his mind didn't want to acknowledge, *I'm already out, I'm right here. Can't anyone see me?* Realizing he couldn't be seen or heard was the loneliest feeling he'd ever experienced.

Then, all of a sudden, a flare of optimism lit within him. *Maybe once they get me out, and start to work on me, maybe that's when I'll go back. Yeah, that's it,* he reasoned excitedly, *I've heard of things like this before. I'll be pulled back, like I'm supposed to be. I'm not dead yet,* he thought hopefully.

Within a few minutes, the firefighters had cut away the door and then, the steering wheel and dashboard that had pinned him. Gingerly they removed his limp body from the car. Two paramedics lifted him up, while a third placed a backboard under him. They laid him on the asphalt and started to work feverishly to save him.

Michael stared at his mangled lower half, but avoided looking directly at his face. He watched in horror as the paramedics failed to find a pulse. They started CPR and several IVs. About ten minutes later, the paramedics stopped all their efforts.

"That's it, the driver's expired," one of them declared, with a mundane finality that was not lost on the deceased.

All Michael could do was stand there in dazed disbelief. The man's conclusion was incomprehensible. *Expired? Like a gallon of old milk?* For a few seconds, he froze in shock. *I can't be dead. How the hell can I be dead?*

Now, panic overtook him. Tremors hit both his knees and he shouted, "No! I'm not dead!" Pointing at the paramedic crouched near his corpse he screamed, "He's wrong! You can't just stop! Help me!"

Of course, no one answered him.

"He's young, check his wallet. See if there's an organ donor card," one of the paramedics called out.

"Yeah, it says he is on his driver's license," was the response. "He's young, so have the hospital notify the next of kin first. Quick though, we haven't got much time."

Organ donor? This was the last straw. His last glimmer of hope faded. *You know it's over when they start talking about parting you out like a totaled car.*

For the first time, he gathered enough courage to look at his own face and he couldn't believe it was his. This guy was grotesque and repulsive. Glass was embedded in his skin, his eyes were shut and his face was ashen, punctuated only by a few red streaks of blood. Altogether, the man lying there was a very frightening sight to behold. *That can't be me.*

As they covered his body with a white sheet, he pleaded with them. "No, no...you have to help me, I can be saved. Try again, damn it!" he swore angrily.

Sensing the utter futility of his own words, he lowered his voice to barely a whisper, "I don't want to die. I'm too young to die." Right beside his lifeless body Michael dropped to his knees, looked up to heaven and pleaded with all his might. "No, *please God, no.* This can't be happening. Please!"

Much to his despair, he heard no response...from anyone.

• • •

Karen went outside to wait by the ambulance entrance. Now that she knew Melissa was okay, the tightness in her chest had eased up a little. She took a long drag off her cigarette, hoping to steady her nerves. Guilt nagged at her for not telling Melissa what was going on, but she certainly couldn't tell her Michael had been in an accident. At least, not until she knew more, she rationalized.

She tapped out the cigarette with her shoe, encouraged as she heard sirens approaching. Dead on arrivals never need the sirens. The ambulance pulled into the rotunda and two paramedics got out.

Before the men could even get to the back of the ambulance, Karen called out, trying to sound calmer than she felt, "Hi Jim, Ed, is this one from the accident on 206?"

"Yeah," Jim replied. "He's the driver of the rig. Got a few lacerations, nothing major. In his fifties though, and overweight, so he'll need an EKG."

"How about the other driver?" she asked, a little too anxiously now. She knew they would have brought the worst case in first. *Was it too much to hope, could Michael have only minor injuries?*

"Nah, he didn't make it," Jim replied in a matter of fact tone. "Mark and Keith are bringing him in. Probably died instantly," he started to say, as he and Ed opened the back of the ambulance. "Ribs went through his heart and..." Jim stopped abruptly when Karen's face turned several shades whiter.

"Karen, are you okay?" Ed asked.

"I...I'll be okay," she stammered. She thought she might be sick on the spot, but managed to force out the question she dreaded most of all, "Do you know his name? Is it Michael Andrews?"

"Yeah, Karen. What's wrong?" Jim asked, realization dawning on his face. "Did you know him?"

"Yes, uh…my daughter did, he was…um…a good friend. He was…a great kid." She wanted to add more, but found it too difficult to speak.

Ed touched her shoulder lightly. "Karen, we did everything we could, honestly."

In a heartfelt way, Jim added, "I'm really sorry."

"I know," she replied with deep regret, "me too."

•   •   •

At that very moment, his mother had just arrived home and picked up the note Michael had left for her earlier. As she read the words, she suddenly had the strangest feeling of dread and fear. Her stomach cramped and a touch of vertigo made her queasy. She tried to shake it off, but she couldn't help feeling like it reminded her of something. Like something's gone missing, or gone very wrong. When her boys were little, this same instinct used to make her search for them when the house had become too quiet. She didn't know why, but something was wrong and she needed to check on Michael. She reached for the phone, but it rang, startling her.

"Hello?" she asked tentatively.

"Mary…it's Karen. I'm over at the hospital," she said and then paused, barely able to dislodge the words from her paralyzed tongue. She took a deep breath, trying to control her emotions, "Michael was in a very bad car accident, they're bringing him in now," she said, her voice cracking.

Mary listened to her friend on the other end of the line, but she might as well have been a million miles away. She could hear the anguish in Karen's voice, and immediately she knew what her friend could not say. Somehow, she knew Michael was already gone.

Karen found the next few moments of silence unbearable. Finally she said, "Mary, I've sent a police car over to your house to bring you here. I don't want you to drive, okay?"

"Yes, I understand," Mary replied, her words full of meaning. Lips trembling, she said as calmly as she could, "I'll be right there."

Life can change in an instant, Mary knew this all too well. It had happened before with her husband, and now, it was happening again. She had been strong when Eric died, because she knew she had to be for Michael and Chris' sake. But this...how on earth would she be able to live through this? This was every parent's worst nightmare. This was the phone call every parent prays they'll never get.

Mary's surroundings wobbled and blurred out of focus. Her whole body shook uncontrollably. The receiver slipped from her hands, clattering to the floor. For the moment, it was more than she could take, and she collapsed into the chair like a marionette that's been dropped. With no one around to hear her, she started sobbing, the deep mournful, gut-wrenching sobs of a mother. A mother whose heart has just been splintered into a million pieces by the loss of a child.

CHAPTER SIX

HOME

NOT KNOWING WHAT to do, Michael followed his body into the second ambulance headed to the hospital. Until that moment, he'd been very lucky. His whole life he'd never even had so much as a broken bone. Now, he was taking his first ambulance ride and his last. Unable to take his eyes off the covered body lying on the gurney, the trip seemed to take a thousand years.

Thankfully, the ambulance finally pulled up in front of the ER. The paramedics carefully and slowly removed the stretcher, and he followed behind them through the automatic doors. He caught sight of Melissa's mom walking towards the ER waiting room. A second later, he turned around to see his mother and brother being led in by two police officers.

"Mom! Chris!" Michael cried out frantically, rushing to their side.

As Karen and one of the doctors relayed the grim news of his death, his mother took Chris in her arms and he broke down crying.

"Don't cry, Chris…please don't cry," Michael mumbled. He wished more than anything that his mother could hold him in her arms again. Tormented by his family's pain and

his own, he wanted so badly to cry but for some reason, the
tears simply wouldn't fall.

His mother had always been there for him. Now, more
than any other moment in his life, he wished his mother
could help him. Like a desperate and frightened child he let
it all out. "Mom, I'm scared. I don't know what to do. Mom!
Help me, please!"

Good thing his mother couldn't hear him, for if she had,
the despair and terror in his voice might've killed her on the
spot.

•   •   •

Karen identified his body for his mother, while the police
recounted the details of the accident to her and Chris. The
driver of the truck admitted to having fallen asleep at the
wheel. A few other drivers at the scene had pulled him out of
the truck before the flames completely engulfed the front
cab.

More enraged than he'd ever been in his life, Michael
stormed around the ER, ranting to no one in particular.
"*Great*, so he was saved and I'm *dead* at the age of eighteen?
You've gotta be *freakin'* kidding me. This is *his* fault, and he
gets to walk away with nothing but a few *scratches?* The
guy basically *murdered* me. Isn't anybody going to *do*
something? He gets to live and I have to *die*? It's not fair.
It's just not fair. This can't be the end, it just can't!"

Now, Karen and the Organ Donor Director approached
his mother. They explained that he had been dead too long
for anything but his corneas to be successfully harvested.

But with her consent, at least he could give those.

Being talked about like he wasn't there was already getting more than a little annoying. "Say yes, Mom. Just say yes," he said out loud. "What the hell do I need them for now anyway?"

Without hesitation, his mother agreed and the Director handed her a consent form. Shortly afterward, Karen called her husband. He agreed to pick up Melissa and give her the news. Karen would drive Mary and Chris home and stay the night so they wouldn't be alone. Branchburg Funeral Home would come to collect his body.

Emotionally numb, he followed his mother and brother out of the hospital and got into Karen's car with them. Completely lost and unable to accept his fate, he had no idea how else to get home.

The four of them drove home in depressing silence.

Less than twenty four hours ago, he had so much planned, so much to look forward to, so much life to live. *How could this have happened? It must be some cosmic mistake. Some kind of mix up.* They pulled into the driveway and he saw his house, as he never had before. Everything was exactly the same as when he had left earlier that afternoon, and yet, he would never be walking back in alive. *I'll never be coming home.*

He wanted to cry out, to beg someone to make time go backwards. *If only I could go back to the moment right before I got in the car. If only...* But deep down inside he knew it sounded crazy. His mind felt like a jumble of impossible knots. Like a movie flashback sequence, a myriad of memories rushed at him mercilessly—Christmas mornings, his dad's infamous Fourth of July barbecues, playing baseball in the backyard with his brother, shooting baskets till his hands were raw, taking pictures the night of the prom under the big oak.

Unable to move and not ready to go inside his house yet, he let everyone else exit the car first. Finally, he gathered his courage and for the second time today, he walked through the door of a car. As he slipped through the front door unseen, Sam stood up and barked at him. Not menacingly, but like she was trying to alert his mother and Chris of his presence.

"Can you see me?" he asked his old canine friend.

Samantha tilted her head as she always did when she was trying to interpret human speech. Michael peered at the German shepherd, just as puzzled. In the authoritative tone he always used with her he commanded, "Sam, sit."

Much to his surprise, she instantly obeyed and sank to the floor.

Can the dog really hear me?

"Good girl," he said with affection, as he bent down to pet her. But the instant his hand made contact with her fur, Sam gave a small yelp and quickly jumped up, whimpering as she fled to the living room. She lay down on the carpet and began a low mournful howl.

So much for man's best friend, Michael thought, deeply stung by her behavior. Her recognition had been a small, but all too brief, comfort.

As he walked around the house, he started to pay more attention to his surroundings. Too distracted and upset to notice before, he realized for the first time that he couldn't feel his feet hit the floor. The floorboards didn't creak in places where they usually did, and his feet left no impressions in the carpet. Everything felt different now, as if nothing around him was solid. His sense of touch was only a faint echo of what it had been when he was alive.

Slowly ascending the stairs, he retreated to the sanctuary of his bedroom. Everything was exactly as he had left it earlier that day. Yet, in only a matter of hours so much had changed. He had left all of this behind.

He glanced around the room at the remnants of his ordinary life. All of his trophies sat on their shelves above his desk. In the corner of his room, next to his music stand, his guitar lay waiting to be played. Basketball pictures and his varsity letters were pinned to the corkboard on the wall, along with his letter of acceptance from Pitt. The detritus of a life well lived. *But now it's over.*

Passing his long dresser, he caught a glimpse of himself in the large mirror above. He came back to stand directly in front of the glass and couldn't believe his reflection. *No cuts, no blood streaks, no crushed torso. I look almost the same as when I left the house earlier.* Only slightly paler and somewhat see-through, his body even appeared to be three-dimensional. He could turn all around in front of the mirror while watching.

As he stood there, he reached his hand up and brushed his hair back from his forehead. *Holy shit, I can actually feel my body.* Slowly touching his face and then his torso, he could swear he was as perfectly solid as he had been when he woke up that morning. He was even wearing the same clothes he had put on after his shower. He could touch them, move them, feel them and see them, both in his hand and in the mirror. *It makes no god-damned sense at all. How the hell can that be?* He struggled to understand but got nowhere. *At least I'm not walking around buck naked,* he thought with morbid amusement.

He lay down on his bed, but it didn't hold the same comfort it usually did. For one thing, he was on top of the bed, but it didn't seem like he was lying on anything but a cushion of air. He wondered why he didn't fall right through it. *Why should only my body feel solid to me, but nothing else?*

Tentatively, he put his hand over his heart. The silence and stillness of his chest was unnerving. No beat, no breath. No life. He would do anything to even just bleed again, to feel warm blood rushing through his veins. Life had a pulse he could only appreciate once it had ceased.

I guess that's it then, I'm dead. Really, truly, officially dead. Here one minute and gone the next. That about sums it up, he thought bitterly. The day's events played back in his mind like some surreal circus.

Wait a minute, wasn't my life supposed to flash before my eyes, or something like that? Shouldn't I have seen some bright tunnel of light or something? I don't remember anything like that happening. Did I somehow miss where I was supposed to go? He thought about that old saying his mother had repeated so many times "when one door closes, another one opens". *So, how the hell do I find this second door?*

Instead of finding answers, he found himself trapped in an enigmatic nightmare, where nothing made sense and from which, he couldn't wake up.

Wait a second, maybe that's it. Maybe I'll go to sleep and wake up, and this'll all have been some horrible nightmare. Problem was he didn't feel like he needed any sleep. Instead, for some unknown reason, his entire body felt extremely energized and restless. His leg trembled uncontrollably as he tossed and turned on the bed. Great. His ADHD had even followed him into the afterlife.

All night, he stared into the darkness, wide awake and thinking. Wandering the corridors of his mind, he left no door unopened. He remembered in vivid detail every holiday, every happy birthday. Freeze frames of triumph, tribulation, and jubilation. He also recalled all the little moments sprinkled here and there, that had added spice and flavor to his life.

Still he was dead, unequivocally, irreversibly, dead. *Dead. Dead. Dead.* Now, he thought about all the things he would do differently if he had the chance. Without question, the first one would have been to tell the people he loved, every day of his life, how much they meant to him. Too late now.

Life wasn't fair, he knew that. Losing his dad so young, had taught him that lesson. *But why me, and why now?* He had had so many expectations for his life. Things he had wanted to do, to see, and places he would've gone. *My God, I'll never go to college, play basketball, get married, or be a father.* So many dreams and accomplishments would go unfulfilled.

What about his family and friends? How would his death affect everyone else? *Melissa...she must know by now. I should go see how she's doing, but I can't watch her cry. I just can't. And what about Chris? My brother's going to grow up without me. Christ, he'll grow up without any male role model at all. That sucks. And my mom...my poor mom. I can't believe I've done this to her. This is all my fault. I should've been driving a car with air bags. How could I have been so stupid?*

As he lay there, he started to realize something else odd. Time itself wasn't behaving as it should. Like some erratic, out of control conveyor belt, time kept speeding up and slowing down. He glanced at the clock at what seemed like regular intervals, and sometimes only minutes would pass, but sometimes several hours would go by.

His circadian rhythm was also completely mixed up. It felt more like day than night, and yet he knew exactly the opposite was true. *This isn't making any sense, but why should this be different than anything else?* Time simply had no measure or meaning. In fact, it was as if time no longer existed.

Though he didn't understand this peculiar phenomenon, he wondered if he might eventually learn to be grateful for it. After all, how many earthly, living souls yearn to be free from the cursed shackles of time?

CHAPTER SEVEN

FUNERAL

BY EARLY SUNDAY morning, his father's sister, Susan, had driven down from Massachusetts. Together, his Aunt Susan and Karen made the necessary phone calls to other family and friends. They called the funeral director and made preliminary arrangements. They notified Mr. McClure, the high school principal who said he would arrange for grief counselors to be on hand Monday for the students.

News of the tragedy propagated quickly across the tight-knit community, and for most of the day, Michael lay in his bedroom listening to the endless parade of people downstairs. In and out, in and out they trudged. As if every shoulder his mother cried on could carry away some of her pain along with some of her tears.

Michael had expected this. He remembered what it had been like when his father had died. It's different when it's about *you*, though. Feeling guilty for everyone being so sad and melancholy, he wanted to tell them all to stop. Stop sobbing, stop crying, and stop wringing their hands. *When the hell is this cry-a-thon going to end?*

Later that night, he followed his mother as she put Chris to bed, hearing her say sweet things to soothe him. She was trying to be strong and not cry too much in front of his brother. Once Chris was in bed, Michael followed his mother downstairs and listened to her conversation with his Aunt Susan. His heart was breaking, but like a spectator at a disaster, he felt compelled to watch.

"First Eric, now Michael. It's more than I can take, Susan," his mother said, as she broke down sobbing in her sister-in-law's arms.

"I know, I know." Susan replied, tears streaming down her cheeks. "He was too young…too young."

Michael put his hand on his mother's shoulder, but suddenly she shuddered as if she had caught a chill. Quickly pulling his hand away, it felt slightly warmed and strange, as if he had touched warm, molten wax. He wanted so much to give his mother a hug, to let her know he was there, but he didn't want her to be repulsed by his touch like the dog had been. He was sure he wouldn't be able to stand it.

•　•　•

Light streamed from his windows as a new day dawned, but Michael had no particular inspiration to move. Only when he heard noises from his mother's bedroom, did he get up. He went down to the kitchen and she was there, as always, preparing breakfast. If it wasn't for the fact that he was dead, this could've been any typical Monday morning.

Michael almost couldn't bear to look at her. He never doubted his mother's love, not even for a second. She had always made him feel incredibly loved and protected. So many times she had said he was her treasure. Every day of his life she worked tirelessly to take care of his every need, ensuring that he was happy, healthy, and most of all loved. And even though he stood right next to her, he missed her like crazy.

For the entire morning, he wandered around bewildered by his predicament while his mother made funeral arrangements. She was going through the motions, fulfilling her responsibilities, doing her duty.

He felt exactly the same, like he was on autopilot. By noon, his mother returned home and Michael followed her around the house as if attached by an umbilical cord.

His mother went about the house tidying and cleaning everything in sight. She vacuumed and dusted every nook and cranny. She wiped down the already spotless shelves in the refrigerator. His mother was shattered of course, but only Michael could see it fully. He'd seen her do all of this before, the night after his father died. It was her comfort mechanism. She was trying as best she could to put life in order, as if a little Windex and Mr. Clean would fix everything.

Several friends and neighbors stopped by to drop off food and his mother thanked them for their kindness. She tried in vain all afternoon to get his brother to come out of his room and have a bite to eat.

Finally around four o'clock, Chris came downstairs. He didn't touch his meal. Instead, he picked up the newspaper and, out of habit, searched for the sports page. He stopped abruptly when he stumbled upon an article about the accident.

As Chris began reading, Michael read the headline over his brother's shoulder:

SCHOLAR ATHLETE DIES IN COLLISION

Residents in the small community of Branchburg are mourning the loss of a star athlete who died in a weekend accident. Michael Andrews, 18, Co-Captain of Branchburg High School basketball team was killed Saturday when a tractor-trailer struck his car.

According to Montgomery police, Michael Andrews was driving southbound on Route 206 at about 2:45pm when the driver of the tractor-trailer apparently fell asleep, lost control and swerved into the oncoming lane, hitting Mr. Andrews' vehicle head on. The driver's compartment of the vehicle was crushed by the impact. Paramedics pronounced him dead at the scene.

William McClure, principal at Branchburg High School called the news of the young man's death "devastating" for students, neighbors, and everyone that knew him. "Michael was a charming, polite, and talented boy. He was a model student. This is unbelievable, just unbelievable," McClure said.

Michael was to have attended University of Pittsburgh in the Fall. On behalf of the University of Pittsburgh community, Ryan Murphy, Athletic Director, offered his condolences on Michael's death just weeks shy of his graduation. "I cannot begin to fathom the grief his family, classmates and the faculty of Branchburg High School must feel at his loss, a grief intensified perhaps in losing him at what would have been one of the milestones of Michael's young life. Today our hearts and prayers are with Michael's family, friends and loved ones," he said in an issued statement.

During a moving candlelight vigil Sunday night, fellow teammate, Shawn Kerber, said, "Michael loved life and lived it to the fullest, always with a big smile and a positive attitude."

Meredith Nickels, parent of another teammate, described Michael as very well-liked, pleasant, and well-rounded. "It's a very sad day for everyone. The whole community is just crushed. It really makes you wonder why. Why does something like this happen?" Nickels said, wiping away tears.

The driver of the tractor-trailer was issued a violation for reckless driving and has been suspended by the trucking company that employs him. Records indicated he had been driving for nearly 20 hours nonstop from Florida on his way to Albany, New York. Police commented that his exhaustion, in their opinion, definitely contributed to the crash. More charges may be filed, pending an investigation.

The truck driver was also found to have been driving with a suspended license in NJ, as well as, having traffic citations in five states. The safety group, Americans for Safe Highways, commented on yesterday's tragedy, saying that, more than 100 people a week are killed in large truck crashes in this country. They are calling for legislation to reduce how long big rig drivers can work without rest.

The opinion of the safety advocacy groups is that safety is taking a backseat to the profit of the trucking industry. Last year alone, nearly 5,600 deaths and more than 112,000 injuries were reported by the NTSA.

Over three million registered tractor-
trailers are on the road in this country,
with roughly 15 million commercial drivers
licensed in the US.

Bitterness slammed Michael, as they finished reading nearly simultaneously. Chris threw down the paper in disgust and looked up at his mother.

She stared back for a few long seconds.

Come on, Mom. Say something.

His mother opened her mouth, but unfortunately the words seemed to freeze in her throat. Michael couldn't blame her. What could she say this time that might make Chris feel better? *Obviously, she has no idea. I have no idea, either.*

For a few moments, the silence hung between all of them like dead air.

Michael reached out to put a hand on his brother's back, but before he had the chance, Chris mechanically rose from his chair and went upstairs to dress for the viewing.

• • •

The next day, Tuesday, dragged on and on. His family spent most of the day at Branchburg Funeral Home for the viewing, again. The outpouring of grief from the community was touching, but he just wanted it to be over. Not for his sake, but for his family's.

Meanwhile, he wandered around the house alone, being careful to avoid Sam. If he got within twenty feet of her, his dog would howl relentlessly. It was seriously unnerving and completely annoying. What was it about his presence that bothered her so much?

Finally, Wednesday arrived, overcast and threatening rain. Perfect weather for a funeral day. He had to go. *How can you miss your own funeral?*

On the way, he sat in the front seat of the limousine next to the driver. Grief and sadness hung in the air like palpable smog.

Walking around the funeral home, Michael's stomach was gripped by phantom pains. *I can't believe this is all real. This has to be a nightmare. I just need to wake up.* His mother and brother seated themselves in the front of the room. The quiet anger on his brother's face could've turned anyone in the room to stone in an instant. Michael was surprised it didn't.

Many of the same faces, he'd seen at his dad's funeral. This time though, nearly the entire town turned out. Some people looked only vaguely familiar, and he wondered who they were that they would be crying for him. *It's funny how you never notice those people in your periphery who care about you, until tragedy brings them into sharp focus.*

The rest of the people he recognized right away. His high school principal and the school superintendent were there. His whole basketball team and most of their parents came to support his family. Many of his classmates came to pay their respect. They appeared especially lost, all of their faces displaying shock and sorrow. Michael knew why. They were just learning a fundamental truth—life is nothing but a delicate balance of tenuous circumstances, all swirling on the head of a pin. *The slightest nudge can throw everything off balance and life can change in an instant.*

His three closest friends, John, Craig, and Shawn huddled together in the farthest corner from where the casket lay. He'd known all of them since he was about five and he'd never seen them like this. They were a complete mess.

The people mingled with one another and Michael walked around the room listening as they talked in hushed voices and low whispers. Fragments of conversations fell upon his ears from every direction.

"Tragic…"

"He was so young…"

"He had so much going for him…"

"What a shame, such a wonderful young man…"

"I feel so bad…"

"I have no idea what to say to her…"

The scene before him was like watching a documentary about someone else's death. No one wanted to see an innocent young person cut down in their prime. *I just can't believe it's me they're talking about. I wonder if anyone will update my Facebook page to say I'm gone.*

Inevitably, he wandered over to where his body lay in the corner of the room, surrounded by more flowers than he'd ever seen. His knee quaked as he stared down at the familiar stranger in the casket. The dark suit made him appear older and stiff, but they had done a great job with his face. *So peaceful and serene, as if I'm simply asleep. Would anyone really believe I'm standing right here beside them, feeling so utterly undead?*

Turning away, he saw his basketball coach, Mr. Feldman, and his English teacher, Mr. Knox, whispering in another corner. He was one of the most gossipy members of the faculty. Obviously talking about something juicy, Mr. Knox kept raising his hand up to cover his mouth as he spoke.

Curious about their conversation, Michael walked over.

And he couldn't believe what he heard.

"What a stupid, *stupid* mistake," Coach remarked with a shake of his head.

"I'm telling you," Mr. Knox mumbled behind his cupped hand, "speed or alcohol *had* to have been a factor in the crash."

More unbelievable still was his coach, nodding in agreement like some idiotic bobble head doll.

Michael's hands automatically curled into fists.

They had absolutely no basis for such speculation, yet there they were, demonstrating the less laudable qualities of two men he'd once admired and respected. He found it incomprehensible that not all people say the kindest things, *even when you're dead*.

His frustration boiled over, and without thinking, he took an angry swing at his teacher. His arm sailed through the man's head so quickly, Mr. Knox didn't even seem to have gotten a chill.

Great, they can say anything they want about me and I can't even set the record straight. Had he been alive, he was sure he would have felt nauseated.

Just then, an odd prickling danced up the back of his neck. He knew right away what it was—that natural instinct that tells you to turn around because someone is either looking at you, or has come up behind you. Whirling around, he found no one there. He scanned the room, but of course, no one was watching him. *No one can see me, so who the hell would be looking at me? I must be* completely *losing it.*

After a short memorial service at the funeral home, everyone, including Michael, left for the funeral Mass at Saint Ann's Church.

Moving cautiously, he navigated around the crowd gathering at the back of the church, being careful not to touch or bump into anyone. Afraid of what might happen if someone walked completely through him, he wasn't ready yet to find out. He listened as Father Anthony delivered his eulogy.

"A church is a focal point for the happiest and the saddest events of life. The full and complete circle of life happens in a church. Unfortunately, today we are all here for one of those very saddest of moments. This morning I come before you to reflect on the life of Michael Andrews, a young man who was smart, talented and honest. Indeed, I can say this about him because I knew him well. He was no stranger to our parish. His circle of life began on this altar when he was baptized. He attended church regularly with his family and received all of his sacraments here at Saint Ann's. As a boy scout, he did community service hours by helping to build the booths for the summer carnival each year."

Father Anthony paused before continuing, "That's exactly what makes this all the harder to understand. Why a promising young man, such as Michael, would be taken away from us? Many times, even as a priest, I find it very hard to understand why the Lord allows tragedy to strike, but we must all rely on our faith. We have to remain steadfast in our belief that God must have a higher purpose, a greater plan. Then, we will find solace and comfort in the fact that Michael has gone on to a better place in heaven, a place of everlasting peace."

Wait a second, why didn't I move on? Why am I still here? As if coming to terms with his own death were not enough, these thoughts unsettled him the most. *Did I do something wrong? Am I being punished for something? Didn't I live a good life?*

During the entire service almost everyone was crying. He wanted to cry, but still no tears would come. His aunt read the twenty-third psalm and the ashes to ashes verses. Just then, the choir broke into a song he'd heard before at his father's funeral—something about being raised up on eagles' wings.

Wings? Good point, where are *the angels? Where* is *that sweet chariot, comin' for to carry me home?* He mused bitterly. *Did I take a wrong turn, miss a connection or something?* The only time he'd ever been this upset in church was when his father had died.

Frustrated and distraught, he dropped down to his knees. "Dear Lord, please, *please* help me. I don't know what I'm supposed to do, or where I'm supposed to go."

Completely penitent, he cast up a desperate prayer, a final plea, "*Please* God, I'm sorry for anything I've *ever* done wrong. I know I was angry with you for taking my dad from me, but I didn't mean it, I'm *sorry*. I'm so sorry."

When nothing happened and no answer came, the sadness and confusion proved to be too unbearable and overwhelming. Michael got to his feet, gave one last fleeting glance at the cross hanging above the altar and ran straight through the doors of the church.

CHAPTER EIGHT

BURIED

ONCE OUTSIDE, MICHAEL sat down on the church steps trying to calm down. Over the last three days, he had ample time to reach the obvious conclusion. *Death is permanent.* He grasped that reality, and now, all he wanted was to move on. With his ADHD, patience had never been one of his strengths and he simply couldn't stand any of this another second.

But, how does someone move on? Is it like hailing a cab or catching a bus? No matter how he tried to make sense of his predicament, he kept coming back to the same question. *Why the hell am I stuck here?*

An idea skittered across his mind, sparking some hope. *Maybe my soul will be able to leave when my body is buried. That's it! Of course! I have to be laid to rest.* Wasn't that the whole point of that expression? The more he thought about it, the more convinced he became that he had figured it out. *I bet that's all that needs to happen, and I'll be ready to go.* As he considered this possibility, relief flooded through him. It made perfect sense. After all, he had heard of spirits not being at rest until their remains were properly buried.

So he followed his family to the cemetery for the burial, fully expecting this would be his last hour or so, on earth.

Raindrops the size of raisins pelted the congregation assembled and a hundred black umbrellas popped open around his gravesite.

Of course, the rain passed right through him. Standing there, waiting for the whole ordeal to be over, he lifted his face to the sky, wishing, pleading to feel the rain on his face. *Did I take life for granted? Except for losing my dad, I had a pretty damn good life. Did I not appreciate everything enough? Am I being punished for that?*

As the service began, Father Anthony moved to the foot of the casket and spoke to the throng of people assembled.

Michael tuned him out. Instead, he stared at the gaping hole beneath his recently sealed coffin. A chill ripped up his neck. *I can't believe I'm looking at my own grave. I'm only eighteen.*

He bit the inside of his cheek and bowed his head, taking a sidelong glance at his mother. She leaned heavily on Chris, whose eyes were as blank and as lifeless as his own.

His mother had loved him very much, no doubt about that. Every day of his life she had told him so. She had her own silly, loving expressions like, "you're 129% angel" and "you're my treasure". He never told her so because of course, he was way too mature, but he loved when she said those things. Now, he wished like hell that he had.

His mother wobbled over to the closed casket, but as her shaking hand placed a white rose on top, she suddenly tilted, collapsing on one knee. Her black dress covered in mud, she sobbed uncontrollably.

"Michael...Michael," she choked, in between gut-wrenching sobs.

He ran to her, but Chris took her arm and pulled her to her feet. The two shuffled away, clinging to one another.

Melissa was next to place her rose on top of the casket and say goodbye. Tears streamed down her cheeks, destroying her mascara, but she was still as beautiful as ever. She looked so much like a distraught widow that he agonized over what she might've looked like as his lovely bride. Obviously, as he was learning, emotions could be just as painful without a corporeal body.

Roused from his thoughts, the priest's words caught his attention.

"Michael is with his father now in heaven."

Wait a minute, that's right, where is my dad? Why hasn't he come to get me? Aren't all my dead relatives supposed to be here, ready to greet me as I cross over?

He scanned the rows and rows of gravestones. The only people around the cemetery were living, breathing ones. Could his father be nearby? Watching? Waiting? The thought of seeing his dad again was the only bright spot he could find in all the pain.

So, he waited. And waited. And nothing happened. The service ended.

Eager to escape the rain, everyone tromped quickly to their cars. Soon, the last one pulled away.

Completely alone beside his grave, he debated staying with his body and came to the obvious conclusion. *This is freakin' pointless.*

• • •

Not knowing exactly what to do next, he followed Melissa to her house. He needed some distance from his family. Another minute of seeing their pain would've been impossible to bear.

Trailing Melissa up to her bedroom, he darted in behind her as she shut the door. She sat down in front of her dressing mirror and started brushing her windblown hair. His heart ached as he watched her from across the room. He would do anything to hold her again. Desire seized his chest with a crippling pain. If he could just fold her in his arms, even for a moment or two, smell her hair, one last time...

Taking a few steps closer, he reached out.

At that same moment Melissa paused, put down the hairbrush and picked up a picture frame leaning against the mirror. It held their prom picture, taken a month earlier. Tears welled up in her eyes and she blinked them back, dropping her head.

Can she sense I'm here?

With a sudden trill, Melissa's cell phone rang and she picked it up.

"Hi, Kevin. Yes, I just got back."

Kevin Manfreda? Great. The one player from his basketball team that he didn't get along with. Jealous and resentful of Michael's talent, Kevin did all he could to undermine him with his teammates. It didn't work, but the fact that Kevin tried to, really pissed him off.

Even worse, Kevin had always had his eye on Melissa and every other girl in school. The guy was a male whore. He'd caught him trying to big time flirt with Melissa more than once, though she barely gave him the time of day. *I bet he's only calling to try to take advantage of her while she's vulnerable. He's probably gonna use this to try and get in her pants. What a son of a bitch. Classic Kevin. I'm not even buried a whole day yet and he's going after my girlfriend.*

"Yes I will, thanks for calling." Melissa's tone was polite and civil as she hung up.

A feeling of pride…and emptiness filled him. So she was loyal. She was being loyal to a dead guy. But how long would that last? This was going to happen again…and again. He would have to stand by and watch helplessly while someone else made a play for her. *How long before she falls for someone else?* He sat down on the bed and hung his head in his hands, heartbroken. She was always his.

A second later, another painful fact struck him. *I never did get to be with her.*

Well, that's a monumental epic fail. She looked amazing at the prom, too. We should've been together that night. Only, he hadn't wanted to push her into anything. All of his friends assumed he'd slept with her anyway, though he never told them one way or the other. He couldn't stand those losers who needed to brag about every sexual exploit. He never really felt the need to strut his testosterone like some fool.

Melissa wasn't just any girl; she deserved better than that. They had been friends since the second grade. She had been there for him when his dad died. She had clutched his hand tightly during the funeral, giving him the strength he needed to not lose it completely in front of all those people.

If they were going to be together, he wanted it to be because she was ready. When it did happen, he wanted her to have no regrets, only fantastic memories. If anything, he'd thought of prom night as a test. Passing that test had proved to him how much he cared for her. Besides, it didn't make any difference when they had sex. They had done everything else. There was no rush. He had always thought there would be plenty of time. Some of his friends acted downright desperate, spending hours text messaging sexual innuendo to every girl they knew. *Pathetic.*

Melissa got up from the chair and started to undress. She unbuttoned her blouse and laid it on the bed.

He wanted so desperately to touch her, even just one more time but she would probably tremble under his touch, like his mother had done. As the seconds passed, the more clothes she took off, the more uncomfortable he grew, as if he were doing something wrong. *I feel like I'm invading her privacy and to be perfectly honest, I am! What am I, some kind of frickin' pervert? I respected her in life. Why should that change now?*

With his conscience nagging at him, he left her bedroom quickly, running down the stairs to get out of her house. As he reached the landing at the bottom, however, he realized something extraordinary.

Hey, I missed most of those steps! I think I can sort of float when I want to. Lightly, he pushed off the landing and drifted down the three remaining stairs. *It's like being on one of those inflatable Moon Bounces at the county fair. How long have I been floating around without realizing? This is cool as hell.*

Once outside, he tried his new skill in the front yard. He took a step with his right foot and then pushed off. He floated forward slightly like a balloon caught in a breeze and then landed on his left foot. It reminded him of the video he'd seen of Neil Armstrong walking on the moon—one small step for man, one giant leap for ghostkind. *Man, this is weird. I'm not quite weightless and I'm not quite flying. But, I don't seem to be completely held down by gravity, either. So, why don't I just drift off into space?*

Marveling at his newfound ability for a little while longer, he practiced in Melissa's front yard pushing off and floating from tree to tree. *Damn, this sure would have come in handy on the basketball court.* The feeling was exhilarating, almost better than the first time he drove a car. Almost. If only it wasn't for the being dead part.

A cluster of thick clouds shifted, revealing a bright moon and a starry night. The light struck him, sending a tingle throughout his ghostly body. Glancing up at the heavens, reality grounded him once again as his feet met the earth. Enough playing around. Time to contemplate his next move. He needed a game plan.

Unfortunately, he had no idea where to go next, or what to do. Only one thing he knew for sure. The pity party was over. It wasn't his thing.

He searched the stars above, hoping for an answer and trying to think about his situation logically. *My father must be in heaven, so that's where I have to get to. I don't want to be stuck here, but there must be some cosmic reason why I am. I just have to figure out what that reason is. How hard can that be?*

CHAPTER NINE

FEAR

HIS BEST MOVE would be to get away from his family and friends for a little while. That way, he might be able to think more clearly. The decision of where to go was a no-brainer. His favorite place in the world was the Jersey Shore. *Why not? It's as good as any other place for a ghost to hang out. Geez, that's almost comical. Is that what I am, a ghost?*

He walked along Route 539, the familiar back road which snakes through the Pine Barrens. The dense pine forest is scarcely populated compared to the rest of the state. This late at night, most of the local roads that lead through these woods are devoid of all but the occasional vehicle. He'd never thought about it before when driving through, but without a doubt, *this place is dark, deserted and definitely creepy.*

Presently, he came upon a row of small houses set back a little way from the road. Large yards fronted each home and any number of items littered the grass. One house had a couple of old cars parked on the lawn. Another was decorated with dozens of tacky lawn ornaments, plastic flamingos and small garden gnomes. *Gotta love those South Jersey Pineys.*

Passing a fenced in yard, a loud snarl erupted and he

whirled around quickly as a large, black dog leaped off a darkened porch. The crazed animal now barreled straight towards him, viciously barking its head off.

"I may be dead," Michael said out loud, "but I'm still glad there's a fence between you and me, buddy." This only incensed the dog more.

The Doberman hit the corner of the fence closest to him, growling and snarling nonstop. Michael quickened his pace and the ferocious dog followed along the fence as he passed by. The slobbering beast continued to bark in his direction, even after he walked past the other corner of the yard.

Michael turned around to stare back at him. *So, dogs must be able to see me or, at least, somehow sense my presence.*

The last of the houses faded in the distance behind him. Walking down the road enveloped in the darkness, a strange uneasiness slowly came over him. *This is ridiculous*, he almost said to himself out loud. *Get a grip. You're not afraid of the dark!* Still, he started wishing the road had more than the occasional street light. *Don't they believe in street lights around here?*

Michael walked on and on, further south and deeper into the Pine Barrens. Mostly gliding along, he barely touched the road now. As he went, he discovered the darkness was the same in death, as it had been in life—limitless, impenetrable, and unnerving. His eyes didn't need to adjust, for he no longer had that physical issue. Yet, the inky darkness surrounding him was growing ever blacker by the moment. A twinge of fear crept over him. *Is it my imagination, or is this forest closing in around me?*

Still, he pressed on and after a few moments, his

fearfulness struck him as funny. His knee tried to wiggle, but he tensed his leg in response. He let out a chuckle. *Why should I be scared? I'm the ghost!*

No matter how he tried to joke about it though, he couldn't shake the feeling someone, or some*thing*, was watching him from the darkness. He stopped and stood stock-still, listening.

A malevolent murmuring rushed through the trees, coming from not only one source, but oddly, from all around him. Was it simply the voice of the wind talking to him in whispers? Or, something else?

The further he went, the worse the feeling became. An oppressive heaviness hung in the air around him, clawing at his throat like a tightening noose.

The whispering grew louder.

Detecting movement out of the corner of his eye, he spun around to see shadows moving and swirling behind him. All his energy now trembled with a distinct sense of danger, and for the first time in his afterlife, he was afraid.

Very afraid.

Afraid of the dark.

And he began to fly.

CHAPTER TEN

SEASIDE

WHEN HE WAS young, like most people, Michael had vivid dreams of flying. But this was no dream. Fear propelling him, he sped forward a few feet off the ground, then higher and higher. Within seconds, he rose up into the night sky, quickly gaining altitude. He glanced over his shoulder. Whatever those shadows were, they hadn't followed him.

The veil of clouds hung directly over his head, but this was high enough. He wasn't exactly afraid of heights, *but let's not get crazy*. The houses and trees whizzed by below. He arched and banked like a bird on the wing. Stranger still, flying came just as naturally to him. He stretched his arms wide and tried a barrel roll—*exhilarating*. Almost better than a breakaway drive down a basketball court. Almost.

Before long, the road led to a stretch of highway more populated and built up. He descended and slowed down to a walk again. Flying was incredible, but he preferred his feet on the ground.

The old movie-theatre that had been there as long as he could remember was a familiar and welcomed sight. Restaurants and stores of all kinds lined both sides of the highway. A bank sign up ahead displayed the time—*10:14 pm. Somehow I managed to go a hundred miles in only ten minutes?* Crossing the bridge over to Seaside Park he watched a seagull dive low over his head. *Was I really going that fast, or was it the odd movement of time again?*

Now that he was here, his mood lightened up. He loved the Jersey Shore. Every square foot of the place held great memories for him, like a time capsule full of comfort. His family had been coming down to the shore since he was a tiny baby and he'd been raised as a true Jersey beach bum. Surfing, sailing, body and skim boarding—he'd done it all. And he certainly was going to miss it all.

He headed for the strip to take a walk on the boards. For mid-June, the boardwalk wasn't very crowded. The rain earlier in the day must have kept some tourists away. At least there were some people here though, even if they were strangers. Already, loneliness was beginning to gnaw a hole in his gut. It was difficult to ignore.

Lost in thought and staring at the ocean, he wasn't paying attention as a young woman walked straight into him. He gasped as their shoulders and arms went right through each other. Suddenly a very warm, but pleasant sensation radiated outward from where they had collided, coursing through his body. As the woman moved past him, he glanced back over his shoulder to see her reaction. She shivered as if she had gotten a chill, exactly as his mother had done.

Noticing the same thing, the man holding hands with her inquired, "Are you getting cold, Hon?" Draping his arm over her shoulder he offered, "Do you want me to go back to the car and get your jacket?"

"No, there's just a little breeze coming off the ocean," the woman replied, while the man rubbed her arm. "I'll be fine."

As Michael continued walking along, it was difficult to stay out of everyone's way. He hated the way others reacted to his touch, so he made a game of darting between bunches of people clustered here and there along the boardwalk.

For a moment, he stopped and stood next to a girl having her picture taken by a friend. He laughed a little, flashing his best smile. *I bet it would really freak this girl out if I showed up in the picture. I wonder what I'd look like if I did?*

Eventually, he came to one of the long piers extending off the boardwalk. Over the years he'd been on every one of the rides hundreds of times. Everything from the Tilt-a-Whirl to the Gravitron, affectionately referred to as the Vomitron. Tonight, children of all ages were enjoying the attractions, and a cacophony of laughter, screams, and squeals filled the night air. The happiness and excitement cheered him up a little. *This place is so full of life.*

He sat on an empty bench off to the side of the carousel, watching the people go by. The carousel started again on its rotation. Spinning around and around. Over and over again, in an endless circle. This reminded him. *Hadn't Father Anthony mentioned the circle of life?* He felt more like the child who's been sent flying off the merry go round before the ride is over.

Roused from his reverie, he saw a short, skinny woman approaching with a stroller. Inside sat a chubby and cute baby boy with curly blond hair. He couldn't have been much more than two and his large, blue eyes darted about taking in every bit of sensory input the boardwalk had to offer.

The woman now pushed the stroller closer to the bench

and Michael locked eyes with the child. For a few seconds, he could've sworn the boy was staring right back at him.

Can he see me?

As the stroller passed in front of him, he leaned forward and made a funny face at the toddler just to see what might happen. Right on cue the baby started to giggle, reaching out to touch Michael's cheek.

Where the tiny fingers trailed over his face, he instantly got a shock of warmth.

I think he really can see me! He was almost sure of it, as the child even craned his head around to peer at him once the stroller had passed. For a few fleeting moments, Michael put his hand on his cheek, comforted that someone had seen him, even if he couldn't understand how it was possible.

For the first time, he took notice of the carousel music. Basketball had been his first love, music his second. As he sat listening, the tune affected his whole spirit. A pleasant energy rippled through him with each sound wave, rejuvenating him and resurrecting some of the joy that had disappeared with his body. *So far, music is the one thing from life I'm able to fully experience and enjoy.*

Unaware that he was being drawn toward it, he reached the side of the carousel as it began to spin again and slowly pick up speed. Taken by a sudden urge to ride, he reached for a horse as it swung by, but the reins slipped through his grasp. The painted horses passed right through him, riders and all, as he stood by, impotent.

He would never ride on the merry go round of life again. His ride had ended all too soon. All he could do was slowly walk away, while the truth spun dizzily behind him. Cleaved from life and thrust into an unfamiliar world, Michael suddenly felt utterly and completely lost.

CHAPTER ELEVEN

TOM

THE MOON WAS high in its nightly traverse across the sky, so it must've been getting on toward the early morning hours. The rides had long since stopped and the amusements, stands and shops had all closed for the night. Michael walked along the beach near the water's edge, with no idea how he had gotten there. He felt so strange, so ethereal. *I'm as irrelevant in this world, as I am invisible.*

Even though he loved the Jersey Shore, tonight it didn't hold the same joy. On a beautiful night, such as this, the windswept beach should've made him feel alive and exhilarated. Instead, he was completely numb. He couldn't feel the sand between his toes, or the waves licking his feet. At least, not completely, not in the physical sense. He had a vague recollection of what that should feel like, and he tried hard to remember, to force himself to feel it. Unfortunately, he failed miserably.

Up ahead, Michael saw two sets of footprints, as yet, undisturbed by the tide. Evidence of a late night stroll by a couple, no doubt, and a painful reminder. *That should've been Melissa and me.* Suddenly, it occurred to him to turn around and check if he could see his own footprints behind him on the beach. Not surprisingly, he discovered the sand untouched. *Not a trace. No evidence I'm even here. I don't exist anymore. I am nothing.*

The moon peeked out from behind the clouds, making the ocean sparkle and dance. But he was too preoccupied to even appreciate the beauty of the moonlight competing with the starlight. Looking out at the vast, dark ocean stretching to the horizon, it no longer seemed majestic. So completely lost and alone, he started to wonder if he would forever be a sad, lonely spirit, wandering aimlessly. A black hole of emptiness grew inside him, threatening to swallow him whole.

For the first time in his life, he questioned if there really was a God. He was mad as hell after his dad died, but he had never doubted the existence of a higher power. *Until now.*

Maybe all he'd ever believed in was a lie, or just a trick of the mind, to give some kind of explanation for life or false hope. *Maybe there really is no God, no heaven, and nowhere to go after death.* Sadness and despair struck him like a rogue wave, sudden and severe. It was as if he were spiraling down, into a deep, dark abyss.

Up ahead in the distance, movement caught his attention. A man stood by the surf, turning in his direction. Much to his surprise, the stranger waved. Michael's phantom heartbeat rocketed as if shot with adrenaline. *He can see me! He can definitely see me!* Michael bounded across the sand, his feet barely touching ground, in a quasi-run-fly pattern. As he drew closer though, he saw the man more clearly now. More precisely, he saw *through* him.

The ghost was somewhat shorter and definitely older, judging by the gray hair around his temples. Michael stopped a few feet from him and any idea of what to say immediately flew out of his head. *What do I say to a fellow ghost? Should I be afraid? Why though, he's a ghost too, right?*

A moment or two passed as they stared at one another, considering each other. Then, exactly as if they were meeting in life, the stranger reached out to shake his hand. Relief washed over him as he took it and, as their palms connected, a slight sensation like static electricity passed between them. *Oh my God, the guy's hand actually feels solid.*

"My name is Tom...Tom Wright," the man said in a welcoming voice.

"I'm Michael Andrews," he replied, so many questions churning in his mind. "You're a ghost too, right?"

"I've been like this a while now," Tom said matter-of-factly. "How about you?"

"Not that long. I died a few days ago." The words came out of his own mouth, but they still sounded so bizarre and unreal.

"How did it happen?" Tom asked in a genuinely interested tone.

Forcing himself to control his emotions he said, "I was on my way to pick up my girlfriend and take her down here. I wasn't drinking, wasn't speeding...wasn't on my cell phone." He shook his head a little and ground his teeth against the bitterness. "All I remember is coming around a bend, and next thing I knew, my steering wheel was where my lungs should've been."

"I'm very sorry to hear that," Tom responded with a visible sincerity on his face.

"So am I," he replied, a faint, ironic smile crossing his lips. Somehow, finally getting to tell his story had a tremendous cleansing affect. "It's hard not to feel regret for everything I've lost, everything I'll never do…everything I ever did wrong."

Tom smiled back in a compassionate way. "I understand, Michael. I think everyone feels like that at first."

Growing curious, he now asked, "How about you?"

"I died on September 11th, 2001," Tom declared.

He accidentally let out a slight gasp. "Oh my God…I'm so sorry."

Michael fell silent for a moment, not knowing what else to say. Eleven years old when the attacks of September 11th occurred, he remembered it well. How could anyone ever forget? The tragic events of that day touched everyone. *I can't believe I'm actually meeting someone who died that day.* He wanted to ask Tom about the exact circumstances of his death, but thought it might be rude. Why would the guy want to dredge up what must certainly be a horrible memory?

Before he even had the chance to ask, Tom offered, "I died of a heart attack."

"What? Oh…I," he stammered, self-conscience that Tom must've read into his silence. "You don't have to—"

"It's okay, I don't mind telling you," Tom said, as he began to walk along next to him. "I had a heart attack that morning," he paused for a moment before continuing, "at 8:00."

Michael inadvertently blurted out, "*What?*" This made no sense at all. Everyone knew the first plane hadn't struck the towers until a little before nine o'clock.

"Yes, I know what you're thinking…but no, I didn't die in the attacks," Tom said, pointedly. "I had a heart attack in my car, right after I arrived in New York that morning. No surprise really. I was a workaholic and an alcoholic."

"Oh…I…I'm sorry," he replied awkwardly, shocked by the man's bluntness.

"Don't be sorry, son. It was my own fault. I worked long hours under pressure, because that's all I enjoyed. My two best friends were Jim Beam and Johnny Walker. Most of the time I had either a beer or a shot glass in my hand. Nothing mattered to me except making money and meeting deadlines." He paused for a second, a look of regret coming across his face. "I never spent enough time at home with my family, never took a vacation. It wasn't that I didn't love them, because I did. It was just that I had my eyes on the prize."

"And what was that?"

"Well, that's just it," Tom replied, peering off into the distance. "The prize was always out of reach. As soon as I made a hundred thousand dollars, I wanted two hundred thousand, after that I had my eye on half a million. Expensive cars, a luxurious house, nothing was ever enough. I always wanted more. What I really had was a terminal case of possession obsession. I would tell myself I was doing it all for my family and to a degree, I think I even meant it. But looking back on it all, I realize it was mostly the thrill of the chase. I was addicted to greed and high on money."

Tom glanced at him for a second, and then continued. "All the while my heart had been a ticking time bomb. You might as well say I killed myself. I was supposed to have a meeting in the south tower at 8:30 that morning and I wanted to make some phone calls beforehand. If I had made it to the meeting, I would've been killed when the first plane hit the World Trade Center. My wife and son would've collected millions like all the other victim's families. As it was, they got nothing. How's that for irony?"

"Didn't they at least collect some money from your life insurance?"

"I guess they would have, if I had ever thought to get a policy. Unfortunately, I was too busy to see to it that they'd be taken care of if anything ever happened to me."

The honesty and candidness of Tom's story impressed him. He had to say something. "I know it's really none of my business, but you shouldn't beat yourself up. There's nothing wrong with wanting to be successful."

Tom's eyes met his with a look of gratitude. "You're right, but at what cost? In order to truly be successful in life, one has to strike a balance. My life simply had no balance and I paid the price for that."

Just then, Michael did the math in his head and his hopes sank. *Oh my God, this man's been stuck since 2001! Will I be stuck for that long, or even longer? At least this guy might be able to answer some of the questions I've had since this whole nightmare began. He must know something about this side.*

"Would you mind if I asked you a few questions?" he inquired hesitantly.

"I had a feeling you might have some," Tom replied. "Ask anything you want and I'll try to answer as best I can."

He hardly knew where to begin. "Let's see…for starters,

what are we…ghosts?"

"There are many names for what we are…spirit, specter, geist, phantom and soul, to name a few. The most important thing you must understand, Michael, is that you are energy. Tell me, did you have Physics in high school?"

"Yes, of course" he replied, thinking it an odd question.

"Then, I'm sure you'll remember one of the most basic laws of Physics is that energy can neither be created nor destroyed. When you were alive, your body was full of electromagnetic energy. Your brain fired electrical impulses across your nervous system every second of your life. Now that you're dead, your body may be gone, but your energy is still here."

He tried to wrap his mind around this concept. "So, all we are is energy?"

"Yes, exactly. Each person's energy is unique and survives the death of their physical body."

"But why don't we just disappear into thin air?"

"Because our energy has a boundary, our aura maintains that boundary. It's the same reason amputees can itch from an appendage they had removed years before. The aura of their limb is still there, and remembers what it was like to have an itch on that extremity. Sometimes the aura of an amputated part of the body even shows up on an x-ray. The medical community simply explains these images away as anomalies. But they're not anomalies."

Somewhere, Michael had heard of this before, but like most people, he'd simply dismissed it as nonsense. *Maybe I'm going to have to be more open-minded from now on.*

"So where are we, a parallel plane or something?"

"No, we exist right where we always did, among the living." Tom said plainly.

He wrinkled his brow as he thought about this. "So, why haven't I seen any other ghosts yet besides you?"

"Oh, eventually you'll run into other spirits," Tom assured him. "But how many do you think are out there?"

Michael shot him an I-don't-have-any-idea look.

In answer to his ignorance, Tom continued, "With all the people that have lived and died on this earth, down through time, not that many, I can tell you that. Nope, I think most souls must move on, but those who don't can hang around for anywhere from a few hours to several centuries."

"Centuries?" he repeated, incredulous and dismayed. *I can not be stuck for that long. Time to ask the most important question.* "So if there aren't many ghosts around, then where did they all go?"

"Do I *look* like I know the answer to that?" Tom asked, pointing at himself mockingly.

"Right." That was a stupid question. "So, why am I stuck here then?"

"I can't tell you that, Michael. From what I've seen, I think people stay bound to earth for various reasons. I believe it's different for everyone." Tom turned to him with a look of sympathy. "You'll have to figure that one out for yourself."

"Great, I had a feeling you might say something like that," he replied, trying hard not to sound ungrateful. He really did appreciate all the answers Tom had given him so far, but it was difficult not to reveal at least some of his disappointment at this last answer. "Well, have you met other ghosts?"

"Yes…some," Tom said. "I'm sure you'll meet others in your travels, too. But I have to warn you," he cautioned, the expression on his face turning serious. "One thing you must understand, Michael, not all souls are good. Some of them are the spirits of people who were evil in life and they remain so in death. Others are dark, damned souls who have turned evil over time. You must be wary of these souls for they can be very dangerous."

Dangerous? What's there to fear if you're already dead? Michael wanted to ask, but he wasn't sure he was going to like the answer. He didn't need any more bad news right now, so he changed the subject. "There's just so much I don't understand yet. Like, for instance, how come I can see and feel my body?"

"You feel solid, because you feel the boundary of your energy, your aura as I mentioned before," Tom explained. "When I touched your hand, I felt it too."

"What about my appearance? I mean, it even looks like I'm wearing clothes. How the hell can that be?"

"Oh, that's only your mind Michael, your memories. You're remembering and projecting what you last looked like before you died. If you tried really hard to remember yourself when you were, say, nine years old and a cub scout, then that's what you and I would see. How old are you anyway?"

"I turned eighteen on March 16th," he said, "and you?"

"Forty-seven. I died a few weeks shy of my birthday."

"So, you mean you're in your late fifties."

"Nope, I mean I'm forty-seven," Tom corrected. "You have to look on the bright side...at least being dead, you never get any older."

At that, Tom grinned a little and so did he. For a moment, he felt the most light hearted he had since his death. Tom seemed like a genuine good soul. Before he knew it, the two of them walked along side by side, talking as if they had been friends all their lives.

"Where are you from?" Michael asked.

"Before I died, I lived in Warren, New Jersey. It was an easy commute into New York City where I worked. My wife and kids still live there. What about you and your family?"

"I live...lived in Branchburg," he corrected himself. *That'll take a while to get used to.* Talking about himself and his life in the past tense still felt awkward as hell. "My mother and brother are there. My father passed away a few years ago."

"I'm very sorry to hear that," Tom said, sympathetic. "I bet you miss him."

"Only every minute," he answered, wanting to change the subject. He had long ago grown tired of people staring at him with pity in their eyes. "Do you mind if I ask you something else?"

"Not at all. I'm sure you have a million questions and very few answers."

That's the understatement of the millennia. "It's probably a silly question..." he began.

Tom put up his hand in disagreement and reassured him, "There are no silly questions."

"Uh, well…this little boy on the boardwalk…it almost seemed like he could see me."

"He probably could," Tom answered flatly.

"*Really*?" he asked, stunned that he'd actually been right.

"Yes, some children can sometimes see spirits. They are so full of energy themselves and their minds are pure. Little children are able to deflect bothersome, mundane sensory input and experience all reality around them. For this reason, they actually use more of their brain function than adults do, and they're more open to their extra sensory perception. As children grow up though, most lose this ability because their minds become too cluttered with everyday life to be able to pay attention to their ESP."

In some strange way, this made sense. "So, adults won't be able to see me?" Michael asked in disappointment, thinking of his family.

"No, you can make the living see you," Tom replied, "but it's difficult and usually takes several attempts before you can get it right. How well you manifest, depends on how much energy you can harness from the atmosphere and other sources around you. Gather only a small amount, and you will appear only as a faint misty shape, or a black shadow." He paused to look at him directly and then added in a discouraging tone, "But I wouldn't recommend manifesting at all."

Michael frowned in confusion. "Why not?"

"Oh, lots of reasons…for instance, you could scare the living to death," Tom replied sternly.

Pressing the issue didn't seem like a good idea at that

moment, but he would definitely have to figure out how to manifest later.

"What about dogs? I think my dog Sam was able to see and hear me. And I passed a strange dog I didn't know and he acted as if he could see me, too."

"In a way, animals are very much like children," Tom replied. "Most of them are pure forms of energy. They're unfettered by the constraints of human disbelief, so they're open to the possibility of the impossible. They rely heavily on their senses, and the ESP they possess is closely related to their natural instinct. They're probably able to sense the disturbance in energy that you create with your presence. So basically, they expect to see you."

Growing really curious about his very knowledgeable friend, Michael came right out and asked, "How do you *know* all this stuff?"

"Oh, I've been around long enough to have figured a few things out, that's all." Tom answered dismissively.

Michael's next thought was lost, for at that moment, rising above the dunes up ahead in the distance, the top of a lighthouse came into view. The conical tower topped by a black light room with its orange brick façade was immediately familiar to him. *But, this can't be the lighthouse I think it is.* The Currituck Beach Lighthouse in the Outerbanks was miles to the south in Corolla, North Carolina.

As if to answer his question, a pair of wild ponies came galloping over the dunes and veered to the right of where they were walking. Michael came to an abrupt halt. The only place he knew of along the East Coast that had a wild horse sanctuary was in North Carolina.

"Wait a minute," he said, finally taking a good look at his surroundings. The beach houses were much larger and more spread out. Even the dunes were different. "Are we in the *Outerbanks*?"

"Yes, that's where I was when I met you," Tom responded.

"Okay, I'm *seriously* confused. How did I get all the way down here, when I was up in New Jersey?"

"You probably didn't realize it," Tom said, "but as you were walking along the beach in New Jersey, you must've been thinking about this place."

"Yeah, I guess I was. My family and I came to the Outerbanks every summer. We would meet my parents' old college friends down here for vacation. The four families would chip in and rent a huge house in Corolla. Before my dad died, there were seventeen of us all together, eight adults and nine kids."

"Wow, that's quite a crowd," Tom commented.

"My parents started coming down here with their college friends right after graduation. As the families expanded down through years, all of us became the best of friends, too. Coming to the Outerbanks was a blast. We had so much fun down here," he recalled, a smile crossing his face. "I couldn't wait to come back every year. It was a family tradition for all of us." He shook his head a little, still very perplexed. "I don't understand, though. How did I get all the way down to the Outerbanks, when I was up in New Jersey?"

"It's simple. You must have been thinking very hard about those fond memories and they brought you here," Tom said.

Michael stared at him, dumbfounded. "I still don't get it. What do you mean my memories brought me here?"

"You memory traveled."

"What the hell is *that*?"

Tom paused, deep in thought. Finally he said, "You know how they say humans only use seventy percent of their mind's capacity?"

"Yeah, I guess I've heard something like that before."

"Well, now you're going to start being able to use all the rest," Tom explained. "Cessation of the mind's everyday activities enables your consciousness to tune in to a channel normally blocked or obscured by all the chatter. Basically, your mind isn't busy running your body anymore, so it can finally do some of the other things it's capable of. Some of it will take a while to learn and get good at, but slowly you'll find you have more and more abilities. Obviously, you didn't know it, but you just had your first experience of memory traveling. Very soon, you'll be better able to control it and use it only when you want to."

"How does it work, exactly?" he asked, still trying to understand.

"You can go anyplace you've been, that you can remember well enough, as long as you think and concentrate on that place hard enough." Tom answered.

Unbelievable. "So, you mean, if I think really hard about my house, I'll travel there?" he asked in amazement.

"Yes," Tom said simply. "You can travel anywhere along your energy trail."

Michael tried to keep up. "What's an energy trail?"

"When you were alive you left traces of your specific energy everywhere you went."

"Like cookie crumbs?"

"Yes, exactly," Tom replied. "The more time you spent in a particular place, the more of your energy you imprinted there. So, your energy trail will be strongest in those places where you spent most of your time. In fact, you can't stay too long in a place where your energy trail is weak, or you'll grow weak, maybe too weak to leave again."

"So, to get from place to place, I have to memory travel?"

"That's one way," Tom said. "But the best way to conserve your energy is to travel as an energy orb."

His eyes went wide. "An *energy orb?*"

"Yes." Tom grinned with amusement. "You become a small ball of concentrated energy."

"Are you *serious?*"

"As a heart attack," Tom replied with a smirk.

"Well, how do I do it? Is it difficult?"

"No, not really, it's actually very natural," Tom said. "All you have to do is imagine yourself getting very, very small and focus all your energy inward. You won't even realize it happens, but you'll become a small ball of light, an orb, or globule, as they're referred to."

Michael recalled a television show he'd seen a few times. "So, on Ghost Hunters, those things they capture on camera are really ghosts, not just dust specks, after all?"

Tom laughed a little. "No, some of them probably are dust specks and bugs, but I can guarantee you some are spirits. It's how most of us prefer to get around. You can get where you're going much faster and it conserves your energy. You can also draft with another spirit if you wish."

Oh my God, I'm such a newb. I know nothing about being a ghost. "How does that work?"

"Drafting is easy. If you wanted to go somewhere along my energy path with me, all you would need to do, is firmly hold on to some part of my aura as I begin to memory travel. Your energy would be temporarily connected with mine, and you would be transported wherever I went."

Michael thought of all the possibilities drafting might offer. Obviously, Tom had learned quite a bit since his death. *If I can visit other places with him and meet other ghosts, maybe I can learn more about this realm of the dead I'm now a part of. Maybe then I can figure out why I'm still here.*

"Drafting doesn't sound half bad," he replied, thinking to himself, *I feel sort of trapped here anyway.*

"Would you like to try it?" Tom asked.

"Sure, why not?" he answered bravely, even though he definitely had some trepidation about drafting. *Finally, I'm getting some answers. Afraid or not, I need to learn as much as possible from this guy.*

"Alright," Tom said. "I'll take you along, but there's one thing you have to remember. Once you get to the destination, since it wasn't along your own energy path, you can't spend too much time there. If you do, you might grow weak, possibly even too weak to leave."

"Okay, I understand. But, where can we go?" he asked, eager now to draft somewhere and try it out. Excitement rattled through him and he placed a hand on his thigh to stop his knee from quivering.

"Well, as a business man I traveled quite a bit while I was

alive. So, I have many places I could show you." Tom paused a moment, rubbing his chin and deliberating. Finally, he said, "I think I know where I'll take you. Here, grab my arm."

Michael obediently reached out and took hold of Tom's arm. Immediately, he wished he hadn't.

CHAPTER TWELVE

PRISONERS

MICHAEL ENJOYED AMUSEMENT park rides, but he never liked the roller coasters with loops. The sensation of going upside down at a hundred miles an hour, everything speeding past you in a nauseating blur, was exactly what drafting felt like—and he hated it. Luckily, drafting only lasted half as long. Within seconds, they were back on terra-firma, but he had no idea where they had landed.

It was twilight, but still bright enough to see the distinctive shape of a massive building. High turrets rose above a tall stone wall, giving the structure a look like some kind of medieval fortress. Every wall was flaked and peeling, as if some festering disease caused it to shed its skin. The entire place was crumbling in ruin and yet, the building still appeared formidable and ominous.

"Where the hell are we?" Michael asked, as he took in his strange surroundings.

"We're just outside Philadelphia, at the former Eastern State Penitentiary," Tom said. "Have you ever heard of it?"

"No, I don't think so."

"It was the first penitentiary ever constructed in the United States."

He gave Tom a funny look. "So, this was an old prison?"

"Not only a prison, but a penitentiary. The Quakers heavily influenced the design of Eastern State. They believed that given enough time in complete isolation and silence, a prisoner could be made penitent or repentant, hence the name."

Gazing around at the present state of the buildings, he inquired, "How old is this place?" *It looks ancient.*

"Eastern State was finished in 1836," Tom began to explain. "The building was made completely out of stone and rock, and designed in the Gothic style, mimicking early churches and cathedrals in Europe."

Michael gazed up at the exterior wall towering above him and swayed, dizzy.

Tom caught his reaction. "The exterior walls are thirty feet high and twelve feet thick at the base. Everything about the place—the iron gates, the long narrow hallways, and the isolation cells was meant to intimidate the prisoners and have them repent from their sinful and disruptive behavior. The penitentiary's frightening appearance also served to remind people on the *outside* of what might happen to them if they broke the law."

"It's definitely creepy. I'll give you that," he commented. "Stephen King would adore this place."

"It may seem hard to believe," Tom said, "but back in the day, this was the largest and most expensive building in America. Now, it's simply eleven acres of dilapidation."

Of all the places he could have brought me, why here? He wondered. "You traveled on business *here*?"

"Once...back in the late eighties. The company I was working for was in discussions with some developers who wanted to buy the land and convert it to a shopping center. They—"

Before Tom could say anything more, a terrifying scream sliced through the darkness enshrouding the property.

Michael whipped his head around toward the sound, his spine prickling with cold. "What the hell was *that?*" he blurted out.

"That…was the sound of hopelessness," Tom replied quietly. "Come with me, there's something I want you to see."

Instantly, Tom orbed. Michael followed the tiny ball of light, flying straight through the outer wall and up to the highest tower directly in the center of the property. The trees below shrunk to the size of matchsticks.

From the catwalk of the circular tower where they now stood, the skyscrapers of Center City Philadelphia glowed, lit up against the black velvet backdrop of the night sky. The tall modern buildings stood in stark contrast to the dark ruins that surrounded him below. He looked down at each of the long cellblocks radiating from the central hub like spokes on a wheel. All of the buildings had fallen into disrepair. Every bit of plaster was crumbling and water stained. Every piece of metal was rusting and corroded. Trees poked through the collapsed roofs in some places and vines crawled up the walls, as if nature were reclaiming the structure, ready to pull it back into the earth.

Michael stared out at the cold, empty darkness surrounding them. Was something there? An icy touch of foreboding crept over him, but he wouldn't dare say anything. *I don't want Tom to think I'm scared. He might not take me anywhere again.*

Tom stretched his arms out wide. "This was the central rotunda. From here, the guards had constant surveillance of the entire prison." He gestured downward. "As you can see, each eight by twelve foot stone cell had no windows. The only lighting was a narrow opening in the ceiling, called the Eye of God. The prisoners were given nothing to do, no work and no reading materials, except for a bible."

Pointing toward one of the cells, Tom said, "You see that small, roofless pen."

He nodded.

"Those were the exercise yards. Prisoners were allowed only one hour a day to roam in that tiny space."

Michael cast an incredulous glance at him. "Man, this place makes Alcatraz look like the Ritz-Carlton."

"You haven't seen anything yet," Tom commented darkly. "Let's go inside."

Reluctantly, Michael followed as Tom descended the stairs, entering the first cell block. A long narrow hallway with an arched ceiling stretched out before them. The stone walls surrounding them were leaking, peeling, chipping and deteriorating, as if they'd finally succumbed to despair. The fetid air was thick, oppressive. Like being in a tomb. A very dark, dank tomb.

At the very end of the long corridor, black shadowy figures stirred restlessly. Their indistinct shapes undulated, as if molten, but they appeared vaguely human.

"Are those other ghosts?" Michael asked, trying to hide the anxious edge to his voice.

With a sorrowful expression on his face, Tom replied, "Yes, they're the souls of people whose misfortune it was to have been locked up in this place at one time."

"Why are they all black?" he asked, apprehensive. "Why don't they manifest completely?"

"Those spirits appear only as dark shadows, because that's how they see themselves, as black and nearly formless." He lowered his voice. "They have forgotten their identity and their very humanity."

This explanation disturbed him a great deal and a chill raced up his arms. But he didn't say anything. Instead, he walked down the hallway, passing the first cell. The doorway to the chamber only came up to the height of his chest.

Standing there completely perplexed, he turned to Tom. "Why is the cell door so damned short?"

"So that the inmate was forced to stoop down in humility, like a penitent man."

Michael opened his mouth, but the sound of laughter and whistling, echoing down the hall, snapped it shut. Shadows danced on the wall as several ghosts hovered closer, drifting in and out of different cells. Some darted about chasing one another; a childish laughter erupted as others played hide and seek.

Struck by the nonstop cacophony of the spirits, he asked, "Why are they making so much noise?"

"Because they weren't allowed to when they were alive. Inmates here were forbidden to communicate with anyone. In fact, they couldn't make any noise at all. If they were caught whistling, singing, or talking, even to themselves, they were either deprived of food and water, or taken to one of the punishment cells."

"*Punishment cells?*" he repeated in disbelief. *As if these weren't punishment enough?*

"Oh, yes." Tom said gravely. "Eastern State had all sorts of creative ways to ensure an inmate's compliance. If you broke the rules, you could be whipped, tied in a straitjacket for hours, or chained outside naked, under a stream of ice-cold water, until parts of you froze. If that didn't convince you, then you'd be put in The Hole."

Michael stared at him in shock. "I'm not sure I want to know, but…what was 'The Hole'?"

"The Hole was a pit that had been dug under Block 14. You would be put in that completely dark, dirt hole for weeks. You had to fight the rats and the bugs for the cup of water and slice of bread you were graciously given each day."

As they turned the corner into another of the cellblocks, Michael silently contemplated the misery and horror these walls must have witnessed. No matter what these men had done, the place seemed unusually cruel and inhuman.

"This is Block Eight." Tom said matter-of-factly, just as the low strains of a waltz filled the hall.

They approached a cell on the left and a man's voice suddenly cried out over the music, "Leave me alone Jimmy!"

Full of curiosity, Michael shot a questioning glance at Tom.

"This is Al Capone's cell. Back in 1929, he spent eight months here on a weapons charge shortly after the St. Valentine's Day Massacre in Chicago. The man he's referring to, James Clark, was one of the victims who got brutally gunned down that day. Since Capone ordered the hit, the story goes that Jimmy started haunting him even before Al was dead. I don't think they get along so well now, either."

Michael peered into the cell and couldn't believe how different it was from all the others. Decorative paintings and fine furniture graced the usually bare walls. A large mahogany desk sat on one side, across from a small bed and nightstand, upon which sat a tiffany lamp. The music seemed to be emanating from a wooden cabinet that housed an old-fashioned radio receiver.

The ghost sitting on the bed surprised him the most. The jet-black hair behind a receding hairline. The round face, puffy lips and bushy eyebrows. Every caricature of a gangster had been modeled after this man's face. The man in the plain white t-shirt and navy pinstripe pants with suspenders was, without a doubt, Al Capone.

At first, Capone didn't see them come in because he was holding his head in his hands. When he did look up, ferocious black eyes pierced Michael with such hatred that for a moment he was stunned. Then the mobster's face softened into that of a broken man.

Tom strode forward with his hand outstretched. "Hi, Al...I'm not sure if you remember me. I'm Tom Wright."

"Sure, sure, I know you." Capone rose from the bed to grasp Tom's hand. "It's been awhile. Where've you been?"

"Oh...around I guess," Tom answered jovially. "I brought a friend to see you."

Throwing his shoulders back, Capone said in a deep

voice, "So, he wants to meet the celebrity prisoner, eh?" He extended his chunky hand. "How ya doin' kid?"

As Michael took the man's hand, a strange sensation roamed into his fingers, somewhat different than the one he'd felt when he'd first shaken hands with Tom. Al Capone's touch was colder, radiating less energy. He had no idea why this handshake should feel so different, but it did.

He was barely recovering from the handshake when Capone asked him, "Do you like the music?"

"Uh…yeah, it's very nice," he replied awkwardly. He wasn't quite sure why, but the famous gangster already intimidated him.

Capone affectionately ran his hand over the fine finish on top of the wood cabinet. "She's a beauty, ain't she?" he said, as he threw him a threatening glance over his shoulder.

Feeling obligated to respond (or undoubtedly face his wrath), Michael swallowed hard and said, "Yes, sir."

Capone sat back down on the bed. "The radio belonged to my grandmother. The warden let me bring it in. He was always real nice to me." Puffing out his chest again he added, "That man had a lot of respect."

Michael had no idea what to say to that, so he looked around, pretending to admire the place. "Is this what your cell…uh room, looked like?"

"Yeah, it's a reproduction, so they can show the people who go on the tours of the penitentiary. I like it here. For the most part, it's peaceful and no one bothers me."

Michael couldn't fathom why this man would say he liked it here, but suddenly a question dawned on him, "Are you saying you're here by choice?"

Capone's eyes grew cold, distant. "Of course, I'm staying here as long as I can."

"I don't understand. Why don't you want to move on?"

"And go to my judgment before I have to, are you *kidding?*" Capone stared at him as if he'd just asked why he didn't want to wear lipstick or a dress. "Do you know all the things I did? Gun smuggling, bootlegging, *murder.* Nah, I'm staying right here until they come for me," he declared, his tone defiant and dangerous. With a hearty laugh the mobster now joked, his voice booming from deep within his wide-barreled chest, "Hell, they'll probably send that bastard Eliot Ness to come and get me!"

Would *anyone come and get him? Or, was* this *already the gangster's punishment?*

"Mr. Capone, can I ask you something else?"

"Sure, kid, what do you wanna know?"

"You were from Chicago weren't you?"

"Actually, I was born in New York, but it's true, Chicago was more of a home to me than anywhere else really. Why do you ask?"

"Because, I don't understand. Why do you stay *here*? Why wouldn't you choose somewhere a little more...*happy*?"

Capone leaned forward and cocked his head to the side, again in a way that came off unmistakably as a threat. "You think I have a choice? I don't have a choice. Even if I did, why would I want to be anywhere else? This was the last place I can remember where I was truly happy because I was still calling the shots," he said gruffly. "I was the big guy, the boss."

Almost as soon as the words came out, confusion blanketed Al Capone's face. He was an old man struggling to find the lost thread in a conversation, his mouth agape searching for words. Finally, after he seemed to forget all about Michael, he turned to Tom. "I like it here. The warden lets me have my cigars and my Templeton rye. He even sneaks a girl or two in for me every now and then. He shows me a lot of respect," he said, sitting upright and squaring his shoulders.

Michael gave Tom an inquiring look. He couldn't help but notice Capone now spoke in the present tense, as if he believed he was still alive.

"The only problem I have is that damned Jimmy," Capone cursed. With a sudden movement, he rose from the bed and shouted angrily, "He won't leave me alone. That bastard won't leave me in peace!"

Tom backed up slightly toward the cell door and whispered to him, "I think we had better go."

Michael couldn't have agreed more.

Pacing around the cell as paranoia overtook him, Capone shook his fist in Tom's direction and blurted out, "You're not a friend of Jimmy's *are* you?"

•   •   •

After they left the cell, Tom explained what had happened to Al Capone. "Once they put him away in Alcatraz for tax evasion, he basically grew more and more confused and disoriented by syphilis. That's probably why this is the last place he remembers."

Continuing down the corridor, they came upon a ghost sitting in a cell all alone. The man appeared to be in his thirties, his clothes torn and faded. The inmate's face was stark and expressionless. Michael took a good long look at his eyes. He'd never seen eyes so totally blank and devoid of emotion. The man barely acknowledged him, and no sound came from his lips. No whistling, no weeping, not even a whisper. It only took a moment to realize why; the man had obviously gone totally crazy.

Almost as if he had read his thoughts, Tom commented, "Most of the inmates here were eventually driven insane by the solitary confinement, not to mention the physical and emotional torture. And if they didn't succumb to insanity, then disease eventually got them."

Up ahead in the darkness, something slithered across the hall. Moving closer to investigate, Michael suddenly stopped short and his chest contracted in horror.

The ghost of a man with swollen, bluish–black limbs was slowly crawling along the narrow corridor towards him.

Appalled by the ghastly sight, Michael pointed with a shaking hand at the poor man near his feet. "Why is that guy on the floor like that, and why are his arms all black and blue?"

"This man is remembering being punished in the Mad Chair," Tom replied in a grim tone.

"The *Mad* Chair?" he repeated in disbelief.

"It was similar to the straitjacket, except this time the inmate was bound to a chair with chains and leather straps so he couldn't move at all. They left you in the Mad Chair for days until your limbs swelled from lack of circulation. Most of the time, you couldn't walk or use your arms properly for weeks afterward."

More ghosts lingered up ahead. The haunting cadence of their cries filled the air. One spirit drifted closer, stopping directly in front of him, his face expressionless. Then, the dead man smiled, revealing horribly stained teeth and a discolored tongue.

The next instant, the ghastly spectre was in his head. Macabre scenes flashed before him like movie clips. Memory and reality folded into one and Michael couldn't decipher one from the other.

He'd been caught again, throwing a note to another inmate over the wall of the exercise yard. They slipped the black hood roughly over his head and dragged him quietly from his cell. *What would it be this time?* He grappled with the mounting fear as his stomach cramped in agony. *The straitjacket, the water cure?*

Thrust into a chair, terror seized his very core. Pain shot through him, as the guards pulled his arms up tight and tied them behind his neck.

"No, no!" He screamed in desperation. "Not the Gag! Please!" Before he could protest any further, a five inch piece of metal was forced into his mouth and over his tongue, and then fastened to his hands by a chain, locking it in place. *I can't move an inch. If I move at all, the gag will go deeper into my mouth.*

Time had passed now. His arms were getting too heavy and they began to slip. The gag thrust deeper into the back of his throat and his mind thundered with panic. *I'm choking! I can't breathe! Someone please help me! Dear God, I can't breathe!* As he struggled for survival, he heard a distant, yet familiar voice. He could swear it sounded like his father's.

"Michael, it's not real," the voice pleaded. "It's only a memory."

Tom now turned on the spirit of the inmate and sternly commanded, "Let go of his mind."

And just like that, Michael was back in the corridor. Slightly disoriented and still terrified, but he was back.

"Michael...can you hear me?" Tom asked, sounding concerned.

He didn't answer him at all. Instead, he flew out of the penitentiary straight through the outside wall. Near the main gates, he stood clenching his fists. Furious as a wet cat, he couldn't control his leg from twitching. He wished he'd never met Tom. Worse yet, the bastard had followed him.

Michael rounded on him angrily. "Well, that was *disturbing.* Why the *hell* did you bring me here?"

Tom sighed heavily. "Like I said, I was here once in life," he answered gently, "but also once in the afterlife. Someone brought me here, to teach me the same lesson I hope I've just taught you."

"And what *exactly* was *that?*" he asked with a caustic tone.

"Some ghosts, such as you, are very aware that they're dead, others are not. They may not realize, or want to accept that they're dead. They may replay or relive the final moments of their lives over and over again."

"Why the *hell* would they want to do *that?*"

"Sometimes they're hoping for a different outcome," Tom answered, "and sometimes they're simply trying to demonstrate their tragedy to others."

In spite of his anger, he asked out of curiosity, "How is that even possible?"

"The dead can show anyone, living or dead, their memories of the past. They can replay like a movie projector—their life, their hardships, even their death. As if reliving it could change anything." He shook his head slightly left and right. "In truth, it changes nothing."

"That's *great*," he fumed, "but I still don't understand why the *hell* you brought me *here!*"

In a patient, fatherly way, Tom put his hand on his shoulder and said, "Son, these men are prisoners of their own making. They punish themselves by not letting go of the past, or the pain. They think only of the suffering they endured here, and they long for a restitution and restoration that will never come. They will not forgive, and they cannot forget. At the same time, they deeply regret the choices they made in life that brought them here. Michael, listen to me carefully, because I *must* tell you this. Enough regret can crush any man, living or *dead*."

Michael simply stared and listened intently to the diatribe from his new friend, the weight of his words pressing down on his soul.

"I wanted to show you this place," Tom continued, "because I think it's important for you to understand the fate of some spirits. When a man loses hope, he loses everything. These men have trapped themselves. Despite what you said before, you are not trapped, not unless you allow yourself to be. On the contrary, as a spirit, you have a freedom most people can only dream of."

Tom extended his arm and reluctantly, Michael once

again drafted with him. Within seconds they arrived back at the beach in North Carolina. It had been a long strange night, but his anger had subsided, somewhat.

The first brilliant sunbeams peeked over the horizon, bathing them in a warm sea of light. Instantly, he felt exhausted, as if he had just walked off the basketball court after playing an incredibly grueling game. He wondered if the reason was the return of the light again, or the traveling, so he asked Tom about this.

"It's probably a little of both, but the light is definitely the biggest reason. You'll always feel less energized in the light."

"Why is that?"

"I can't tell you exactly, but let me explain what I've figured out," Tom said. "You can't tell if a lamp is on in a bright sun-filled room, can you?"

"No," he replied. "I guess not."

"Energy is actually very similar. Think of it this way." Tom knitted his fingers together to form a sphere. "Light is made up of bundles of energy. Too much energy, and a spirit gets lost in it, like a drop of water in a pool. It becomes impossible to separate the drop from the rest of the water. And, it's the same with you. Staying out in so much light makes you work harder to keep your energy defined, so it's exhausting to keep oneself whole. For this reason, you'll come to learn you have the most energy and are strongest at night."

"So...I'll want to rest during the day, but I'll be more energized at night?"

"Yes, exactly."

"Great, so I'm doomed to wander the night like some god-damned *ghoul*," he remarked bitterly.

Tom turned to face him, gazing directly into his eyes with such a piercing look that Michael actually flinched.

"No, don't misunderstand me," Tom said in a very serious tone. "You mustn't think of yourself that way. You are *not* a creature of the night. You are a light in the darkness, which is why you are more well-defined there."

Michael opened his mouth to reply, but before he could say another word, Tom raised a hand in farewell and began to disappear.

"Wait! Where are you *going?*" he shouted in exasperation. "How will I *find* you again?"

"Call me," was Tom's only reply.

CHAPTER THIRTEEN

GRADUATION

AFTER TOM'S ABRUPT departure, Michael had no choice but to memory-travel back home. He considered flying, but he was afraid there might be limits to how far he could travel. So, he closed his eyes, trying to focus. *I have to remember,* he told himself. *Concentrate and remember,* he commanded his mind. Within seconds, he stood on the front porch of his house.

As painful as it was to be there, he simply had no idea where else to go.

The next few days were rough on everyone, including him.

By day, he lay in his bedroom thinking, considering what to do and listening to the endless parade of people still giving their condolences. When no one was visiting, the house was deafeningly quiet. His mother and brother hardly said two words to each other.

By night, he shuffled around the house energized, but with no particular direction to go in. He considered talking to Tom, but he wasn't sure how to find him again, or if he even wanted to. *I can't tell if that guy's gonna lead me out of trouble, or into it.*

On Monday, his brother had to go back to school. Michael needed to get out of the house too, so he followed

Chris onto the bus. Most of the kids stared at his brother in uncomfortable silence, but as Chris took his usual seat, a few of his good friends lightly acknowledged him.

Michael remembered the terrible awkwardness the first day he went back to school after his dad died. The pity in everyone's eyes had been especially hard to deal with. *I don't envy Chris, that's for sure. It's gonna take a helluva lot of bravery to get through today.*

He turned out to be right, but fortunately his brother did manage to survive it.

Every day that week, Michael followed Chris to school. Wandering the halls of his high school, he watched painfully as everyone tried to get on with life.

In the first couple of days, the students and faculty who knew him well were still relatively quiet and somber. As the week went on though, the mood gradually lightened and the school days seemed more normal. He avoided the hallways and classrooms where Melissa would be, but a few times he did see her. She still appeared depressed, but his other friends were starting to laugh again.

This was the hardest part—watching life go on without him. Bipolar emotions threatening to tear him apart, he felt on one hand somewhat relieved, and yet on the other hand, resentful as hell.

The next week, the seniors were all wound up and excited, anticipating graduation. They had all been suffering from senioritis for weeks and now most class work was finally over. Even the lower classmen bounced from class to class, infected with summeritis. *Everyone's having such a good time. I only wish I could say the same.*

An ache, just for normalcy again, echoed in his hollow stomach.

At the end of the school day on Tuesday, the afternoon announcements came over the PA system. "Weather for tomorrow looks fine, so we anticipate having graduation ceremonies on the football field as planned."

He'd completely lost track of time. *Graduation is tomorrow already? Should I go? I don't know if I want to see that or not. Maybe I shouldn't go?* A minute passed while he wrestled with his emotions.

No, he resolved. *My family's gonna be there and I deserve to at least see graduation.*

• • •

Sluggish and melancholy, Michael dragged himself out into the bright sunlight and into the car with his family. A few wispy clouds hung in the sky, the only break from the intolerable light. *Great, it's a beautiful day for graduation. Unless, of course, you're dead.*

Rows and rows of empty folding chairs had been set up on the football field and the stands were full of anxious parents.

Trying to stick to the shadows, he stood below the bleachers and watched in silence as the marching band opened with "Pomp and Circumstance". One by one, the graduates shuffled forward in their black caps and gowns, all smiles.

Just then, that odd sensation assaulted him again, as if pins and needles were poking the back of his neck. *Someone is definitely watching me this time.* He spun around looking in every direction but there were so many people. He searched the sea of faces. About to give up, he spotted a man standing near the end of the bleachers. For a second, the stranger's eyes seemed to connect with his own. *Is it my imagination, or is that guy down there staring at me?*

As he took a few steps towards the man, the band finished playing to a loud roar of applause. Momentarily distracted, he turned to the field. When he looked back again, the man had vanished. *He couldn't have been watching me. It must've been my imagination. But why the hell do I keep getting this feeling?*

He glanced over at his family sitting a few rows up the bleachers with all the other parents and a fresh sadness swept over him. His mother looked exhausted, numb. His brother's face was blank, zoned-out. *Why did they even want to come? I wish they didn't have to suffer through this.*

Next, came all the familiar faces of the students. Spotting John, Craig, and Shawn, he was actually relieved to see them talking and laughing.

He caught sight of Melissa in the crowd. Her face was somber and puffy, as if she'd been crying. *She doesn't really want to be here. Her parents probably forced her.*

Mr. McClure, the principal, now took the stage, adjusted the microphone and addressed the gathering.

"I would like to welcome you all to the 23rd commencement ceremony of Branchburg High School." For a few moments, cheers and clapping filled the air.

Mr. McClure continued, "We ask that you bow your heads for a short prayer and then we will observe a moment of silence for Michael Andrews." Instantly, a hush fell over the crowd of parents, students and faculty.

Wonderful, what a buzz kill, he thought, irritated and embarrassed.

With head bowed and voice solemn, Mr. McClure began, "Dear Lord, bless this day and these graduates, as they turn the page on this chapter of their lives. Guide them as they embark on their new journeys, wherever they may lead. We also pray for Michael Andrews, a wonderful young man, whom we shall all miss dearly. We ask that you grant Michael and his family the peace they deserve."

A minute of silence dragged on forever. Finally, the principal called up the valedictorian, Stephen Cho, to give his speech. It was long-winded and full of the usual cliché, but thankfully Stephen mentioned him only briefly. "Each moment of life should be cherished as a gift and not squandered."

Michael couldn't have agreed more. *He sure as hell nailed it there.*

Finally, the time rolled around that the students had waited for. In alphabetical order they proudly stepped forward onto the stage and accepted their diplomas. About two dozen names in, right after Abers, Allen, and Amin, he heard his name called, "Andrews, Michael."

Simultaneously, his brother Chris rose from his seat and approached the stage, as Mr. McClure announced, "Michael's degree will be accepted posthumously by his brother Christopher." The principal handed the diploma to Chris, who limply shook his hand.

Michael clapped his hands lightly, as if he were watching

a golf tournament. *Oh joy, I earned my high school diploma.*

The principal handed out rest of the diplomas and the marching band played the school song. That was the cue for all the graduates to carefully move their tassels from left to right on their mortar boards. As if it really mattered, for a moment later, the song ended and the hats went straight up into the air, amid shouts and screams. Everyone was moving now, congratulating each other, laughing, and hugging.

A happy moment, unless of course, you're dead.

Families converged on their children now. His mother and brother descended from the bleachers, and quietly left through the adjacent gate. They had no one to greet.

After graduation, Michael lingered around the school parking lot, watching all the kids and their families leave. Groups of families clustered together. Pictures snapped. Laughter and happy conversations wafted on the air around him. Many people mentioned going to parties and celebrations later that night.

Wonderful, I've never felt so left out.

• • •

For the next few hours he wandered aimlessly around the school, thinking about how much he had taken for granted.

Tom's warnings lingered in his mind. *Regret can destroy the soul.*

Nearing the gym, he stumbled upon a makeshift memorial. His basketball jersey was pinned on an easel next to a display board crammed with pictures. Several oversized poster boards were also hanging up for students to write their feelings about their missing classmate. The space was filled. For a long time, he stood there reading what everyone had written about him.

Yeah, this is all very touching, but years from now, will any of them even remember or think of me at all?

Tired of feeling sorry for himself, he glided through the double doors into the gym.

As he walked around the basketball court, a memory tiptoed around the edges of his mind, trying to go unseen. It was too late though, for he'd already caught a glimpse of it.

The memory was from eighth grade, right after a big game. Tucked behind the bleachers, Kathy Mitchell, the cutest cheerleader on the squad, was leaning against the wall and congratulating him. He'd made the winning shot in a crucial game against Hillsborough. She'd never paid too much attention to him before, but tonight was different. His braces had finally come off, his acne had cleared up, and recent growth spurts had already put him at five-eleven. As far as he was concerned, he felt ten feet tall and bullet proof.

On a whim, he put his hand on the wall beside Kathy's head and leaned in close. He wasn't even sure if he liked her and he had never kissed a girl. But, she was flirting like a horny, intoxicated prom date. *What the hell.* With his knee shaking, his heart pounding through his chest, and his stomach performing some really annoying barrel rolls, he planted his lips on hers.

She responded by leaning into him, something he hadn't exactly anticipated, so he was aroused before he knew what hit him. He just went with it though, praying she wouldn't notice. That first real kiss was one of the most incredible moments of his life. One small step for a young man and a giant leap toward manhood.

A few seconds later, the spell was broken and the memory faded, as the door to the gym creaked open. Monty, the old janitor, shuffled in and started sweeping the floor.

Standing at the foul line, Michael ignored him and pretended to make some free-throws, then some lay-ups.

After a few minutes, he turned to the janitor and asked out loud, "Wanna shoot a few?"

Oblivious to his presence, the old man kept pushing his broom.

"Oh well, I guess you're too busy," he said, putting up another perfect shot. He was used to one-sided conversations.

"You know what I liked most about the game?" At least he could act like the janitor heard him. He politely paused before answering, "The finesse, the synergy of the team and the magic you could make with just a round leather ball." Spinning the imaginary orange sphere on his finger, pure enthusiasm for basketball raced through every inch of his ghostly body. "The thrill of making a three-pointer that puts your team up by one and cements a momentum change. The roar in the bleachers as the winning basket falls." Like someone tenderly recalling a lost lover, he said, "God, I loved this game."

All of a sudden, the janitor remarked out loud, "Christ, no wonder they can't save any money around here." Shaking his head back and forth the man grumbled in disgust, "Feels like they still have the damned air conditioner on full blast. It's freezing in here."

For an instant, Michael thought the janitor was speaking

to him, but the man never even looked in his direction. *The old guy must be talking to himself. But...am I somehow making the room feel cold?*

He went back to shooting and dodging imaginary guards while the janitor swept. He recalled the championship win this past year. *That game was the zenith of my career. I can't believe I'll never get to play basketball again.*

Driving backwards to the basket, he pulled up short for a turnaround jumper from almost three-point range. As he did, the loud, familiar squeak of his sneakers ricocheted off the walls of the gym. He froze, just as the spectral sphere left his fingers.

And he wasn't the only one. The janitor stopped suddenly and turned toward the sound, too.

The ghostly ball hissed as it sailed through the air, arcing gracefully toward the net and making that familiar swishing sound as he nailed the bucket. Only, the net didn't move, and the ball disappeared as it dropped through the hoop.

Making the shot didn't surprise him, but the expression on the face of the janitor who was now staring bug-eyed at the basket, sure did.

Could he see the basketball, too?

A split second later, Michael got his answer, as Jake, the other night janitor, walked into the gym.

"Monty, are you done in here yet?" Jake asked, and then paused when he saw the strange look on the old man's face. "What the hell's the matter with you?"

Monty hesitated, and then in an unsure voice said, "Um, nothing...I thought I heard some noises or something. Like someone was in here playing basketball."

So, the old guy obviously couldn't see it, he only heard it. But, how did I even do it?

"You old geezer." Jake snorted. "You really *are* losing your marbles."

Monty made a sour face. "No, I'm *serious*. Don't you sometimes get the feeling there's someone else here with us?"

"*No*, not *really*." Jake gave a little laugh. "Are you trying to tell me that you seriously think this place is *haunted?*"

"I don't know," Monty said slowly, as if trying to decide. "It's just a feeling I get, ever since that kid from the basketball team died."

"Christ, Monty, you sound like a *nut*." Jake laughed loudly, taking the broom from Monty's hand.

Walking toward the double doors, right past Michael, the janitor declared emphatically, "You old *loon*, you know there are no such things as ghosts."

"Yeah, no such thing," Michael parroted behind him, smirking.

CHAPTER FOURTEEN

LESSONS

CURIOSITY ABOUT EVERYTHING that had happened at the gym was killing him. He drifted back and forth, over and over, barely skimming the ground. Only one person might have the answers—*Tom*. After the experience at Eastern State though, did he really want to talk to him again? He deliberated a while and finally shrugged, unable to come up with any better ideas. What choice did he have?

Since he'd met Tom at the beach in North Carolina, it probably was the best place to try to find him again.

It's about time I try that orbing thing, no matter how ridiculous it sounds. If Tom could do it, then he could too. So, he did exactly as Tom had instructed and imagined himself becoming a small ball of light. All those years of learning how to focus his mind because of his ADHD were coming in handy. *I have to concentrate. I'm getting smaller and smaller and smaller... but stronger and stronger and stronger.* All of him now thrummed with an intense energy. Unable to hold it together any longer he zoomed off, a small firecracker exploding through the night air. Within seconds, he stood on the deserted beach in the Outerbanks.

Cool, it worked! I can't believe it! That was so easy, hundreds of miles, just like that!

The moon was high in the night sky, so it must have been shortly after midnight. With no one living or dead anywhere in sight, he spent several minutes pacing around in frustration, trying to decide what Tom had meant by "call me". *Couldn't he have been a little more specific?* The only thing he was sure of was that Tom probably didn't mean on the telephone.

Then an idea occurred to him. *Could it really be that simple? Could it be similar to memory traveling? Maybe that's all I have to do? Concentrate on my memory of Tom and call his name?* Feeling utterly idiotic, he closed his eyes, concentrated hard and called out loudly to the empty air, "Tom Wright?"

"Boo," Tom replied as he materialized right behind him.

"Eek," he responded, acknowledging the joke and feigning fright. And actually, he was a little surprised. He hadn't really expected calling Tom's name to work.

"What's doin'?" Tom asked.

"Nothin' much," he said, trying to be nonchalant, "just chillin'." Desperate for answers, he still didn't want to act like a needy child. Making it sound off the cuff, he asked, "How did you know I called you?"

Tom paused for a few moments and said, "Any earth bound spirit can summon another spirit, by concentrating the same way you did and calling them with your mind. Have you ever heard that sometimes people can sense something has happened to someone they know, like a loved one or a close friend?

"Yeah, I guess I've heard that before."

"That's because energies become familiar with one

another—connected in a way. So, as far as I can tell, now that we've become acquainted, our specific energies are somewhat connected. So when you summon me, my energy will sense the disturbance and orb there automatically."

"Oh, sorry," Michael said, being a bit of a smart-ass. "I didn't catch you in the shower or anything, did I?"

Tom chuckled a little, "No, and if I hadn't wanted to come, all I would have to do was ignore your summons."

"Well...um...thanks for coming," he said, anxious for answers. "I have a bunch of questions about something that happened at my school."

"Go ahead," Tom encouraged and with that, Michael related the events that had taken place at the gym.

When he finished with the whole story he said, "It was cool, but I don't understand how I did it."

Walking alongside him, Tom explained, "You can project any sound you're familiar with, any sound that you remember vividly. Those sounds are strong memories for you, so you're able to project those auditory memories with your mind, the same way you can with your visual memories. Did you ever play the flute?"

Michael puckered his face. *A flute? That's a girl's instrument.* "No, I played the bass guitar since seventh grade."

"Then you would probably be able to project the sounds of a guitar quite well, but not the sound of a flute playing. Does that make sense?"

"I think so."

"You also projected the image of the basketball because it's an object very familiar to you. If you had concentrated even harder, the janitor might have seen it too."

"So, why did the room get cold?" he asked, curious.

"The room got cold because you were inadvertently drawing energy from your surroundings to help you project the memory of the basketball. In your mind, you wanted so badly to see the basketball that you made it happen."

Michael gaped at him. "But how could I do these things without even knowing I was doing them?"

"It's actually quite common to project sounds without realizing. Happens with footsteps all the time. You know what it should sound like to walk on the floor or squeak your sneakers on the court, so you're expecting to hear them," Tom explained. "Remember I told you, you have certain abilities because you're energy. At first, things like this will happen by accident, but soon, you'll learn to control and manipulate the energy around you."

Jolted by reality, Michael remarked out loud, "Christ, I can't believe it. I really *am* a ghost."

Tom suddenly stopped walking and turned to face him. "Why is it so hard to believe you're a ghost? Didn't your parents teach you to have an imagination?"

"Of course they did," he answered, getting defensive. "Harry Potter, Luke Skywalker and Jack Sparrow were all good friends of mine growing up."

Tom grinned at him. "Then why are you so shocked? Didn't you believe in the possibility of an afterlife?"

Michael was thrown by the question. "I guess...no...I don't *know*. I never really gave it much thought. I mean, when my dad died, it was so...final. I knew he was gone. I wanted to believe he went to a better place...heaven, I guess…or…wherever." He stared at the ground uncomfortably for a moment and then looked Tom straight in the eye. "Now I don't know what to believe. Obviously…this *isn't* heaven," he said sarcastically. "So, I have no *choice* but to believe in ghosts now."

"Really though, you must've had some knowledge of ghosts, right?"

Michael pursed his lips tightly in a thin line. "I was a ghost for Halloween when I was eight, does *that* count?"

"Come on," Tom said, with a touch of impatience. "Don't you know anything about ghosts?"

"Well, let's see…I've been on the Haunted Mansion ride at Disney and I saw a few episodes of Ghost Hunters on TV, but that's about it," Michael replied, purposely being facetious. "Oh, and I watched Field of Dreams with my brother once. We both thought it was a pretty good movie."

Sounding a bit annoyed, Tom said, "Seriously now, how about someone you knew, like a relative, or friend who had a paranormal experience?"

"No, not really." He shrugged. "You said yourself, there aren't that many ghosts around. But…then again…" He hesitated, remembering a long forgotten incident from his childhood. "I guess now that you mention it, I did have an experience myself once. But I don't even understand what it was."

"Go on," Tom encouraged. "What happened?"

"I'll tell you," he said, pointing his finger in a pre-emptive reprimand, "but you have to *promise* not to laugh."

"Of course," Tom promised very sincerely, while he made the sign of the cross over his heart.

"Okay," Michael began, "when I was seven, my parents threw me a surprise birthday party. I had no idea they were planning it. When I woke up that morning I came out of my bedroom, went into the hallway, and caught a glimpse of some balloons and streamers downstairs. All of a sudden, I realized they were setting up for my party. I was so surprised and excited that I started to run towards the stairs, but I somehow tripped on the top step. I must've gone tumbling down head first, over and over again.

"My mother and my aunt were standing near the landing, but it all happened too fast for them to react. When I finally stopped at the bottom, I heard my mother say my head had hit every step. But I'll never forget this—I couldn't understand why she was saying that. As far as I knew, someone had carried me down those stairs. Just as I hit the floor, I had the strangest sensation. I can only describe it as feeling like I'd been washed up on shore...except, I was washed back into my own body. Still, I could tell by the look on my mother's face she was scared to death."

"Very interesting," Tom commented. "What happened then?"

"My dad heard the fall from down in the basement and came running upstairs. As he looked me over, everyone kept repeating, "Oh my God, Oh my God. Where's he hurt? Where's he hurt?" But they checked every inch of me and couldn't find a thing wrong. I didn't have so much as a bump or a scratch anywhere. They couldn't believe I wasn't injured."

He continued in earnest, "Even my dad, who was hardly ever an alarmist, said maybe they should take me to the hospital for an x-ray. He was worried I might have a concussion or something. But I knew I wasn't hurt. How could I be? So when I heard him suggest that, I told everybody I wasn't hurt. I remember clearly what I said next. As always, I told them the truth, that someone had carried me down the stairs. In fact, I couldn't understand why they were all so concerned. As far as I knew, I hadn't hit a *single* one of those steps. I felt as if I'd floated down in someone's arms, and it had happened in slow motion, too."

He scanned Tom's face to gauge his reaction. Since Tom didn't laugh or smirk, he continued with his story. "Even though I never saw the person's face, as surely as I knew my own name, I knew I'd been carried down those stairs by someone."

Tom nodded silently and then said, "What did your family say when you told them that?"

Michael laughed. "They looked at me like I was *crazy*, of course. I think they were even more worried about my head than before. But I seemed fine and started running around the house like nothing happened, so they decided to go on with the party."

"Did your family ever say anything more about the incident?"

"Well, later on, I heard my mother mention to my father what I had said about being carried. You know...I got the feeling she believed me, but I was too embarrassed to ever ask her. My dad thought I must've imagined the whole thing or made it up, maybe because I didn't want to have to go to the hospital and miss my party."

"But I didn't imagine it," he said, shaking his head

slightly, "and I didn't make it up. To this day, I can honestly say I don't know what it was, but I know it really happened. In fact, every once in a while I would think about it and wonder who carried me down the steps. Was it a ghost? Was it a miracle? I don't know, you tell *me*."

"I can't answer that one Michael, but I do believe you," Tom said sincerely. "So, you thought perhaps your mother believed you?"

"I think so." He nodded. "My mother knew I'd never lie about anything and she always had an open mind about unusual things. She used to say nothing would surprise her. As far as she was concerned, anyone who believed in God had to believe anything was possible."

"Smart woman, your mother," Tom said, a tiny smile crossing his face.

"Thanks," he replied, touched by the compliment to his mom. *I'm really beginning to like Tom.* He couldn't believe how easily he was opening up to this man, who was nothing more than a friendly stranger, really. The only other person he ever told that story to was Melissa. Maybe it was because Tom was older and, in a way, seemed almost fatherly to him.

Still, he worried about what Tom thought of his crazy-ass tale. *I hope he doesn't think I'm a wacko.*

Unsolicited, Tom replied, "No, I don't think you're a wacko."

Tilting his head, he bugged out his eyes, completely taken by surprise. "*What* did you just say?"

Tom gave a tiny smirk. "I said, I don't think you're a wacko."

His mouth fell open. "Did you just *read* my mind?"

"Yes," Tom answered simply.

Staring slack-jawed at him for a second, Michael couldn't decide how he felt—intrigued or violated. "Have you been doing that the *whole* time?"

"Pretty much."

"So, you've been reading my mind since we *met*?"

"Yup."

Michael thought back to when they first met. And, he did recall a time or two when it seemed as if Tom had known what he was thinking. *Well, that explains a few things.* "Why didn't you tell me?"

"You didn't exactly ask."

"Very funny," he retorted. "You *still* could have told me."

"Technically, Michael, if you remember, I did tell you once that I knew what you were thinking."

He did recall this, but still shot him a disgruntled look anyway. "Can you read the thoughts of the living, too?"

"Of course," Tom said, with a slight shrug of his shoulders.

"How come you can read people's thoughts and I can't?"

"Because I've been practicing longer than you. Like everything else it takes time to perfect the skill. All you have to do is give it a try." Tom glanced up the beach, and pointed to an old man a short distance away, beach-combing with a metal detector. "Let's take this man here for instance. Do you remember what I told you about tuning in to a channel your mind was never able to before?"

He wrinkled his brow. "Yes."

"This is much the same. Try to concentrate on the man's energy, especially around his mind."

Michael had no idea what Tom wanted him to do, but he tried anyway. Finally, after a few minutes, he said in exasperation, "I don't hear anything."

"What are you listening with?"

"My ears!" he snapped back impatiently.

"Then, there's your problem. You don't really have those anymore, now do you? You need to listen with your mind and your soul. Now, *concentrate*," Tom ordered.

Skeptical and annoyed, he tried to focus hard and think. Soon, he did begin to pick up something, a feeling, an emotional vibe.

"The man seems...sad, something about missing someone." He turned to Tom. "That's the impression I get anyway."

"Very good, you're right," Tom agreed. "He's actually thinking about his daughter Trish, who recently moved away to California."

"You really heard *all that?* All I got was a vague feeling of loneliness or...abandonment."

"That's exactly how it'll start, as a series of impressions. You'll be able to sense emotions, especially if they're strong ones. Then the more you practice, the better you'll become at tuning in directly to a person's thoughts. Before long, their thoughts will become as clear as words."

Tom opened his mouth to say something but then closed it in a tight line. He got a peculiar look on his face as if listening to a distant sound. "I've got to go," he said in a hurry, "but practice that while I'm gone." He faded quickly without even waiting for a response.

"Alright," he answered tersely, somewhat agitated by Tom's weird behavior and abrupt departure.

What is the deal *with him?*

. . .

Over the course of the next few days, Michael went to the local Mall and followed around a few living strangers, practicing. Listening in on his mother or brother's thoughts was out of the question; that would've felt too much like intruding.

At first, he was only able to sense vague emotions. Then, finally, after days of practicing, he met with success.

Following a middle-aged woman for over an hour, he was about to give up and try someone else, when the woman got a call on her cell.

The woman listened for a few moments and then exchanged a few heated words with the caller, "I'm not doing it. Take her yourself." With that, she hung up.

As he was walking away, he thought he heard something, a muffled sound coming from far away. First, it came as a whisper and then, grew stronger.

Finally, the woman's thoughts and emotions came through loud and clear. *The nerve of my sister. Why doesn't* she *take Mom to the doctor this time? Mom's probably faking again anyway. Let her cater to that damned hypochondriac. I have better things to do.*

A second later, he knew he was right, because the woman called her husband and repeated exactly those words.

I can't believe I did it. I finally heard the thoughts of a living person!

Elated, he orbed and went directly to the beach at the Outerbanks. As before, he closed his eyes and called out in a loud voice, "Tom Wright."

Appearing on his left side, Tom said loudly in his ear, "Boo."

"Eek," he said with a little smirk at their silly, inside joke. Without hesitating, he launched into the story of his success. "I did it," he said, smiling proudly. "I was able to hear someone's thoughts."

Tom shot him a smile of approval. "That's great, Michael, I'm glad. You're learning."

"Yeah," he said. "Being a ghost is sorta like figuring out how to walk all over again. I feel like such a newb at everything."

Tom laughed. "It's going to take time to adjust." He gave him a reassuring squeeze on the shoulder. "You're doing fine."

"Thanks," he replied, truly grateful for everything his new mentor had taught him so far.

"You're welcome," Tom said. "You listen and you learn fast though, so it's easy to show you things."

Just then, a funny notion ran across his mind. "Hey, do you remember the movie Beetlejuice?"

"I think so. Why?"

"Is there anything like a Handbook for the Recently Deceased?"

"No," Tom answered, sounding slightly amused. "Sorry, no handbook that I know of."

"Damn it," Michael grunted, "I could really use one."

"You're doing just fine without it," Tom commented, his voice trailing off. As if straining to listen to something in the distance, that strange expression flickered on his face again.

This reminded Michael of Sam's behavior. Like all dogs, she would sometimes perk up her ears when she heard a sound or sensed something he hadn't. Tom almost behaved the same way. Tempted to ask Tom about his bizarre behavior, he decided against it. He sensed that this too, was something his friend was being purposefully vague about. Not wanting to push him too hard, he merely said, "Let me guess, you've got to go."

Tom glanced at him with a meaningful look. "Yes, but if you need anything, call me."

As his friend slowly faded, Michael replied, "Don't worry, I will.

CHAPTER FIFTEEN

SARAH

"NOW WHAT DO I do," Michael wondered aloud. *I guess I better keep moving. I should go somewhere. But where?* Not home again…at least, not yet. That had been all too intense and depressing. His family's moping and the dog's constant howling was getting on his nerves.

A little time away from all that might be what he needed to figure this whole thing out. Then an idea came to him. *My meeting Tom was a godsend. If I can find other ghosts to talk to, maybe I can learn even more and find the answers I'm looking for.* After all, his father had always told him— ask the right questions and you'll get the right answers. Questioning other ghosts would be the most logical thing to do and at least taking action, any action, might be a step in the right direction.

He could think of only one place rumored to be haunted by a bunch of ghosts—Cape May, an old shore town he'd visited many times with his family. At the southernmost tip of New Jersey, Cape May was one of the most charming resort cities on the East Coast. The town was home to hundreds of beautifully restored Victorian homes, hotels, and Bed & Breakfasts. And, as he now remembered, supposedly home to a number of restless spirits, as well.

Each time his parents had brought them down to Cape May, he and his brother had gotten a kick out of going on a walking ghost tour around the town. At the time, he hadn't really believed in ghosts, but it'd been fun to hear the many stories of phantoms, specters and supernatural phenomenon. *I sure hope it wasn't all bullshit.*

Closing his eyes and concentrating hard, he orbed, landing on a corner surrounded by Victorian shops. An old-fashioned white horse and buggy came to a stop, only steps from where he now stood on Washington St. An older man and his wife got off, and a young couple climbed aboard for a romantic carriage ride.

Michael joined them to see if he could find some ghosts around town. Careful to leave a little space between his knees and theirs, he sat down in the seat across from them. The way these two were cuggling, they were obviously out on a date. He and Melissa had loved snuggling and cuddling so much they had even coined their own word for it.

A pretty brunette in her early twenties, the woman kind of reminded him a little of Melissa. A twinge of pain flared in his ghostly heart, especially when the guy planted an intimate kiss on the girl's lush red lips.

Feeling a bit awkward and annoyed, Michael said a little too bitterly, "You know? I could've had a dozen beautiful girls like you."

Of course, neither one of them responded. They hadn't heard him. He hated that, but at the same time, he was beginning to get used to it.

If they're going to ignore me, I'm going to ignore them. He turned halfway around in the other direction, not really wanting to watch their tongue-fest anyway.

As the carriage weaved through the lamp-lit streets of pastel-colored, gingerbread-like houses, Michael kept an eye out for any sign of another ghost. After a while, he grew bored and discouraged. *Maybe all those stories of ghosts down here were just made up?*

The carriage now proceeded down the street alongside the ocean and away from the heart of the Victorian district. The driver took a sharp left at the corner where a handsome old restaurant stood. The sign out front read, The Peter Shields Inn. The carriage continued further down the block and he caught sight of an enormous building as it emerged behind the restaurant.

Spread out on his right was the largest and most spectacular Bed & Breakfast he'd seen so far. A bright, colorful painted sign on the lawn read, Angel of the Sea. The driver stopped out in front and began to explain to his passengers a little of the history about the inn.

"The Angel of the Sea consists of two buildings that appear to have been built at an odd angle to each other and almost mirror one another," the driver said. "In reality, the two halves were originally part of one building which was split, allowing for it to be moved to its present location. Upon arrival however, it proved impossible for the construction crew to join the two halves together again. Now, a large walkway separates the two structures and leads to a small garden in between. Each floor of the grand Victorian building has wrap around porches adorned with white lights and ornate scrollwork. The turrets, balconies and Mansard roof are all classic Victorian architecture."

But it wasn't the grandeur of the place that got Michael's attention.

Pointing to a small brass plaque below the large painted sign, the driver said, "The Angel of the Sea is famous for having its own resident ghost. The sign below details how a young girl fell to her death and is believed to still haunt the place."

Michael jumped down from the carriage to read the whole inscription:

In 1965, a young Irish girl by the name of Sarah McConnell died tragically from an accident, while staying here at the Angel of the Sea. She will forever be our 'angel', for her playful spirit walks these halls still.

Interesting. If any place down here had a real chance of being haunted, this was it. *They're practically advertising they have a ghost.*

Movement on one of the floors above drew his attention. Sure enough, as he glanced upward, he saw the ethereal vision of a young woman gliding across one of the topmost balconies. Dressed in a flowing white gown, her thick red hair falling softly onto her shoulders and in waves down her back, she moved like a delicate ballerina. She was about his age and quite attractive, her curvy body evident behind her thin gown. He watched for a moment or two magnetized, as the woman moved gracefully above him. *This has to be the girl who died here.*

She didn't see him gazing up at her, for the girl was too preoccupied playing with the old wooden rocking chairs on the porch. If anyone alive had looked up at that moment, they would've thought only the breeze caused the chairs to rock, but Michael knew better.

Having been skeptical it was even possible to move anything, he watched her, growing more envious by the second. *How does she do that?* Now that he saw her doing it, he was desperate to learn. He'd wanted to ask Tom about this, but hadn't gotten the chance. *Maybe she'll tell me how?*

Before he could call out to her, the girl disappeared into the building through the screen door. Making his way into the bottom floor of the second building, he looked around and listened. Not a single sound. *All the guests must be out or asleep.*

Ascending the stairs, he wanted to see if the girl was still on the second floor. Even though he technically could've floated right up through the floor above, he still preferred to come and go like a living person as much as possible. It felt more normal. Reaching the second floor landing, he halted in his tracks.

Twirling round and round at the far end of the hall, the girl startled when their eyes met. She stared, dumbfounded. Then suddenly, she whirled about and ghosted straight through a door into one of the guestrooms.

"Hey, come back!" he shouted, bolting after her. He stopped in front of the door she had disappeared through. "*Please* come back," he implored her. He paused for a moment, and then more soothingly he said, "Please, I want to talk to you."

At that, her disembodied head slowly peeked back out through the door, and she asked him softly, "Who are you?"

"My name's Michael. I saw you out on the balcony. I just wanted to talk to you."

"Sorry, I didn't mean to act that way," she said, stepping back into the hall. "My name's Sarah. I'm sorry. I wasn't trying to be rude. I'm not used to visitors." Her long eyelashes fluttered shut. "Not visitors who are like me, anyway."

"That's okay, I understand," he reassured her. "Am I the only other ghost you've met?"

"Yes," she said shyly, dropping her gaze to the floor. "I don't like to go very far from the Angel of the Sea. I feel safe here. Mostly, I hang around this place...doing different things."

"Like what?" he asked, trying to be friendly.

"Like annoying the guests," she replied, a devilish little smile crossing her face.

She took a few steps up the hallway and he followed beside her. "Why annoy the guests?"

"Well, at first I did these things because I was angry, now it's just a fun way to pass the time."

As she continued down the hall, she stopped near the door at the end of the corridor. She laid her ghostly hands on the lock and to his amazement he heard a distinct click as she unlocked the door.

He frowned, completely perplexed. "Why did you do that?"

"I don't like locked doors," she stated firmly.

"Why?"

"I just don't like them, that's all!"

He couldn't understand what she was getting so angry about. "But what if those people get robbed while they're gone?"

"I was robbed of my life because this door was locked!" She gestured toward the keyhole. "Okay? Happy? Now you know!"

Michael wished he could take back the question. "Oh…I'm really sorry."

She calmed down and said, "It's okay. It's not your fault."

"Will you tell me about it?" he asked gently.

Her expression softened. "Sure," she replied, as if she didn't mind sharing. "Back in 1965, I was working as a maid for Reverend McIntyre at the nearby Christian Admiral Hotel. The Angel of the Sea was being renovated, so they let us have a room here for very cheap. My shift at the hotel ended and I needed to come back to my room, so I could shower and change for prayer services."

She sighed regretfully before continuing, "But when I got to the Angel, I realized I'd left my keys at work. I wouldn't have had enough time to go back and still make it to church on time, so I decided to try to get in through my window. I thought I would crawl out of that small one." She waved her arm toward the end of the long hallway. "See it?"

"Yes," he replied and nodded to say go on.

"There's a ledge right below it that leads around the back of the building and under my room's window, directly above the walkway between the buildings. I crawled along the ledge, but when I got to my window I'd forgotten there was a screen on it. I tried to pry the screen from the window frame, but it suddenly let go. I fell and landed in the walkway near the back of the building. I don't remember anything until the groundskeeper came along. I must've already been dead for a long while when they found me, because they didn't even try to revive me."

"That's terrible," he said sincerely. He could definitely relate—*accidents suck.* "I really am sorry."

"It's okay, how about you…,"she asked softly, "how did it happen to you?"

He told her all about the car accident and the truck driver. "I died a few weeks ago."

"It's so unfair," she said, looking into his eyes. "Isn't it?"

"Yeah," he replied heavily, "you can say *that* again."

They were both silent for a long moment, as neither one of them knew quite what to say next. *She looks pretty damn good for being a classic. Wow, 1965…she's been stuck even longer than Tom.* If time moved so strangely on this side, did Sarah even know how much time had passed, especially after as many years as she'd been lingering?

"Do you know what year it is?" he asked her delicately, not wanting to upset her again.

She glanced down, as if she couldn't face the truth. "Yes, I know it's been decades. I look over people's shoulders at the newspaper every once in a while to see the date."

Curiosity gnawed at his insides. "So, does it seem to you like it's been a long time?"

"It didn't at first," Sarah replied. "I'm sure you've noticed the difference in the way time moves for us."

He nodded. "Yeah, I've noticed that. I'm sure that must help a *little*," he said, full of hope.

"Well, like I said, at first it didn't seem so long." She paused to draw in a deep phantom breath. "But now…every time I find out the date, then it does seem like an awfully long time, you know?"

MARLO BERLINER

"Yeah, I can understand that." He hesitated. "Sarah, why do you think you didn't go on?"

"I don't know," she answered, her eyes full of pain. "Sometimes I wonder if God thinks I committed suicide. Maybe He doesn't know my death was only an accident."

Michael twisted his face into a frown. "Honestly," he said, "that doesn't make sense to me. Do you really think the big guy wouldn't know the truth?"

Sarah's eyes locked with his, almost pleading. "Then, why didn't I move on?"

He wished he knew the answer so he could take away her sadness. *Eyes so beautiful shouldn't be so sad.* "I don't have any idea," he replied regretfully.

For a moment they simply looked at each other, realizing they were both two lost souls. Then, as if fearful of being overheard, Sarah asked in a whisper, "Michael, do you even still believe in God, or heaven?"

His ghostly breath caught in his throat. That very question was slowly beginning to torment him too. He had to answer her truthfully. "I'm not sure," he confessed, revealing his own doubts. "Right now, I'm questioning *everything* I ever believed in. How could I not?"

"Thanks for being honest with me," Sarah replied in a quiet voice. "These thoughts are difficult to admit to myself, let alone someone else. Sometimes I hate myself for even thinking them." And like a sinner released from a burden of guilt, she began to cry.

Empathy flooded him. Her frustration and confusion mirrored his own. He'd been angry with the man upstairs for taking his dad. That was for sure. Yet, the existence of God

134

wasn't something he *ever* thought he'd question. *But now?*

Instinctively, he put his arm around her and drew her close. *Oh, thank God, she certainly feels solid enough.*

As she cried softly into his shoulder, their energies connected a little. Everywhere their auras touched became slightly warmed. He couldn't believe how good it felt. *Almost better than being alive. Can she feel it too?*

After a few moments Sarah collected herself. "Why do you think you haven't moved on?"

"I honestly have no clue," he said with a heavy sigh.

CHAPTER SIXTEEN

DEMON

SARAH SEEMED GRATEFUL to finally have some company. Even though he'd met Tom, the last few weeks had filled him with loneliness too, so Sarah's friendship was like turning on a light in a dark room. It was bright, extinguished the blackness, and filled him with hope.

The two of them spent the next few days getting to know one another. Sitting on the rockers out on the porch balcony, they talked all about their childhood, their families and their hometown. The conversation came easily, and before long, they were like two old friends catching up.

Michael pointed to a large heart-shaped pendant that hung from her neck. "Do you have any pictures inside that?"

She touched her hand to her neck. "Oh...of course," she replied, slowly opening the locket. "My parents on this side and my little sister on the other."

He stared at the gold heart with the pictures, fascinated that she could conjure the memory of it so vividly. Wondering if the locket would feel solid, he reached out to touch it.

His fingers lightly grazed her chest and she drew in a phantom breath. *Amazing*, he thought, as he held the locket in his hand, *it actually feels solid*. He even closed it on its hinge. Running his thumb over the heart, he asked, "What's this symbol on the front?"

Sarah blinked and finally let out the ghost of a breath she'd been holding. Her hand went not to her locket, but to the spot on her neckline where he had touched her. "Oh," she said, seeming slightly distracted. "It's the Celtic cross...an Irish symbol."

He couldn't help but grin a little at her cute reaction. "So, what part of Ireland are you from?"

"I was born and raised in Mornington, not far from Dublin."

"Is your family still there?"

"I imagine so," she said. "It was only me, my sister, my mother and my grandmother. My father died suddenly when I was fourteen. He passed away within weeks of finding out he had pancreatic cancer."

"I'm really sorry. I know how that feels. I lost my dad suddenly a few years ago."

Her emerald green eyes held him, nearly melting his soul. In a quiet, sympathetic way, she said, "How did *your* father die?"

"That's a great question. I used to think my old man was invincible, you know? Unfortunately, so did my dad. He'd been having some dizziness and shortness of breath, but he wouldn't go to the doctor, even after he had this one really bad episode."

"What happened?" Sarah asked in a soft voice.

"He was coaching my brother's baseball game. All of a sudden, he turned white as a sheet and collapsed on the field. Two of the other coaches had to carry him to the bench. My mom and everyone else at the game begged him to go to the hospital, but he wouldn't go. My dad could be really stubborn when he wanted to be." He shook his head slightly. "For the next few days my mom argued with him about seeing a doctor, but he refused. He kept saying he was fine and told my mother she was making a big deal out of nothing."

He paused for a long moment, eyes pinned to the floor. The memory rattled him, like a tremor in his soul. "I'll never forget the way my mother screamed my name when she found him in the backyard. I had never heard my mom scream like that before. I raced to the back yard and saw my father slumped near the lawn tractor." He clenched his jaw tight, remembering the awful scene and struggling to push it from his mind. "I ran inside and called 911. My mother and I tried CPR but he was already gone," Michael said, his voice dropping low. "They said it was a massive heart attack. I was glad my little brother wasn't home when it happened."

Reaching over, Sarah laid her hand gently on his.

A warm tingling instantly roamed up his arm and settled into his chest.

With understanding in her deep green eyes she said, "I'm really sorry, Michael."

Several hours later, they were still talking. In the past, he'd had his share of heart-to-heart talks with Melissa too, but never like this. Sarah was incredibly interesting and he wanted to know everything about her.

"How come you don't have a strong Irish accent?" he asked her.

"Oh," she said, slipping into a thick Irish brogue, "you

mean, why don't I be sowndin' a wee bit like an Irish brrat?"

He laughed out loud. "Yeah, why don't you sound like that?"

This time, with only a hint of Irish in her voice, she replied with a giggle, "I think it's because I've been listening to Americans for so long." Her mouth spread into an enchanting smile that lit up her whole face.

He looked away, realizing he was staring at her lips.

For a moment, they sat in hushed silence watching the first rays of morning light breaking over the ocean. The hotel was quiet, the guests obviously still asleep. Magic hung in the air and he fell under the spell of the inn, the dazzling sunrise…and Sarah.

Suddenly, she jumped up from the rocker full of energy. "Would you like to have some fun?"

"Hell, yes," sprang to his lips before he even realized he had formed an answer to her question. *What kind of fun can ghosts have?*

• • •

"I think some of them know I'm here," Sarah said playfully, as they walked down the first floor hallway.

"Really?" he asked, his curiosity peaked.

"Yeah, I'm pretty sure at least some of the staff does."

Michael thought of the plaque out front. "How do you know for sure?"

Before Sarah could answer, a stocky Jamaican woman lumbered around the corner carrying a bucket full of cleaning supplies. She pulled a large ring of keys out of her apron pocket, unlocked one of the rooms in the middle of the corridor and went inside.

Sarah motioned for him to follow, walking further down the hall, until she reached the room the maid had entered. Together, they floated into the room unseen and watched as the old black woman stripped the bed linens, leaving them in a pile on the floor.

"Let me demonstrate," she said mischievously. She walked across the room and stood beside the television set. Then, putting her hands together she began to rub them vigorously. After a few moments, she touched the on/off switch on the television, the tips of her fingers disappearing slightly behind the power button. As the television flickered on, the sound slightly startled the old woman, but only briefly.

The maid glanced at the television for a moment and then went right back to changing the bed. With a casual, friendly air she spoke to the empty room in a thick island accent, "No tricks today, Miss Sarah. Ol' Ruby has too much work to do, child. Those people in room eighteen, oh, what a mess they made for ol' Ruby. It's gonna take me hours to get that room cleaned. You go run along now and leave ol' Ruby to do her chores."

Sarah rubbed her hands obediently, touched the television once again and immediately it shut off.

"That's a good girl, Miss Sarah," Ruby said, as she dusted one of the antique bureaus in the room.

Sarah turned to him. "See, I told you some of them know I'm here."

"And they're not afraid?" he asked wide-eyed.

"Most of them aren't," she replied. "Ruby definitely isn't, she's kind of a friend actually. I like her, she's sweet and understanding. I play tricks on her sometimes, but she's a good sport."

"That was *amazing*. How the hell did you ever figure out you could turn on the television?"

"By accident, actually," Sarah explained. "One day, I happened to walk through one of the television sets on the first floor and it suddenly turned on. I knew I must've caused it somehow, because no one else was around. At first, I couldn't get it to happen again, so I started trying different ways to direct my energy. None of them worked, until one day I happened to see one of the guests rubbing their hands together after coming in from the cold. That gave me the idea and it wasn't long before I discovered rubbing my hands together did the trick. Now, I can turn on lights, televisions, radios, just about anything electric. If I concentrate and go slowly, I can even put the volume up and down. That *really* freaks them out."

"I'm *sure*," he said, laughing. The prospect of letting someone know he was there was intriguing as hell. "I want to try it."

"Alright," she said enthusiastically. "I'll show you."

Gliding up to the second floor, they went into another room. A young man and woman lay sleeping on a large four poster bed.

"The first thing I do is pull energy from the room around me," she said. "It's kind of like sucking in air. Just use your mind and think about it, and it'll come naturally. You'll feel it enter and fill your body, as if you're inflating with energy."

He had no idea how to do what she was asking, but he was sure if it worked for her, then he must be able to do it, too. After everything he'd seen, nothing seemed impossible. So he closed his eyes, stretched out his arms and concentrated on pulling energy from his surroundings.

At first, nothing happened. About to give up, he exhaled. But a faint tingle started at his fingertips and shot like lightening to his core. The atmosphere around him now shivered with more sparks, settling upon his skin. As if charged with static, an electrical hum enveloped his entire aura. Slowly absorbing the energy, he let it accumulate for a couple of minutes and then turned to Sarah for guidance.

"Now, rub your hands together and touch the power button," she directed, her beautiful, emerald eyes sparkling with excitement.

Michael rubbed his ghostly hands vigorously for several seconds before letting his fingers penetrate the television. Instantly, it came on with the volume blaring into the quiet.

Completely terrified, the two guests bolted upright in bed, flailing and clawing at the blankets. They exchanged a questioning glance between them and then stared at the TV in bewilderment.

He and Sarah convulsed with laughter as they watched the man hop out of bed in his boxers and scramble over to the television. Sounding disgusted at having been awakened so early the man blurted, "I don't believe the electrical surges in this old place!"

"It's a wonder they don't have a fire," the woman commented groggily, flopping back onto her pillow.

The man paced for a second before going into the bathroom. Through the door he called out, "And why is it so damn cold in here? Did you crank the air conditioning way down?"

Michael laughed hysterically all over again. This was the happiest he'd been since before his death. "What else can you teach me how to do?" he asked excitedly.

"I know how to move things a little," she offered.

"Show me."

Sarah glided down the hall and stopped directly in front of the room she had unlocked before.

"This was my room," she said, drifting through the solid wood door.

He floated close behind her, taking in his surroundings. Larger than the others, this corner room was furnished with antique walnut furniture and adorned in flowery forest green wallpaper.

Sarah walked over and stood in front of a pink fainting couch that lay against one of the walls. A large mirror hung suspended from a nail above the couch.

"It's just mind over matter," she declared, as she placed her ghostly hand on the wooden frame of the mirror. Closing her eyes and pulling energy from around her, ever so slowly, the mirror started to shake on its hook.

His eyes went wide. "That's *fantastic,*" he said with wonder. "You can move anything you want?"

"No, not exactly. I can push objects, but I've never been able to lift anything up. All I can do is slide or slightly jostle things that are easy to move, like the rocking chairs on the porch, or this mirror. I've also figured out I can push doors because they already swing on a hinge. Does that make sense?"

"I guess so," he replied slowly, still a little perplexed. "I don't really care why it works. I just want to be able to do it." Eagerly, he began to harness energy from his surroundings. As before, the charge slowly flowed into him. Minutes later, thrumming with energy, he touched the frame of the mirror. To his amazement and excitement, it lightly wobbled beneath his hand.

"Wow, you're good," she exclaimed, obviously impressed with his success. "It took me a lot more than one try."

Breaking into one of his notoriously charming smiles, he replied, "I have a great teacher."

• • •

Michael got an enormous charge out of being able to affect the living world again, if only in some small way. For the rest of the day, he ran around the Bed & Breakfast practicing his new ghostly skills with Sarah's help.

As they amused themselves by playing tricks on the guests, he told her all about Tom and the experience at Eastern State Penitentiary. He also told her what he had learned about energy paths and drafting along with another spirit.

"That sounds incredible," she concluded, finding it all quite fascinating.

"Then why don't you come with me?" he suggested. "We can go to my hometown and I can show you around."

"Oh...I don't know," she replied hesitantly. "I never really go too far from the Angel." She twisted her knotted fingers nervously. "I...I'm frightened."

"Please trust me," he pleaded, slowly reaching out to her.

Sarah answered him with her trust and cautiously took hold of his hand. Wrapping his arm around her waist, he drew her closer before concentrating on his house on Fieldpoint Drive. Everywhere their auras touched, flared with warmth and tingles. His ghostly breath quickened, and so did hers—*she feels it too.*

A moment later the two of them stood on his driveway. Lights shone from the kitchen and one of the upstairs bedrooms. *They're home.*

Sarah spoke first. "That was *amazing*," she said, awestruck. "You're so lucky you can go home anytime you want."

"Yeah, I guess," he replied sullenly. For some reason, he couldn't bring himself to go inside the house. *What if I see my mom or my brother, and I get emotional or something? I don't want her to see me get upset.*

She must've read his conflicted thoughts, because she suggested, "We can go somewhere else if you want."

He let out a sigh of relief. "You know," he said in his most mischievous voice, "I was thinking I'd like to try the trick with the lights at my school."

She smiled at him. "Sounds like fun."

"Do you want to walk or draft?"

"If it's okay," she answered timidly, "I think I'd rather walk."

"Of course it's okay," he reassured her, as he confidently took her hand in his.

. . .

Standing in the foyer of the high school, they decided to go into the science lab first. Michael gathered some energy, rubbed his hands together and touched the light switch on the wall. Immediately, the incandescent bulbs overhead flickered to life and he flashed a wicked little smirk at Sarah.

Not to be outdone, she walked over to the book shelf along the wall which held a row of textbooks. Concentrating hard and garnering her strength, she gently nudged the book on the end. With a loud crash, several of the volumes smacked the floor.

She glanced over at him for approval and something in him snapped. Suddenly, all he wanted to do was go crazy. Running around wildly, he pushed anything he could off the counters and lab tables. Glass test tubes and vials crashed to the floor, shattering into billions of tiny shards. He knew damn well it was destructive, only he didn't care. *I was good all my life and look where it got me.*

Laughing and joking, they flew from room to room now, knocking down anything that would move, turning lights on and off, and generally wreaking havoc. They didn't do it to be malicious. They were simply doing the only thing they could to have some fun.

Releasing all the frustration of the last few weeks, he let himself get completely out of control. Like a man on a wilding, he was drunk with recklessness.

Sarah was just as bad. With devilish glee, she darted about toppling anything she could to the floor.

He'd never met anyone as energetic as Sarah. Even dead, she was still so full of life. *She must've been an amazing person to be around when she was alive.*

They entered a large classroom at the end of the hall and Michael started playing with the lights, flicking them on and off repeatedly.

Sarah was pushing a pen cup over the edge of a t eacher's desk, when the door suddenly flew open with a loud bang.

Monty, the janitor, walked in just in time to see the cup move the last few inches and hurl itself off the side of the desk. Screaming like a little girl, he spun around and took off out the door.

This, of course, sent them into fits of laughter. They hadn't meant to scare the poor old guy, but it *was* hilarious.

A moment later, Monty returned, pulling Jake by the arm into the room and babbling faster than an auctioneer.

"I'm telling you, the lights came on by themselves and then the pencil holder flew right off the desk!" the old janitor yelled, pointing down at the mess.

Jake looked at the pens scattered on the floor. "So, there must be some kids in the school," he said emphatically. "We'll call the police."

Throwing his arms up in frustration Monty shouted, "I'm telling you there was *nobody* in here!" Then, with a furtive glance around the room, he said more quietly, "Nobody alive anyway."

Jake scowled and shook his head. "You're not going to

start that nonsense again, are you, Monty?" his friend scoffed.

"Look, I saw what I saw," Monty replied indignantly. "And last time, I heard what I heard. No one's ever gonna convince me otherwise!" He stormed out of the classroom with Jake close behind.

Michael and Sarah glided through the door and back out into the hall, while the two janitors continued to argue whether or not to call the cops. *This is hilarious. They have no idea we're only an arm's length away.*

Raising an eyebrow Michael said, "Should we prove it to him?"

"No, we better not." Sarah giggled. "They'd probably both have heart attacks and drop over."

"Yeah, you're right," he said, feigning disappointment with a pout. Putting an arm around his partner in crime, he walked with her down the hall and away from the two screeching janitors. He turned the corner. They were now alone in another wing of the school. Without even thinking about it, he stopped and hugged both arms around her. As they embraced, an almost magnetic force pulled him towards her and a flow of electricity ever-so-slightly passed between them. *Whoa, talk about being attracted to someone.*

Enjoying the warmth of her aura, his eyes locked with hers. *What would it be like to kiss her? Would it feel the same as when I was alive?* Suddenly, he forgot where they were. He forgot they were dead. He forgot about anything other than wanting to kiss a beautiful girl. Slipping his arms down around her waist, he leaned closer.

Sarah's eyelids fluttered shut and her lips parted expectantly.

Just about to press his lips to hers, his gaze strayed to a picture on the bulletin board behind her—the student council photo with Melissa in the very front row.

Staring at those brown eyes he knew so well, he couldn't go through with it. Melissa was watching him cheat. As a wave of guilt washed over him, he pulled away from Sarah so suddenly she seemed almost frightened.

"What is it?" she asked, sounding hurt and confused.

"Nothing…I think I should take you back to the Angel of the Sea," he said, a little more mean than he intended to sound.

Sarah looked crushed and embarrassed. "I guess I am getting a bit tired," she lied.

Carefully avoiding her eyes, he reached out to take her hand.

Limply, she gave it to him.

Closing his eyes, he concentrated hard on his memory of the old Bed & Breakfast and within seconds they stood on the steps of the Angel of the Sea.

There was a moment of silence as she let go.

Finally, he took a step away from her, surprised at how difficult it was to put distance between them. "Thanks for everything," he said, immediately hating how lame it sounded.

"You're welcome." Her words came out hollow and nonchalant. She opened her mouth to say something else, but apparently lost her nerve.

He didn't give her the chance to change her mind. "I'll

see you around," he said, fading out quickly.

The second he left, he had the urge to go back. But he stopped himself. He didn't want to lead her on. As futile as it was, he knew one thing for sure. He couldn't cheat on Melissa.

He was still in love with her.

Damn it, I hate being dead.

. . .

Curious to see if the two janitors had indeed called the cops, Michael returned to his high school.

Sure enough, a black and gray squad car sat parked out front, while two officers scoured the school's perimeter with flashlights.

Smirking, he went inside to find Monty and Jake still bickering about the night's events. *This is better than a comedy routine.* After a while, though, boredom got the best of him.

As he ghosted through the back door, the comforting sound of nearby church bells drifted through the night air. Was it a sign? *No, probably not.* He'd already been in church and prayed. It didn't do any good. *So, why does that music sound so sweet and comforting?*

Walking across the parking lot of the school, that odd, unpleasant feeling came over him again—almost as if someone were watching him. And waiting. He could've sworn whoever it was had to be behind him, but then a figure materialized just a couple feet in front of him.

Whoa!

He took a few quick steps backward, as the ghost's sudden appearance startled him. Somehow, he was sure that had been the stranger's intent.

The man was a little shorter and not much older, maybe in his mid-twenties. With fair skin, jet-black hair and dark brooding eyes, something about the guy instantly put Michael on alert. For some reason, he had the unmistakable feeling of being threatened, especially if he looked directly into the man's eyes. So, he straightened up and squared his shoulders. His knee bounced for a second, but he willed it to stop.

The guy extended his hand up in a greeting gesture. "Hey, my name's Matt."

"I'm Michael," he replied stiffly.

"You used to go to Branchburg high school?"

"I would've graduated this year," he answered awkwardly. "How about you?"

"I was class of '09. I died the summer after graduation in a car wreck," Matt said in a matter of fact way. "Man, I must've drunk at least a gallon of vodka at my friend's party that night." He laughed, but it didn't sound genuine. "I was practically blind when I got in the car," he bragged.

"Oh," Michael replied, slightly pissed. He certainly didn't feel much like making friends; especially, when this guy acted so trite about having caused his own death. For some reason, it seemed like some sort of act. *How can he laugh about it?*

"So, how about you?" Matt pried.

"Uh…yeah…just like you," he replied, "a car accident." He avoided his gaze and glanced down uncomfortably at the ground instead.

A beat passed and then Matt said, "It's a bitch coming back isn't it?"

"Yeah, you could say that," he replied, an edge of bitterness on his tongue. His mood was dark. He was feeling awful about having sent Sarah away.

Out of nowhere, Matt boldly asked, "You didn't get your eternal reward, *did* you?"

"What?" he asked, thrown off guard by this non sequitur.

"I said…you didn't get your reward, did you?" Matt repeated facetiously. "See the tunnel of light, pearly gates and all that?"

"No," he answered, beginning to get angry at the direction of the conversation. "So what?"

"It's all bullshit," Matt said flatly.

He frowned at him, agitated and short on patience. "*What's* all bullshit?"

"Heaven," Matt said, stretching his arms out wide. "You don't see heaven around here anywhere, do you?"

With his mouth clamped shut, he eyed the stranger suspiciously. *I don't know why, but I suddenly feel like I'm being baited.*

Matt moved a little closer. "I can take you to a place that's a lot more fun," he said temptingly. "Wine, women and song all the time, man."

"Oh *yeah*, where's *that* exactly?" He tossed his head back to show his sarcasm.

Matt thrust out his hand for him to draft along. "Follow me and I'll show you."

Already in a foul mood for having hurt Sarah's feelings, Michael had been growing increasingly frustrated with the lack of complete answers from Tom. *Maybe I should try listening to someone else. What have I got to lose?* He reached out for the guy's arm, but at the very last second, some childhood instinct kicked in and he froze. Overcome by a sudden sense of mistrust and foreboding, he could almost hear his mother's words, "never, ever, go with strangers." *Stranger danger.*

"Uhh…no thanks, I think I'll pass," he said, taking a small step backward.

But it was too late. The mysterious stranger grabbed him by the arm, pulling him closer with such strength that he could do little to resist. The second his hands made contact, a sensation shot through his ghostly body as if he'd been tasered. The man's touch hurt like a thousand tiny knives stabbing him all at once. Instantly, his mind became disoriented and his limbs grew weak. As his knees buckled, the man started to bind him, wrapping tendrils of electricity around his arms like an invisible chain.

Michael struggled to free himself but it was no use. *How the hell can I fight what I can't see?* Unable to move, neither fight nor flight was an option at this point. His mind thundered with panic. *Tom, I'm in big trouble here! You've got to help me!*

A nano-second later, Tom manifested and threw the man back with some unseen force that seemed to emanate from his outstretched arms.

Reeling backward, their enemy got off a shot of his own, thrusting forward an invisible surge of energy from his own ghostly hands. Dreadfully accurate, the powerful bolt missed Tom, hitting Michael directly in the chest.

Immediately, a flash of strange and unpleasant energy swallowed his aura. Then, everything went black, as he dissipated into nothing.

CHAPTER SEVENTEEN

MARKED

NEXT THING MICHAEL knew, he was lying on the grass with Tom standing over him as if the whole incident had never happened. Fully regaining consciousness, he was unsteady and shaken. His head pounded with pain, worse than any hangover he'd ever had.

"What's going on? Where've I been?" His own voice sounded distant and oddly unrecognizable. "It felt like I blacked out or something, but that's not possible, is it?"

Tom offered a hand for him to stand. "In a way, it's actually very similar. You lost your consciousness because he disrupted all your energy."

Michael got to his feet. "Alright, I'm confuzzled. How the hell did he do that?"

"Let me put it this way," Tom said, his tone deadly serious. "There's a reason for that old Irish saying, may you be in heaven an hour before the devil knows you're dead."

A tremor of worry moved through him. "What do you mean by that?"

Tom's expression was one of dread and concern. "That being was a demon."

"A shape-shifting demon?"

Tom laughed a little. "You've been reading too many horror novels. It was a demon, plain and simple. Do *not* romanticize them. They're evil energy and they can do a lot more than shape shift," he said gravely. "They don't even need to take a form. They can become the wind, a sound, a voice, almost anything. That's why they're so dangerous and hard to dispel."

"Dispel? Don't you mean destroy?" he asked, hopeful. "Didn't you destroy him?"

"No, Michael. Like us, demons are energy. And as I've told you, energy can neither be created nor destroyed. They're evil energy and so...like us, their energy can be disrupted. Unfortunately, the effect doesn't last forever. He'll reconstitute his energy, regain his strength, and most likely be back to cause more mayhem. And...he'll be back for *you*."

Recalling the awful pain, Michael shot his friend a terrified look. "*Me?* Why?"

A worried expression crossed Tom's face. "Because, I think you've been marked."

"What the hell does *that* mean?"

"It means for some reason, you're an important soul the devil wants very badly. I've heard of this kind of thing before. The devil's assigned this demon to specifically come after you."

"How *special*, so he's like my own *personal* demon?"

"Yes," Tom replied, "I guess you could see it that way."

"Great, I feel so privileged. Death just keeps getting *better* and *better* every minute." He didn't even trying to mask his sarcasm and resentment. "Not only do I have to figure out *why* I'm stuck…now I have to do it before a *demon* catches up with me."

Tom pursed his lips. "Every man must defeat his demons, Michael. Alive or dead, it makes no difference. You see, once he's been sent for you, he'll pursue you relentlessly. He has no choice. Demons are souls that have given themselves over to the devil—they're the devil's mercenaries. The tale I've heard is the more evil work they do, the less tortured they are in hell. It's a heck of an incentive isn't it?"

"Wonderful, so what can I do?" He hoped like hell Tom had a good answer.

"Once, you've been marked, you have to keep moving because they'll be tracking you. If you bounce around, and keep alternating between memory traveling and drafting, that'll make it harder for the demons to trace your movements. Only go back to your trace energy path when you have to."

"But how long can I be away from my energy trail without getting weak?"

"Usually a spirit can last a few weeks off of his main energy path without much effect," Tom explained. "Tell me, did you sense anything different about him?"

His soulless eyes. "Yeah," he replied slowly, "I think I did."

"Have you ever had that feeling before tonight?"

Remembering the last few weeks as a ghost, he said, "Yeah, now that you mention it…a few times, I had almost exactly the same feeling."

"Good," Tom said introspectively, "that means you're already able to sense the presence of an evil entity. It's a start." He hesitated for several moments, deliberating something. Finally he said, "Come with me," and he extended his arm for Michael to draft with him.

Seconds later they stood in the waiting room of what appeared to be a hospital. Michael read the sign on the wall, *Eighth Floor—Psychiatric*. A long reception desk sat next to two large double doors that lead into the ward. A nurse carrying a clipboard walked right past them and swiped an identification card through a device on the wall. With a loud click, one of the doors automatically unlocked and swung inward. The door closed behind her as she proceeded down the hall. They glided after her and went straight through the doors unimpeded.

In the first room on the right, a middle aged woman was lying in bed all alone. Crying softly to herself, she clutched her pillow as if it were a life preserver. In the next room, another woman with bedraggled hair was alternately talking and moaning to herself—the wrenching moans of a person locked in battle with their own mind. In the last room they passed, a man rocked back and forth in a chair facing the wall.

They came to the end of the hall and a second set of double doors led into another part of the ward. These doors were marked *Hospital Staff Only—No Visitors Allowed*. They crossed over to the other side and immediately an uneasiness descended upon Michael like a heavy weight.

"These are the schizophrenics," Tom said.

Great, just what I want to see. As if those people down the hall weren't depressing enough.

Tom put his hand up, indicating Michael should go no further. "We don't want to be seen," he instructed.

"Who would be able to see us?" he wondered aloud.

"I'll show you," Tom said in a hushed tone.

As they peered around the corner and into the room, a disheveled man in his fifties was being strapped to a gurney. Two hospital personnel were struggling to restrain him. Wild eyed and writhing madly, the man spouted a torrent of obscenities and threats. Except, his tirade wasn't directed at the hospital staff but instead, at the third person near him— an entity so foul Michael sensed his presence before they'd even come into to the room.

Whispering very closely in the patient's ear was a demon. This one was hideous and thankfully, so far, oblivious to their presence. Short and somewhat hunched over, he had a distorted, mangled face. *He hardly seems human.*

Unseen by the hospital personnel, the only tangible hint of the demon's presence was the fluorescent light above him, flickering ominously under his power. The staff also couldn't hear him, but the demon was commanding the patient on the gurney to hurt the two orderlies. The demon kept trying to convince the poor man on the bed to strangle them with the straps.

"So, the voices this guy's hearing are *real?*" Michael whispered, casting a furtive glance back over his shoulder.

Absorbed with his devilish task, the demon wasn't yet aware that they were so close by.

"Unfortunately, yes." Tom answered.

"Is that true of all the crazies in *every* psyche ward?"

"No, not exactly. But you know those times, when you hear on CNN of someone who did something unspeakable like go on a killing rampage, and they say the devil made them do it?" Tom paused long enough for him to nod. "Well, keep in mind…they just might be telling the truth."

All at once, as Tom finished speaking, the man on the gurney succumbed to the voices in his head. He lurched forward, pulling hard on the straps and taking the two orderlies off balance. In an instant, he wrapped one of the straps around the neck of the man to his left and pinned the arm of the man on his right. With one arm and seemingly inhuman strength, the schizophrenic tightened the grip, as the panicked orderly started turning purple. The other orderly shouted for help and tried frantically to help his coworker with his only free hand.

"Do *something*!" Michael snapped at his friend, who didn't move.

Sounding all too detached, Tom said, "We can't get involved."

"What do you *mean?*" he shouted, incredulous this time. "You're going to *let* that man *kill* him?"

At that, the demon, who until that moment had been playfully hopping up and down in sheer delight at the chaos he'd managed to cause, discovered their presence. Now, he stopped and rounded on the two of them. Clearly not wanting anyone to interrupt his devilment, he suddenly lunged at them.

Tom stepped in front of Michael and threw the demon back with a beam of pure energy that shot from his open arms. The demon recoiled as if hit by a grenade blast. A split second later, the creature shrunk into a tiny speck of green light and streaked out of the room passed them.

In complete awe, Michael asked, "How did you do that?"

"Practice," Tom said with a broad smile.

CHAPTER EIGHTEEN

PRACTICE

OUTSIDE THE HOSPITAL, Tom led him to one of the empty parking lots adjacent to a sitting area with benches. "One of the first things you have to understand, is there are many demons at work here on earth," he said. "Some demons are stronger than others, but all of them are dangerous. I'll have to teach you how to deal with them for your own protection." He paused, pointing right in Michael's face. "But if I teach you, you'll have to promise me that you will *not* try to use this power all by yourself...at least, not yet. If you encounter a demon, you *must* call on me for help. Don't try to take one on all by yourself. Do you promise?"

"Yes," he replied obediently, but somewhat pissed. *He's treating me like a little child.*

"Alright...using a concentrated energy surge to dispel a demon is a very difficult skill to master and it takes some time to learn how to control it. For a long time, you may be prone to unstable surges of power. The first few times you try to use your energy, it may make you very weak."

"Okay, I understand," he said, impatiently. "So, what do I do?"

"First, you have to project your energy toward the object you want to hit," Tom instructed him. "You must focus all your power, but instead of pushing it inward, like you do when you become an orb, you have to send it surging out of you and converging on a single point. Use your hands to help guide the path of the surge." Backing away from him slightly, Tom said, "Now, give it a try and let's see what happens."

Michael raised his hands and a pathetic first attempt barely rippled through the air.

Still, Tom seemed pleased. "Not too bad."

"Yeah, *right*," he said, slightly discouraged.

"Look," Tom tried to reassure him, "some spirits train for years to be able to control or use this force deliberately." He paused for a minute, thinking. "Okay, this is what I want you to do. Remember in basketball when they taught you to visualize yourself making the shot?"

He nodded.

"It's the same thing in a way," Tom said. "You have to see yourself hitting the target. You have to believe you're powerful, Michael." In a low voice, he murmured to himself, "And believe me, you are. You just don't know it yet. Now try again."

This time, he took a moment to think and concentrate before his attempt. Then, he let it out. Immediately he met with success, as the shot exploded out of him, hitting a nearby bush and setting it afire.

"Whoa, that was great!" Michael exclaimed. *That wasn't really all that difficult.* So, why didn't Tom try to stop that demon right away? Had Tom been afraid or did he really not want to get involved? Would he have let that man die or had he been waiting for the right moment to jump in? Either way, something about the whole incident didn't sit right with him, and he couldn't shake a slight feeling of suspicion.

Tom interrupted his train of thought, "Okay, I believe it's time you learned the ground rules. We need to visit The Elders."

"*The Elders?*" he asked, mocking. "You're *kidding* me, right?"

With a look of annoyance, Tom said, "Young man, you have a lot to learn about respecting those that can help you."

"Sorry," he apologized in a feeble mumble.

"It's okay," Tom responded, with a slight scowl on his face. "Now…we're going to use a ley line to get there. That's the easiest way and we'll expend the least amount of energy."

"What's a ley line?"

"Criss-crossing all over the earth are paths of high magnetic energy which can be used by spirits as virtual highways. They can take you very quickly from one place along the ley line to another."

"So…it's kind of like an astral autobahn?"

"Precisely. A ley line is also the only way for a spirit to cross a large body of water, like an ocean."

This didn't make sense to him. "Why can't a ghost cross an ocean?"

"Because the chemical properties of water can disrupt energy even if you fly over it. Crossing a stream or small lake may not be difficult for a spirit, but crossing an ocean is nearly impossible."

Huh, who knew? "So, how do we travel on a ley line?"

"First, we have to get to the beginning of one," Tom replied. "Here, grab my arm."

Michael complied and in a flash, he and Tom stood at the top of a tall skyscraper overlooking Manhattan.

Michael's jaw dropped open when he recognized where he was. "The Chrysler Building?"

"Don't be so surprised." Tom grinned. "Ley lines are hidden everywhere, in plain sight."

"Amazing," he commented, shaking his head in disbelief.

"We have to be facing Northeast," Tom said, gliding in that direction. Once they got to the edge of the observation deck, Tom stepped out onto the giant metal eagle adorning the corner and turned to look at him. "Can you feel that?"

The air crackled with a certain electricity. Michael sensed the current of energy coursing through him. "Yeah, I think I *can*," he answered excitedly.

"Good." Tom motioned for him to come closer. "Now, close your eyes, jump off with me, and fly," he commanded. "Your mind and the current, will take you where you need to go."

Stepping onto the ledge sixty-one stories in the air, his mind spun in every direction possible. His right knee bounced up and down wildly. This time, he didn't even bother trying to control it. There was no point.

I'm jumping off the Chrysler Building. Dead or alive…this is nuts.

A milli-second later they leaped off the top of the eagle's head and went soaring over the city. This wasn't just flying like a bird—this was the equivalent of being a jet airplane. In a blur, the ocean sped past below. The current of the ley line pulled them with such speed that within minutes they were halfway across the Atlantic. It was a tremendous rush. *This is what driving a racecar at two hundred miles an hour must feel like.* Every part of his ghostly body trembled from the thrill.

Next thing he knew, they had touched down on soft green grass. They were now perched on the ridgeline of a hill overlooking a lush valley. Behind them stood a large stone structure resembling a table set on nine large pillars. It reminded him of a shorter version of Stonehenge.

"Where *are* we?"

"This is Arthur's Stone," Tom said. "We're outside Herefordshire, Wales."

"*Unreal*," Michael declared. Gazing around at the empty countryside, he asked, "So, where do we meet these *Elders?*"

Tom walked to the front of the stone structure and reaching up, touched the enormous, flat capstone. In a low voice, he said slowly, "We humbly call upon the Elders." Then he retreated several steps.

Immediately, a large u-shaped stone table appeared in front of Arthur's Stone. A second later, eleven spirits, six men and five women, manifested right before their eyes. The Elders seated themselves on invisible chairs behind the semi-circle table. Michael was now surrounded by the strangest collection of people he had ever seen.

Tom leaned toward him and whispered, "Speak only when you're spoken to."

Every elder was dressed differently from the others. Michael decided each ghost must be from a different period of time, for each one of them wore the clothes they'd worn in life. He didn't recognize a single one of them, but somehow sensed they were very powerful.

Tom stepped forward and bowed to them as he spoke out loud, "I have brought you a child who needs to hear the Covenant."

He bristled at being called a child, but kept his mouth shut.

Sitting at the center position of the table was a middle-aged man in an Army General's uniform. Sounding stoic and official the General said, "Very well, he may come forward."

Michael had the distinct impression this man must be in charge, but he didn't dare to ask. He simply moved forward in silence and slightly bowed his head as Tom had done.

The General then nodded to the first person on the left side of the table, a woman with long dark hair, wearing a lavender eighteenth century Victorian gown. With a heavy European accent, she began, "All souls who hear the Covenant shall be bound by the Covenant." She paused, fixing her gaze upon him in a very deliberate way. "One—Interfering with the events of the living is strictly forbidden. Spirits have done so before, with disastrous consequences."

The person seated immediately to her left, a red-headed man in faded farmer's overalls, spoke next, "Two—To possess the body of a living person is strictly forbidden. This is done only by evil, angry spirits and demons."

Dressed in an elegant evening gown, a large black woman next to the farmer continued, "Three—It is forbidden to warn the living of impending disaster for this, again, is interfering in human events."

A young man dressed in a World War II uniform spoke up next, "Four—It is forbidden to harm the living in any way. And the strictest penalty shall be imposed if you either intentionally, or unintentionally, cause the death of a living person."

As each of the Elders spoke, Michael attempted to read their minds but found them somehow blocked. No matter how hard he tried, he couldn't read a single one of their thoughts. *I'll have to ask Tom why.*

An old woman in shabby clothes went next. With a British accent, she said in a frail voice, "Five—Revenge on the living is strictly forbidden." This one sounded a bit redundant with number four, but again, Michael said nothing.

A gray-haired man wearing a modern fireman's uniform firmly declared, "Six—Manifesting oneself in front of the living is not forbidden, but is highly frowned upon, for the obvious reason that the living may be frightened to death. This should only be done in extreme circumstances, and if possible, with prior approval."

Michael wondered. *Is there an official form to fill out for that?*

His attention went next to a beautiful woman with a flower in her hair, and dressed in sixties hippie clothes. She spoke in a lilting tone, "Seven—Falling in love with another spirit is strictly forbidden, for binding oneself too firmly to another soul may keep one, or both of the souls bound to earth for longer than they should be. For this reason, *joining* with another soul is also forbidden."

Her eyes locked with his and suddenly heat raced to his cheeks as if he were blushing. If he didn't know better, he could've sworn he was sweating. *Do they already know about Sarah?*

167

A man wearing a gray Civil War uniform said, with a heavy southern drawl, "Eight—Extreme poltergeist-like activity is forbidden, as it may cause emotional or physical harm to the living."

Michael remembered the mayhem he and Sarah had caused at his high school. *Whoops.*

A thirty-something woman wearing a 1920's flapper dress, spoke in a haughty tone, "Nine—You must learn to part with your past life. Many spirits have become addicted to their former lives. They relive and retrace past events they have lived, until they have worn out their energy path and eventually they fade from this existence. God only knows what becomes of them." Immediately, the memory of those poor souls at Eastern State crossed his mind.

The next man to speak was the strangest looking of all. Tattoos of ivy covered one side of his face and spiraled all the way down his neck and onto his chest. The man wore a toga that came up over his other shoulder, revealing the body art. Around his neck, the tattooed man wore a heavy gold chain that dangled a large red jewel in the middle surrounded by sun-like rays. In a deep, gruff voice he said, "Ten—Be wary of demons in all forms, and all other beings who may be in league with the devil. Never, ever, swear allegiance to Lucifer, the Prince of Darkness, for this is unbreakable once it is done."

Michael wasn't quite sure why, but this last message sent shivers through his soul.

Why do I get the feeling I'm not going to like being marked? The sooner I figure out why I'm stuck and can get the hell out of here, the better off I'll be.

As the last one of the Elders finished, Tom bowed to them.

Feeling compelled to do the same, Michael bent over in a bow. He sensed this would wrap up the proceedings, but he'd really wanted to ask them some questions. *These people might have the answers I'm searching for.*

He opened his mouth to speak, but Tom suddenly grabbed hold of his arm. Caught off guard, Michael hesitated. At the very same moment, all of the Elders and the stone table quickly dematerialized.

Realizing he'd lost his chance, he rounded on Tom and demanded, "Don't I get to ask any *questions?*"

Tom looked him straight in the eye and replied in a short tone, "No. You *don't.*"

. . .

"That's not fair," he muttered angrily, as they arrived back at the beach.

Unable to decipher Michael's mumbling, Tom commented, "You teenagers and your mumble-speak. What did you say?"

"I said," he repeated with a lack of patience, "it's not *fair* that I couldn't ask them any questions."

"Michael...some things you can't be told," Tom said with an air of authority. "In death, as in life, some things you have to learn for yourself."

He rolled his eyes impatiently. "Yeah, well, the only thing I've learned so far is death *sucks.*"

Tom turned to him, with a look of annoyance on his face.

"You know, Michael, some people would say you've got *nothing* to complain about."

"*What!*" he blurted out. "How can you *say* that?"

"It's true," Tom said sternly. "Some people would say you lived the best year's of a person's life. You didn't have to work, grow old or experience too many of life's struggles."

Weeks of frustration came pouring out of him now. "But I wanted to, damn it! I wanted to experience all of it! I wanted to go to college and play basketball. I wanted to accomplish something. I'm sure I would've eventually wanted to get married and have kids. Hell, maybe even *grandkids*. This isn't fair. I won't get to do any of it. And worst of all, I still have *no* idea why I'm stuck here or if there's even anywhere to *go!*"

Tom gave no reaction to his tirade except to calmly ask, "What makes you think you're entitled to all the answers?"

This question threw him off balance and he wasn't sure how to respond. After a brief moment, he said roughly, "Well, I'd like a few *more* than I have right *now*, that's for damned sure."

"You should just be grateful I brought you to see the Elders," Tom replied cryptically. "Not all souls get to meet them, and therefore, they have a lot less information than you do right now."

He narrowed his eyes at Tom. "If not everyone gets to meet them, then how did *you* get to see them?"

Tom paused, as if searching for an answer. "I was fortunate enough to have met someone who brought me to see them."

When Tom didn't elaborate, Michael could sense his friend was holding something back, but he decided not to press the issue. "I still don't get it. Who *are* they? Who are the Elders?"

Tom looked away for a moment before answering, "The Elders are spirits who have made it their job to govern the realm of the dead."

"So, they're like the ghost government?"

"I guess you could say that."

"Let me ask you something. How come I couldn't read their minds?" Michael asked, suspicious. "I sure as hell felt like they were reading mine." He didn't like people who kept secrets, especially when they seemed to know all of his.

"They're not the only ones who can do that," Tom replied. "Any spirit can block another from hearing their thoughts if they don't want them to. It's like putting up a brick wall in your mind. It's actually not that difficult once you get the hang of it."

Yeah, I bet, he thought inwardly. *You seem to be pretty good at it too.*

"Well, let's say someone breaks the rules, what happens then? Do they ever punish people?"

"I believe sometimes they do," Tom answered, again without elaborating.

"But, what *exactly* do they do to you?" Michael pressed.

Before Tom could answer, he got that odd look on his face again, as if listening to a sound far away that only he could hear. "I have to go," he declared abruptly, and without another word, became an orb and shot out of sight, into thin air.

Again, his friend had left him with more questions than answers.

What would the punishment be if he broke any of the rules? Would he relive geometry again, burn in hell, or simply be cast into oblivion forever?

CHAPTER NINETEEN

KISS

MICHAEL ORBED AND within minutes he was back in Cape May. He couldn't wait to tell Sarah about all that had happened and all the things he'd learned so far. He also wanted to ask her opinion of Tom's weird behavior at the hospital.

Searching the Angel of the Sea, he found her in the empty dining room. Afternoon tea and cookies had been set out for the guests. She was standing in front of a buffet table set with silver trays filled with desserts, fine china cups and a silver teapot.

He came up from behind and surprised her. "Why do you torture yourself like that?"

She jumped, but as she turned around her expression softened and she smiled.

He smiled back, incredibly relieved that she still seemed happy to see him.

"What do you mean?" she asked with a look of confusion on her face.

He pointed at the table. "Staring at the buffet," he said, "doesn't it drive you nuts? I'm not hungry, but man, I really miss enjoying food." Rubbing his stomach, he added, "What I wouldn't give to have some French fries, a cheeseburger or a milkshake…anything."

"That's ridiculous." She giggled at him. "I wasn't looking at the food. I was admiring the lovely tablecloth." Tenderly she passed her hand over the delicate fabric. "I would have liked to have had a wedding dress with lace like this," she admitted, as the smile faded from her face.

A face that beautiful shouldn't be that regretful. He had never thought about it before, but it occurred to him maybe Sarah had been a virgin when she died. For some reason, this thought both aroused and saddened him at the same time. He took her by the hand. "Take a walk on the beach with me."

With the moon fully risen in the night sky, the ocean sparkled like an ebony field littered with diamonds, as the two souls walked hand in hand across the white sand.

"I'm really sorry I acted that way at the school," he said. "There's no excuse for my behavior, but I would like to explain. When we were standing there in the school, I saw a picture of my old girlfriend hanging on the wall, and…I don't know what happened. I just suddenly felt so damned guilty for being there with you."

In a quiet voice, she asked, "Did you love that girl?"

He needed to be truthful. "I thought so at the time."

"And now?" Her eyes betrayed her hopefulness.

Stepping closer to her, he said, "Things have changed…in more ways than one. I *really* missed you."

"I missed you, too," she said in a whisper. "I was beginning to think you'd forgotten all about me…or maybe moved on."

"I could never forget you, Sarah." He stared at her lips, longing to kiss her.

She met his gaze and a light flickered in her own eyes.

Instinctively, they leaned closer to one another. As the distance between them dwindled, Michael felt that magnetic pull taking over once again. He brushed one hand gently on her cheek, sliding his other arm around her waist. Slowly, he pulled her close.

Everywhere their spirit bodies touched was instantly electrified with an amazing tingling sensation and warmth. He could tell by her reaction she felt it too.

Now for the moment of truth. He let his lips brush lightly against hers. As before, a pleasurable tingling passed between them. Sarah closed her eyes in a silent surrender and he pressed his lips to hers. Hot and intense, the kiss was better than any he'd ever had. For an immeasurable breadth of time he kissed her, savoring the heat, his mouth moving hungrily over hers.

To be warm again, to tingle again, to feel again, these sensations were so familiar, yet already so forgotten.

Unfortunately, moments later, something changed. He wasn't quite sure what was happening, but the boundary between their energies was weakening somehow, slipping. And it scared the shit out of him. *What the hell's going on?*

Entrancing as her lips were, he forced himself to pull out of the embrace. He remembered the warning of the Elders about the *joining*, and now he had some idea of what they might've been referring to.

Michael arched his eyebrow. "Maybe we should take it slow."

"Yes," she agreed, "that was strange."

Damn it, why do I always have to be so damned responsible?

. . .

Time still appeared to be out of whack. After a while, he stopped looking at clocks at all. There was simply no point. Entire days spent with Sarah felt more like hours anyway. The day of the week never mattered much either. One day just rolled effortlessly into the next.

Even though she never said it out loud, he knew he'd rescued Sarah from her loneliness and isolation. Melissa had never needed rescuing. After his father had died, it had been him that needed her. She'd been his savior, his heroine. Now, it was his turn to be the hero and the role was more natural for him and more satisfying. Sarah hit all the right chords of his soul. He thought he'd felt that way about Melissa, but it was nothing compared to how he felt about Sarah.

The two of them passed the time playing tricks on the guests and the staff at the Angel of the Sea, and taking strolls along the beach. Their conversations lasted for hours and he had never wanted to get to know someone so much in his life. Sarah had a sweet, easygoing nature and with each passing day he was more and more drawn to her.

One particular night after taking a walk, they stopped on the beach to star gaze. Lying on the sand, gazing up at the moon playing hide and seek behind fast moving clouds, Sarah rested her head on his shoulder. A silence of contentment stretched between them and his mind began to wander. Almost as if he were asleep and dreaming, he fell into a kind of trance.

Before he even knew what was happening, memories of their past lives flowed between them. Michael saw images of Sarah as a small girl running across the lush green hillsides of Ireland, the dewy grass cool between her toes. It was as if he were experiencing them along with her. Blowing out birthday candles on a cake. Helping her mother plant flowers in the garden. Making a dollhouse with her little sister. Cursing the cancer that took her father. Dancing at a cotillion. Kissing Ethan McDougall behind the school. Singing in the church choir. Embracing her mother before her flight to the States. Climbing out the window and onto the ledge. All the pages of her life opened before him, as if falling from a book.

Sarah watched as thousands of tiny moments flashed in her mind as well. Learning how to ride a bike with his father's strong hands holding on to the back. Placing a kiss on his little brother's forehead the day he was born. Opening presents Christmas morning. Playing in his first basketball game and falling in love with the sport. Tearing up the surf on his brand new board. Restoring the Mustang with his father and brother. Making out with Stephanie Clark. Puking on Tracy Howell's shoes after a chugfest at Craig's birthday party. Hooking up with Stacy Emmons and Lisa Schroeder. Asking Melissa out for the first time. Getting his driver's license. Rolling the windows down and driving the Mustang by himself for the first time. Playing in his last basketball game. Signing his letter of intent to play for Pitt. Kissing Melissa on the porch. Coming around the bend in the road.

Hours later, with dawn approaching, the spell was finally broken. They'd shared the memories held deep within their souls and they knew each other as they never had before. As Michael sat up, he somehow saw Sarah for what seemed like the first time. She'd been a wonderful person; beautiful both inside and out.

He grimaced in embarrassment though, realizing she must've seen *all* of his memories. Clearing his throat, he said, "That was interesting, kind of like a Vulcan mind-meld."

"A *what?*"

"Oh, never mind, I forgot," he chuckled, "you probably never saw Star Trek."

She smiled, instantly filling him with such a warmth and desire he was surprised he didn't spontaneously combust from the force of it.

Leaning over her, he bent his face slowly to hers and kissed her tenderly on the lips. Moving to her ear, his mouth gently nibbled at her softness. Everywhere they touched seared with heat and electricity. As his lips skimmed her neck, his free hand crept downward caressing the curve of her breast. To his delight, her back arched and her ghostly form rose up against his hand. Again, some kind of electro-magnetic pull took hold and he had no choice but to lean his body fully into hers. Instantly, his mouth was on hers again, his tongue probing and discovering her.

Within minutes though, he could feel their energies slipping together again. *Damn it.*

Pulling himself away took nearly every ounce of his strength.

Sarah tried to yank him back. "What's the matter?" she asked, as she sat up beside him.

He dragged a hand through his hair and steadied himself, regaining his composure. "You have no idea how hard it is to control myself around you."

"I think I know what you mean," she said softly. "I feel it too."

He stroked her cheek. "Sarah, I don't know what'll happen if we go too far," he said with concern. "I wouldn't want to do anything that might hurt you."

She clasped his hand and said warmly, "Then like you said before, let's just take things slowly."

Lying back down on the sand beside her, his eyes roamed the thousands of twinkling stars above. After a minute or two, he remarked out loud, "Now I think I understand why this is against the rules."

In response, she gave him a puzzled look and waited for him to explain.

"All the fun things always are," he concluded with a heavy sigh.

· · ·

Light was breaking on the horizon, the sky taking on a perfect amber glow. Along with it, came the drain on his energy.

"We better start heading back," he said, taking Sarah's hand and gently lifting her off the sand.

Walking slowly along the water's edge, the gabled roof of The Angel of the Sea came into view in the distance. The tall circular turrets rose high above the other buildings on the street. Michael didn't want to rush back. Part of him still wished they could stay out in the sunlight, but if they did, the price would be complete exhaustion.

They had barely reached the sidewalk, when a chilly wind blew against the back of his neck. For a second he thought, *must be the ocean breeze.* Then, a shiver prickled up his spine and a niggling sense of dread made him realize—*I shouldn't have felt that.* He spun around.

About five hundred feet away on the beach, Matt's dark and soulless eyes stared back, two narrow slits. He'd changed since the last time Michael had encountered him. His skin, pulled tight over hollow cheekbones, was turning gray. His teeth had yellowed and his bony hands now ended in fingernails as long as claws.

Michael stepped in front of Sarah, pushing her behind him. "*This* guy again?" he said testily. "Does he just *enjoy* sneaking up on people?"

Matt stood in front of a thick swarm of black shadows massing on the beach. The distinctive shadowy shapes, a tangle of torsos, arms, and legs were human—*they were once human.* A horrible buzzing and whispering, like a thousand tormented voices, emanated from the dark curtain of demons, as they followed close behind Matt.

Is he leading them?

As if to answer his question, Matt and the demons edged towards them.

Michael quickly tilted his head toward Sarah and urgently whispered under his breath, "I want you to get out of here…*now.* We'll go in different directions and meet back at

The Angel." He squeezed her hand and with his mind said, *it'll be okay.*

Her face full of worry, she reluctantly obeyed. Instantly, she orbed, becoming a tiny ball of white light. She darted off to the west, away from The Angel of the Sea.

Matt tracked her with his gaze, but thankfully, he made no move to pursue her.

Michael's thoughts clicked into place. *So it is me he wants.* Pivoting on his heel, he faced the approaching demons. "Matt, *buddy*...you don't look so good."

No direct response, but even from this distance, he could feel the anger, regret, and pain rolling off Matt in waves.

Tensing his leg so it wouldn't tremble, he tried one last time to get him to talk. "What the hell is your problem anyway?"

Still no answer. Matt and the demon horde continued inching closer. The cold, sickening feeling in Michael's stomach grew more intense. They would attack at any moment.

His promise to Tom about not engaging demons in a fight echoed in his head. That left only one other option. "Well, it's been nice chatting with you," he said, backing up slowly, "but I've gotta go."

There was no time to think. He leaped into the air, flying swiftly toward the Victorian District, away from the direction Sarah had taken.

He glanced back over his shoulder.

Matt bore down on him, an evil hatred etched on his face, with the black mass of demons writhing and twisting behind him.

Damn it, this isn't going to be so easy.

In an effort to evade them, he flew zigzag through the streets, but it was no use. They were close behind and gaining.

Michael soared higher trying to shake them, but each time he looked back they were closer still. The cold radiating off them began to burn his skin with snakelike tongues of frost-fire. His eyes searched the ground below for something...anything...

The large white church. Its high steeple loomed a short distance up ahead. Maybe if he could get inside...

His movement had to be quick to catch them off guard. *I need a play fake.*

Suddenly, he plummeted, diving hard right and then, swiftly banking left—straight into the stained glass arch on the side of the church.

Through the window he could just make out the dark shapes on the other side. It worked. For whatever reason, the demons had hesitated.

Now was his chance.

He zoomed out the back of the church at top speed and into a row of shops. Tearing through every one of them as if they had no walls, he came out the other side. Once more zigzagging through the streets, he only hoped they couldn't sense his location, the way he could sense theirs.

Finally, he stopped at the corner near the Angel of the Sea and scanned the area. No Matt or black shadows in sight. He didn't sense their evil presence either. He'd lost them. Still, he made a few more sweeping passes around the block before going inside to find Sarah.

Huddled in the attic between some dusty, old furniture, she leapt to her feet the minute she saw him.

"Thank God!" she exclaimed in relief. "I was so *worried* about you."

He took her in his arms and held her close. "I'm fine. Are *you* okay?"

"Yes, of course," she replied, though her voice cracked a little. "Why didn't you orb and get out of there right away, too?"

"Because," he said firmly, "I had to make sure they didn't follow *you*."

Anxiety and fear drew across her face. "Do you think they could track us to the Angel?"

This thought had crossed his mind, too. A tremor of worry and uneasiness rattled through him. He gave her his honest answer.

"Let's hope not."

CHAPTER TWENTY

ALIEN

ENORMOUS WAVES PUMMELED the beach, driven by a storm off shore. It was time to tell Tom about Sarah. Standing on the beach in the Outerbanks, he summoned his friend as usual.

Tom materialized a few paces away. "Boo," he called out.

"Eek," Michael replied with a grin.

Tom came closer and smiled affably. "What's new?"

This was his chance. He spilled his guts about Sarah as his friend listened carefully.

When he was finished, Tom gave him a distressed look, cautioning him, "I can tell you really care for Sarah, but be careful, Michael. I'm surprised you haven't been summoned before the Elders already."

"I had a feeling you were going to say that." For a moment, he considered asking Tom about the joining, but changed his mind. *That would be way too embarrassing.* He also debated telling Tom about being chased by Matt and the demons, but decided against that, too. He didn't need to hear about how much danger he was in—he already knew *that*.

"I'd hate to see you get side-tracked by Sarah," Tom said significantly.

Putting his hand up, he said, "Spare me the lecture, okay. I won't let my feelings for Sarah keep me here."

Tom gave him a look that said I've-heard-that-one-before, but evidently seeing it was hopeless, dropped the subject. "You said you wanted to ask more questions. Well, I have someone I want you to meet today," he said, extending his arm for Michael to draft with him. "We're going to New York City. He likes to spend his evenings in Central Park, says it reminds him a bit of home."

Curious, he touched Tom's arm and within seconds they had landed next to Cleopatra's Needle in Central Park. Michael recognized the icon immediately. His father had told him all about the needle-shaped stone, an actual ancient Egyptian obelisk made of red granite. The statue was donated to New York by the Khedive of Egypt and erected in 1881. He'd always thought it was one of the coolest monuments in the park.

Tom pointed to a bench about fifty feet away.

He gasped, his jaw dropping wide open. *You've got to be kidding me.*

Sitting on the bench, was the unmistakable ghost of someone definitely *not* of this earth. Blinking in disbelief, Michael turned to Tom. "Is that an *alien*?"

Tom merely smiled, looking all too happy that he had succeeded in shocking him.

They approached the ghost and now he got a better look at him. The bizarre creature was similar to every sketch he'd ever seen of an alien. It had an oversized head with two very large, protruding black eyes that reminded him of the almond shaped eyes of oriental people. Medium gray in color, its skin was smooth and hairless. The being wasn't wearing any clothes and it appeared to have no genitalia at all, so he couldn't for the life of him tell whether it was male or female. Since the creature was sitting down, judging its height was difficult, but he guessed the alien was only a little more than four feet tall.

Tom walked over and introduced them. "Michael, I'd like you to meet my friend Joe."

ET…he brought me to meet the freakin' ghost of ET!

Joe extended a four fingered tentacle and he cautiously accepted the greeting. Nervously releasing the strange appendage, he took a small step backward.

A thrill of excitement danced up his spine and he started rattling off questions. "So, you died here on earth? Were you on a mission or something?"

"Yes, I'm sort of what you would call an astronaut," Joe answered dryly. "I was here to run some tests and bring back samples of soil and plant life to the leaders on my planet."

"Why don't you go back?"

"I would *love* to go back," the alien said, "but I can't. It's too far for me to memory travel because my energy can't reach home. You just don't leave a solid enough energy trail when you travel through the vacuum of space. The imprint of your energy only works on, or near a magnetosphere, like Earth."

Un-befreakin-lievable. I'm having a conversation with a dead extra-terrestrial. "Where are you from anyway?"

"Our planet is called, Donyeh, which means beautiful home in our language. Your people have discovered it, but I hear they've named it *55 Cancri*," the alien said with derision. He sat up a bit straighter and added, "Our planet is forty-one light years from Earth and the fifth from our sun star, which is a little *larger* than yours."

"Forty-one light years away?" Michael parroted. "That's pretty damn far to have traveled, isn't it?"

"Not really," the alien said smugly. "We've learned how to travel on gravity waves."

Michael stared at him blankly.

The alien slapped a tentacle against his forehead, clearly irritated by his human ignorance. "Gravity waves are distortions in the space-time continuum," he said, sounding self-important. "The waves travel at the speed of light, so we get here pretty quickly. But…it's a bitch slowing down, if you don't nail your re-entry just right."

"Sorry about that."

"Oh, it's okay," the strange alien said. "At least my death had meaning."

Michael pinched his eyebrows together. "How so? It's not like you finished your mission, so how could your death have any meaning *at all?*"

A tiny smile played at the corners of the creature's mouth. "I died," Joe said, "so no one else from my planet would have to."

"What do you mean?"

"Well, I'm sure my people investigated the cause of my crash and were able to improve the safety of travel to this planet and others. So, my death probably prevented more of our explorers from dying. After all," Joe said, gesticulating with his tentacle, "there doesn't seem to have been many more crashes since then, so the new visitors have had more success than I. It's at least a positive way of looking at my death."

A pang of regret hit Michael deep in the gut. He only wished his *own* death had some sort of meaning. "I guess you have a point," he conceded to the small gray being with the big head.

While he was mulling over what the alien had said, a young boy raced between them, yanking on a string held high in the air. Overhead, a rocket-shaped box kite trailed behind him.

Wait, am I being punked? Aliens, space travel...it's all real? He couldn't believe what he was hearing. Genuinely interested, so many questions now raced around his mind. "What's it like on your planet?"

Joe closed his black, bulbous eyes as if to picture it in his mind, and then drew in a ragged breath before answering. "It's beautiful. We have dense forests and lush valleys, a lovely purple sky, and our planet is mostly ocean covered like Earth. Actually, it's very similar to this planet, except," and he paused for dramatic effect, "without all the pollution and garbage."

Michael took the rude dig in stride, instead asking a question he'd always wondered about. "Do you guys leave those crop circles?"

"Yes," Joe answered curtly, "we do."

"Why? Is it a way to let us know you were here?"

The strange little alien shook his head. "No, they're a way of leaving important information for the next landing party. The magnetic imprint we leave can last for centuries. And by the way, your government already knows we've been here."

188

"Really?" he asked. "Are you sure?"

"Absolutely. We've been visiting for thousands of years, in fact. Many of your ancient cultures left behind evidence of those first few visits, like the drawings of the Aztecs, and the Nazca lines. Their early knowledge of astronomy, math, and science came directly from those first visitors. We only visited a few times then, but now we come a little more frequently. Your government hides the evidence every time one of our ships is seen or crashes here, like mine did."

"So, that's how you died?"

"Yes," the alien replied. "It's still not a very easy trip to make and I had a serious equipment malfunction on my ship. I crashed in Kecksburg, Pennsylvania back in 1965. My body and my ship were taken in a large Army truck to a secret railway beneath a hotel in New York, and from there I was transported to Washington, D.C. My remains are still in part of an underground bunker right below The Library of Congress."

This is unbelievable. He'd never really taken the possibility of little green men from outer space very seriously. *And yet, here I am...talking to an alien.* Curious as hell, he had so many questions he didn't know where to begin. "If our government knows all about you, and you're not dangerous, then why don't they just tell us?"

"I guess they think your world would be better off not knowing life exists on other planets. Besides, it would probably complicate an already out of control situation."

Michael didn't quite know what the alien meant by that comment. "Why don't *you* let us know you're here?"

The alien gave him the strangest of looks. "Because we're *afraid* of your people, that's why."

"Why are you afraid of *us*? Is it because we look different from you?"

"No," the alien laughed, "your appearance we can handle. It's your violent way of life that we fear."

"What the hell do you mean by *that?"* he demanded. "We're not *violent* people!"

"Oh, no?" The alien questioned sarcastically. "Come on human, wake up and smell the Starbucks. You humans are the most violent beings in all the known galaxies. You rape, torture, and kill each other, practically for sport. You wage war on each other with all manner of guns, bombs, and machines. You let most of your kind starve, while the rest of you consume everything at an insatiable rate. You pollute your planet and destroy your natural resources." He chuckled to himself. "Hell, you've even been known to *eat* each other."

"A few cannibals do *not* represent the whole human race!" Michael shot back, indignant and angry.

"Maybe so," said the alien, "but in my world, great debates rage over whether or not to invade your planet and put an end to all of your evils. Others stress the danger of interfering with such a violent and dangerous people. Still others argue that to let it continue unabated, might cause this wickedness to spread across this galaxy and then, the entire universe. Therefore, some of my people say you must be stopped."

Boy, this guy's miserable. Thank God he doesn't have a blog. "So, you judgmental assholes know everything about us and we're just no damn good, is that it?" He couldn't help it, he was really pissed off now.

The alien shook his head vigorously in disagreement. "Make no mistake," he said plainly, "we Hygons have watched closely as the events of human history have unfolded. We've taken note of the few times humankind has shown promise or hope, like putting down Hitler or Saddam. But it isn't enough. Every time humans seem to take the right course, it isn't long before you slip right back into your old ways again. We see some good, but far too much evil."

"So, you *do* have hostile intentions towards the people of earth," Michael accused.

"No, as I've told you, we're a very peaceful race and we abhor violence. We haven't decided what to do about the problem of the human species yet."

"The *problem? We're* the problem?" Grasping for a clever comeback, he blurted out the only thing he could think of, "Don't you guys kidnap innocent people and do medical experiments on them?"

"Only once in a while," Joe responded dismissively. "We're trying to find out what makes your kind tick, mostly so we can help you. And we don't *keep* anyone. We usually put them back right where we found them."

"Yeah, right," he said acidly. "Then tell me this, aren't you guys responsible for all those cattle mutilations?"

"No," Joe replied, without looking up, "that's those vampires."

Michael didn't respond; it was obvious the arrogant alien was being sarcastic and simply making fun of him. He wasn't going to dignify that with an answer.

Instead, Tom, who hadn't interrupted once during their exchange, now spoke in a friendly tone, "Good to see you again, Joe."

"You too, Tom," the alien replied sociably. "Don't be a stranger."

"It was nice to meet you," Michael said, as politely as he could through clenched teeth. He turned quickly and started walking away.

From behind him, Joe called out, "Hey, Michael, good luck. May the Creator shield you and keep you."

Surprised, he whirled around to face the alien again and stared at him hard. "What did you say?"

"I said…may the Creator shield you and keep you," Joe repeated. "That's how we say goodbye on my planet, and in most of the known universe for that matter."

"So, you Hygons believe in one God, called the Creator?"

Joe laughed at him, "You humans, always wanting to quantify and label things. How can you quantify something that is everywhere and all powerful?" Slowly shaking his head, he faded from sight.

"How rude!" Michael exclaimed, as he turned to face Tom. "He could've at least said goodbye."

Tom looked at him, his expression one of amusement. "Michael, when ghosts fade out, that *is* their way of saying goodbye."

"Whatever," he said coarsely, waving him off. "I still didn't like him very much. What was the point of bringing me to meet him anyway?"

"Oh, I don't know," Tom replied slowly. "I figured you'd

probably never met an alien before." He paused for a second before adding, "And, I wanted to show you that you don't know everything." He smiled. "Not even close."

"I never said I knew *everything*," he shot back.

"No...you didn't." Tom's mouth twisted up on one side in a half-smile. "You didn't have to." Raising his hand in a wave, he began to slowly fade away.

"Wait!" he blurted out. "Where are you always going all the time?"

Tom's eyes stiffened into almost a glare. "That's my business," he answered abruptly and disappeared.

That is starting to get really *annoying.*

• • •

Knowing he was marked, Michael left The Angel of the Sea every few days to be sure the demons couldn't catch up with him. Usually, he would orb or memory travel to his hometown visiting his family and Melissa. Sarah never wanted to go with him. She understood these visits were private and she really wasn't comfortable leaving the Angel of the Sea anyway.

Before long, he began to understand why you had to part with your past life. A person could go crazy. It was incredibly painful to go home and simply be ignored.

Sometimes, he would go back to his house and follow his mother around. He usually left after a few hours; seeing her was too heartbreaking.

Occasionally, he would hang out at Central's field, watching his brother play baseball with his friends. Michael missed him so much, but being there felt exactly like being alone in a crowded room.

Other times, he would pop in on Melissa, staying for hours just to watch her as she went through her daily routine. This too, proved to be unbearable, for the closer he got to Sarah, the guiltier he felt about seeing Melissa.

Eventually, he came to the inevitable conclusion that being unable to talk or interact with the people you love is simply too painful. As time went on, his visits home grew fewer and fewer.

On the other hand, he had Sarah. He could talk with her, walk with her, and hold her.

One afternoon, they lay side by side on the bare wooden floors of the attic, listening to the rain tapping out a spastic yet soothing rhythm on the old gabled roof above. Propping himself up on his elbow, he said to her, "So little girl, what did you want to be when you grew up?"

She glanced over at him, and her face lit up. For some reason, talking about their former lives seemed to make her happy, not sad. "Oh, that's an easy one," she said. "I wanted to be an oncologist and cure cancer."

He made a noise that was half sigh, half groan. "I bet you would've done it, too."

Sarah smiled softly and her eyes were full of gratitude for the compliment. Then, her expression turned to one of curiosity. "What did you want to be?"

He glanced out the window at the rain trickling down the glass, thinking of all the expectations he once had. With a painful stab, the old wound within him ruptured anew—the throbbing ache in the center of his soul. He knew exactly what he'd wanted to be. Turning back to her, he forced himself to crack a smile. "Well...if the basketball thing didn't work out, I was going to be a cardiologist."

The moment he said this, the irony of their similarly tragic motivations struck Sarah as funny and she started to laugh a little.

He couldn't help himself and laughed right along with her. After a minute, he fell silent, content to simply have his eyes on her and listen to the storm.

"The rain sounds wonderful, doesn't it?" she said wistfully. "I don't think I really appreciated everything when I was alive."

"I know what you mean," he said, thinking back to the moment when he'd discovered the very same thing. "I think it's true. No one appreciates what they have 'til it's gone."

She looked up at him, her eyes full of emotion. "In case I haven't said this yet, I want you to know...I appreciate you," she said, sliding closer to him. "I'm so glad you found me."

Raising an eyebrow, he said jokingly, "You mean...you don't care that it's dangerous to be with me? I *am* a marked man, you know."

"Of course not," she replied, her voice a seductive whisper, "it adds a certain element of excitement." Slowly tracing her hand over the muscles on his chest, the warmth of her fingers almost burned his ghostly flesh.

Doesn't she know the slightest touch makes me crave her? "Seriously," he said, gently grabbing her by the wrist. "Maybe this isn't such a good idea."

She stared at him intently for several moments, as if trying to see directly into his soul. "Let me ask you something," she said slowly. "If you could tell your living friends one thing, what would it be?"

He thought for a mere second and said, "Cherish life, it's absolutely precious."

"Exactly," she responded emphatically. "I loved my life…it was just getting started. And I know you loved yours too…but our lives were taken away from us," she said with a glint of anger and urgency in her eyes. "Now that we've been given another chance at happiness, shouldn't we *take* it?"

What can I say to that? Gently brushing a hair from her face, he traced his fingers down her cheek. Desire filling him, he let his hand burn a trail down to her breast and saw his own desire reflected back in her eyes. Any fears he had were swept from his mind. *She's right, we deserve to be happy.* Pressing his lips to hers, he kissed her with the desperation of a man wanting to have his hunger satisfied.

A split-second later, the boundary between their energies grew perilously thin again. *Slipping. I'm slipping. One more second of this and I won't be able to stop…*

"Sarah," he gasped, pulling his lips away from hers.

"I know," she said quietly. "It's happening again."

He nodded slightly, as he held his body over her and struggled to regain his composure. *Ugh, this is gonna be as hard as it was with Melissa. Good thing I've had plenty of practice at controlling myself.* He turned his face up to hers. "We're going to have to work on this."

"Definitely," she purred close to his ear.

I have to focus and stay in control—think about basketball stats or something. His eyes flicked to her lips.

"Good thing we have plenty of time," he muttered, covering her mouth with his once more. This time, he took her lips slowly, carefully. Deliberately taking his time so he wouldn't lose control. Paying close attention to every movement, every touch.

For hours he kissed her, as if it might be their last day on earth.

• • •

It was time to visit Tom again. He'd put it off long enough. Arriving at their usual meeting spot on the beach in the Outerbanks, Michael called out his name.

A moment later, Tom appeared a few paces in front of him and called out, "Boo".

He grinned widely. "Eeek."

"I haven't seen you in a while," Tom said. "Been spending a lot of time at The Angel of the Sea?"

"Yeah, mostly," he said lightly.

Tom gave him a disappointed look. "You *are* getting side-tracked by Sarah, you know that."

"I know," he admitted in a low voice, both to himself as well as Tom. Then, looking him straight in the eyes, he added defiantly, "But I also don't care."

"If you're not going to think of yourself," Tom said, giving him a side-long glance of disapproval, "then consider Sarah. I know you care about her, Michael, but you mustn't keep her here. It wouldn't be fair."

He rolled his eyes. "I know. I *know*."

As they walked near the dunes, a desolate silence

stretched between them, as neither one knew what to say to the other. In principle, Michael agreed with him, but what could he do? Trying not to fall in love was like trying to defy the laws of gravity.

A few moments later, his thoughts were interrupted, as another man slowly materialized up ahead meandering close to the water's edge. When Michael got close enough, he couldn't believe his eyes.

"Is that *Jimmy Buffett?*"

"Yes, I think so," Tom replied, wrinkling up his face. "You know who he is?"

"Yeah," he said excitedly. "My mom and dad used to listen to his songs on vacation all the time. I grew up calling it beach music." Furrowing his brow, he added, "I didn't know he was dead."

"He's not dead," Tom said matter-of-factly. "He's having an out of body experience. An OBE for short."

"Really?" Michael asked, incredulous. "Are you kidding me?"

"No, I'm not kidding. Sometimes a person's astral body can separate from their corporeal, living body for a short period of time. It's called astral projection, or an OBE. The physical body is put on autopilot and the soul is free to wander. An OBE is like a state of consciousness that's neither sleep, nor wakefulness."

"So, it's kind of like...your spirit is sleep-walking, but not your body?"

"Yes, exactly," Tom said. "Jimmy Buffet has always had a wandering soul, so now and again it goes for a walkabout. He really likes the beach, especially down here in the Outerbanks. I've seen him here before."

"Can we talk to him?"

"No," Tom answered. "If he sees us, just smile and wave. Like I've told you before, it's best not to interfere with the living. He's probably asleep and thinks he's dreaming. I'm sure he'll return to his body shortly. An OBE usually doesn't last that long. We wouldn't want to do anything to disrupt his spirit from going back to his body."

Digesting what Tom had said, Michael was struck by a very interesting possibility. "Do you think I can go back?"

Tom gave him a weird look. "What do you mean?"

"I don't know… exactly," he said slowly. "I mean…go back, among the living."

"Honestly, I don't think you'd look very good." Tom grinned. "Your old body has to be in quite a pitiful state by now, I'm sure."

"Very *funny*." He scowled. "No, I don't mean go back as the same person. I mean go back as someone else."

"Michael, you know it's against the rules to possess the body of another living person," Tom said in a stern voice.

"Of course, I know that," he said. "I don't mean that. I mean like…be reincarnated, I guess."

"Why would you want to do that?" Tom asked dismissively.

Frankly, he couldn't even understand the question. "Why *wouldn't* I?" he asked, twisting his face up in confusion.

Tom sighed. "Michael, if you were meant to do that, I think it would've already happened."

"What *am* I meant to do then?" he asked, frustration rising in him again. His anger boiled over and he lashed out,

"I'm not supposed to be a *ghost*! I was *supposed* to be playing *basketball*. I wish this had never happened to me!"

Tom glared at him with hard eyes before he spoke. "So, you would rather have survived the accident and been a *paraplegic* for the rest of your life, unable to walk, and confined to a *wheelchair?*" he said sharply. "Or, how about maybe a comatose *vegetable*, lying bedridden, in a home somewhere, with a nurse moving you every few hours so you don't get bed sores?"

Michael's eyes went wide. "Are you trying to tell me I'm better off being *dead?*"

"No," Tom answered, his voice growing calmer and more sympathetic. "I'm only trying to get you to see the bright side of this."

For a second, he stared at Tom as if he'd just said the most ludicrous thing imaginable. Then he exploded. "The bright side! The *bright* side! You're freakin' kidding me, right?"

Tom took the blunt force of his angry words and replied in his most understanding tone, "I believe there's a good reason for everything that happens."

Seeing the sincerity evident on Tom's face, Michael's anger wavered and subsided. Tom was only trying to help. Deep down, he knew that. "Well...whatever it is," he said begrudgingly, "I'd sure like to see this *good reason* soon."

"I know, Michael...I know," Tom replied sympathetically.

"I mean...how do we really know there's somewhere to move on to? What if ghosts just... fade away or something?" He was about to say something else when Tom again got that look on his face, as if he were listening to voices in his head.

"What is it?" Michael asked quickly. "Has someone summoned you?"

Tom turned to face him, his expression inscrutable. "That's none of your business," he replied in a flat tone.

Great, another unexplained disappearing act. "Why are you always so evasive?" He couldn't but feel vaguely wounded. He always told Tom so much about himself. *So why wouldn't Tom tell him anything?*

"Because it's *my* business, not *yours*," Tom said, as he faded.

Michael kicked at the sand with all his might but not a grain of it moved. "That is *seriously* getting on my nerves!" he shouted out loud to no one.

CHAPTER TWENTY-ONE

SAFE

HOURS AND DAYS slipped away quickly. One day, while looking at a newspaper discarded by one of the guests, Michael made a startling discovery. The summer had flown by. *It's the end of August already? Melissa will be leaving for Pitt soon.*

For a while now, he'd been feeling a little guilty about spending so much time with Sarah. Was he really falling for her? And forgetting all about Melissa?

He had to see Melissa before she left for college or he would never forgive himself.

Standing nearby, Sarah had already picked up on his conflicted thoughts. Before he could even say anything, she said, "I understand, Michael. It's okay…go."

He took her delicate hands in his. "Do you want to come with me?"

"No, like I've said before, these visits are private," she said in a sweet voice. "I know you'll come back to me."

"You've got that right," he said with a smile and kissed her goodbye before orbing home.

Arriving at Melissa's house in the evening, he found her upstairs. One corner of her room was piled with items she had packed for college, a foot locker, rug, desk lamp and posters.

He watched as she cleaned up her bedroom, putting things away, and gathering up laundry. As she laid her purse down on the desk, he couldn't help but notice a little pill pack that spilled out next to Craig's picture—a picture that now sat in place of the one from their prom. *Well, that's new. My best friend...great. Just great.*

It should've come as a shock, but it didn't. Not really. Hadn't they also known each other since they were little? Hadn't they always been close friends? *I guess if I have to see her with anyone, I would want it to be Craig. He's a good guy and she deserves someone like him.*

After a while, she picked up a book and lay down on her bed to read. He stared at her for hours from across the room, wishing he could talk to her. *Does she even still think about me?*

Melissa finally fell asleep and after watching her for another hour or so, the futility of staying became obvious. As he left through the front door, he was surprised to find Tom outside waiting for him.

"What are *you* doing here?" he asked, feeling a little suspicious.

"I came to find you, and when you weren't at the Angel of the Sea," Tom replied, "I had a pretty good idea of where you might be."

"Good deduction, Sherlock." He didn't think he'd sounded all that snide, but he got a hugely disapproving look from Tom. "*What?*"

"I have to tell you something *important*," Tom said in a serious tone. "It's for your own good, and I hope you'll listen."

Michael sensed a lecture coming on. Still sore from their last exchange, he was beginning to get tired of Tom keeping secrets while at the same time doling out advice. "Go on," he replied, already mildly annoyed.

Tom looked at him intently. "I must tell you this, Michael. Men…both living and dead, have wasted away longing for a woman they could not possess."

"*Really?*" He drew out the word, intentionally mocking him.

Tom ignored his attitude. "Yes, and even more to the point, the dead are simply not meant to be with the living in that way."

Deep down he knew Tom was right, but he shot him a please-don't-tell-me-what-to-do look anyway.

"Michael, you have to accept the facts. Melissa will be going to college soon, and she's going to grow up, get married, and probably have kids. Life will move on for her."

"Is this supposed to make me feel *better*?"

"I'm only telling you the truth," Tom said simply. "Isn't that what you'd want for her?"

He knew Tom was right, but that didn't make it any easier. Finally, he conceded with a long, tense sigh. "Of *course*, it is."

"You'll always care about her and I know it's difficult…but you *have* to let her go." Tom put his arm around his shoulder and led him away from the house. "Remember what the Elders said—you need to part with your past life. Visiting home isn't going to help you do that."

"I guess you're right," he said, though his shoulders sagged.

"Listen, I think you need to do something fun," Tom suggested, popping him lightly on the arm. "How about we go to a baseball game?"

He managed a smile. "Alright, why not? As long as it's the Yankees."

Excitement bubbled within him—he felt like a little kid again. He'd always loved going to see the Yankees play. Growing up, his favorite players were Derek Jeter and Alex Rodriguez. His father had taken his family to quite a few games over the years. *Will it feel the same though, going to a game now?*

Becoming two small balls of light, Michael and Tom orbed, seconds later arriving in the Bronx directly in front of Yankees Stadium.

"Do you know they're tearing it down soon?" Michael asked, as they half-drifted, half-walked through the wall near the gates.

"Yes, it's a shame, isn't it?" Tom commented.

"*I* think so," he agreed. "It'll take a while before the new stadium has that feeling of nostalgia like it does now."

"I'm sure the resident ghosts here, feel exactly the same way."

For a second, Michael could've sworn he sounded serious.

•　•　•

They floated down to some empty seats really close to the field, a smidge to the right of home plate. The perfect seats.

"See, I told you there were perks to being dead." Tom grinned. "No need to get a ticket, no need to wait in line."

Michael shot him an I-can't-believe-you-just-said-that look.

The national anthem echoed through the stadium and the two of them sang along with the rest of the crowd. For the first time, he was not a ghost, not the undead, but simply another fan in the crowd.

"Are there any ghost hot dogs or ghost beers? I could really go for a couple right now," he said jokingly.

Tom smirked. "Nope, sorry."

Other than not being able to snack, it felt blissfully normal to be at the game. He and Tom cheered as the Yankees scored twice in the second inning and again in the fourth. By the seventh inning stretch, the Yankees were ahead three-zip. Like everyone else, they stood up to sing along with Kate Smith's recording of "God Bless America".

The eighth and ninth innings turned out to be the most exciting. The Sox came back to score three runs in the top of the eighth, but the Yankees answered with a two run homer by Jeter in the bottom of the ninth to win the game.

At the crack of the bat, they both jumped out of their seats with the rest of the fans, as they watched the ball sail a few inches past the foul pole in left field. In his exuberance, Michael flung his arm up over his head with such force that, as it whipped through the air, it clipped the arm of the man standing next to him. The man had been holding a container of popcorn, and as the cup was thrown up in the air, a shower of popcorn rained down on the fans in front of him.

"I'm so sorry," the man said to the people below, who were now picking greasy popcorn off their clothes and glaring in his direction.

The man's son leaned over to say teasingly, "What a klutz you are, Pop."

"I didn't do it." The older man sounded unsure, inspecting his right arm as if it were defective. "I...I think somebody hit my arm," he mumbled, as he stared at the vacant seat next to him.

"Whoops," Michael said with a grin and a shrug. A second later, he and Tom exchanged amused looks and busted up laughing. They were still snickering, as fans filed out of their seats and headed for the exits. As usual, Ol' Blue Eyes was belting out "New York, New York".

"That was a great game," Tom said.

"Yeah, it was." Yet, a pang of sadness clawed at his insides. He didn't want this feeling of being part of the living world to end. "Hey, I just thought about something. We can go anywhere in the stadium, can't we?"

"Sure, I can't see why not. Where did you have in mind?"

"I would *love* to see the locker rooms," he replied with enthusiasm, "and rub elbows with some of the players."

"Alright, let's do it," Tom agreed.

The hallway leading below buzzed with excitement. The happy voices of the players congratulating one another carried from the locker room.

He turned to Tom to make a comment, and spun around in shock. His friend had disappeared. He searched up and down the hall but the only people milling about were Yankee players and staff. Tom was nowhere in sight. *Where the hell did he go? I can't believe he didn't even bother to say goodbye. Oh well, his loss.*

Thrilled as he glided through the doors of the locker

room, Michael walked around slowly, soaking up the aura of the hallowed place. *How cool, not a single head turned, no one even knows I'm here.*

As he watched the players joking and laughing, his mind rifled through all the greats who had been here before. Walking around the room among the players, he wished he could have a chance to talk to them, to shake their hands. For a moment, he stopped and stood in awe before Thurman Munson's locker, running his hand along the brass plaque. As Michael knew, Munson had played eleven seasons with the Yankees before dying in a small plane crash in 1979. In tribute to their lost catcher, the empty locker with Munson's number 15 was never reassigned. *This is a piece of baseball history most people never get to see.*

A micro-second later, his jaw dropped. Someone definitely knew he was there now.

Another ghost had just drifted through the wall and into the locker room. The round face, the stocky build, the old-fashioned pinstripe uniform—Michael recognized him instantly. It was Babe Ruth, exactly as he had looked in 1923.

"I know you," he blurted out before he could stop himself.

"You a baseball player, kid?" Ruth asked.

"No sir...a huge fan." He extended his hand. "My name's Michael Andrews."

"It's nice to meet you." Ruth took his hand and gave it a hearty shake. "You see them play today?"

"Yeah," he replied with a smile, "it was a great game."

"I thought they were sunk when the Sox got those three

runs late in the game." Ruth gave a little snort. "God help me, but I still hate the Red Sox."

He couldn't help but laugh. *Wow, what would Chris say if he could see me talking with Babe Ruth? If only my brother were here to share this.*

Having heard his thoughts, Babe Ruth asked, "Were you close to your brother?"

Michael broke into a proud smile. "Yes, sir. My younger brother's great. He's a pretty damn good pitcher actually. Who knows, maybe he'll even play for the Yankees someday. Of course, that would be at the new stadium by then."

Realizing what he'd revealed, he stopped short. *What if Babe Ruth doesn't know? What if he's upset?* Cautiously, he asked him, "Mr. Ruth, do you know they're going to be tearing the stadium down?"

"Yeah, we've overheard many of the conversations," Ruth replied. "We all know they're moving across the street. Very little happens here that we're not aware of."

"We?"

"Yeah, Gehrig, DiMaggio, Mantle…they're all here."

"Wow, that's *unbelievable*," he remarked, thinking of all the times he'd been to a haunted Yankees stadium and never knew it. "So, are you gonna miss this old place?"

"Miss it? Of course," Ruth answered, "there's no place like it. You know, people have even called this place baseball heaven. There are so many memories and so much energy wrapped up in that field and in those bleachers. It's in the very walls around us," he said with a grand sweep of his hand. "Still, I've already seen it changed once before. I liked the original stadium best, before the renovations they did in the mid-seventies." Sounding slightly annoyed, he added, "They were disrupting my energy so much I had to spend some time at Shea for a couple of years."

Michael grinned. "So, are you going to be moving to the new stadium when they tear this old place down?"

"I'm not sure yet, it might be a good time to say goodbye," Ruth said wistfully. "I know the fans think we're leaving. The other day I even saw some of them holding up a sign that read, 'Goodbye Stadium Ghosts, Thanks for the Memories, We'll Miss You.' I'm sure they had no idea how close they were to the truth, but it was very thoughtful of them."

"Even if you go to the new stadium, it won't be the same, will it?" Michael now suggested. "It won't really be the house that Ruth built anymore."

"Sure it will be, kid," Ruth said with enthusiasm as he slapped him on the shoulder. "Sure it will be. Every kid remembers coming to his first Yankees game. Why?" he asked rhetorically. "Because, it's not just these walls that we built, it's a monumental baseball tradition. Gehrig, Mantle, DiMaggio, and me—we built a love for baseball and a love for the Yankees. That's what we built, kid. That tradition, that kind of love, is larger than this stadium's walls, larger than all the legends, and larger than all our records combined," he said with a flourish. "Although," Ruth continued with a grin, "I give them credit for trying to take that tradition with them. Did you know they're gonna take pailfuls of dirt from home plate and the pitcher's mound, and take it across the street?"

"No sir," he laughed, "I didn't know that."

"Let me tell you something kid, they can take *all* the dirt they want. That won't be why we come." Babe Ruth shook his head. "Nah...it's the fans. The fans are why we're still here."

Michael nodded silently in agreement, full understanding of the man's words dawning on him slowly. The man they called The Babe had made a choice—a choice to stay. If there really was somewhere else to go, he could probably move on anytime he wanted. But, he wanted to stay right here. So what was really wrong with that anyway? *The man sure seems content.*

A moment later, Babe Ruth got the same, weird look on his face that Tom always did.

Sensing their conversation had come to an end, Michael reached out once more to shake Ruth's hand. "I'm glad to have met you, Mr. Ruth."

"Same here, son. Stop by again, if you get the chance." He smiled as he turned toward the wall to make his exit. "We could always use a few more players on the field."

"Sure," he replied jovially, "sounds like fun."

Michael was about to leave, when he remembered something important he'd wanted to ask the greatest man in baseball. "Wait...Mr. Ruth...did you really call that homerun shot during the '32 World Series?"

Babe Ruth spun around, his eyes glistening. "I sure did, kid. I sure as hell did." And then, with a tip of his cap, he glided through the wall of the locker room once more.

As Michael made his way back down the hall leading to

the dugout, he stopped to read the famous sign hanging from the ceiling. Legend has it every player touches the sign as they make their way to the field. On the sign is a quote by Joe DiMaggio, "I want to thank the Good Lord for making me a Yankee." Reaching up to touch the sign with his ghostly hand, Michael jumped nearly two feet when he saw another spectral hand touch it as well. Startled, he whirled around to find Tom standing next to him.

"Where the hell have *you* been?"

"Sorry, I had something to take care of," Tom said vaguely.

Michael grimaced. *There's that clever avoidance, yet again.* Through gritted teeth he said, "Yeah? Good for you...I just met Babe Ruth."

•   •   •

Still chatting about baseball legends as they left Yankees stadium, Michael and Tom were crossing the street, when a small voice cried out, "Uncle Henry!"

The little girl, no more than six years old, pointed to someone familiar across the street. In her excitement, she wriggled free of her mother's grasp and darted between two parked cars.

"Lizzie! No!" the startled woman screamed in terror.

Michael froze horrorstruck. The little girl couldn't see the car coming at her.

And, paying more attention to the hot blonde next to him than the road in front of him, the driver had no chance of braking in time.

Before Michael could even react, Tom orbed and in a swift rush hit the girl from behind, somehow lifting her slightly off her feet. The car missed her by mere inches, the driver screeching to a halt, finally registering the pink streak that had crossed his path.

The little girl had fallen forward on her hands and knees, with the wind knocked out of her. Catching her breath, she started to wail, just as her mother scrambled to her side.

Relief flooded through every inch of his ghostly body. Michael was grateful Tom had acted so quickly to help the girl, but he was also...confused as hell. "What did you *do* that for?" he said, hurling the question at him like an accusation.

Tom gave him a blank stare and then said in a clipped tone, "I felt like it."

His eyes practically bored a hole through Tom. "I don't get you. I thought you said it was best to avoid interfering with the living."

"I did say that," Tom answered, not meeting his gaze, "but *she* needed to be saved."

He gaped at him, thunderstruck. "How the hell do you know *that*?"

Tom turned fully to him now, his eyes unreadable. "I'm not ready to tell you that yet."

"*What?*" he croaked, as his impatience surfaced. "Why not? What *else* haven't you told me?"

"Michael," Tom said in a calm, steady voice, "I've told you everything so far, that I thought I should."

"How the hell do you expect me to *trust* you," he bellowed, "when you won't tell me *everything?*"

Tom got that far away look in his eyes again. "You're going to *have* to trust me." A split second later, he was gone.

• • •

When Michael got back to the Angel of the Sea, he took Sarah out on the porch and talked her ears off telling her all about the ballgame, Babe Ruth and the little girl Tom had saved.

"What makes you so uneasy about it?" she asked.

Aimlessly, he reached out and set the wooden chair next to him rocking with a swipe of his hand. "I don't know…but sometimes I get the feeling Tom's holding back in his answers. Always choosing his words carefully, like he's censoring out certain information. And he keeps most of his thoughts blocked from me."

"But, he's been so nice to you," she reminded him. "Are you sure you're not just being paranoid?"

"No, I'm not positive," he said with a frustrated shake of his head. "But after what happened with that little girl, I don't know what to think. It's like he knows more than he's telling. He pretty much admitted that, when he wouldn't tell me why he saved her."

"Considering what the Elders told you about interfering with the living that does seem a bit hypocritical," she replied, as the two of them rocked contentedly in the porch chairs. "I don't know him like you do, so I don't know what his motivation could be, but maybe he has a good reason for keeping secrets?"

Michael chewed his lip, thinking it over. Minutes, or

maybe hours passed while they sat in silence, listening to the cries of a few passing seagulls. Finally he said, "I'd love to believe that Sarah, but if there's one thing I've learned, whenever people keep secrets...it's almost never about anything good."

CHAPTER TWENTY-TWO

SECRETS

WITH ALMOST NO distractions, Michael had nothing to do but focus completely on Sarah. So, it wasn't at all surprising, when one day in early October, on a Saturday, at about eleven o'clock in the morning, with a sudden twinge of fear and elation, he realized that he was unequivocally, immeasurably in love with her.

There's a certain moment when you realize you can't live without someone, that is both terrific, and yet utterly terrifying. That's when you figure out that if you were to lose this person for any reason, you would lose your whole world. For Michael, that moment was even more terrifying, for one tiny reason. *I shouldn't have let it happen.*

With a riot of emotions thrashing inside him, more than his knee couldn't stay still. "Let's take a walk," he suggested to Sarah. "I have something important to tell you."

She raised an eyebrow, her interest clearly peaked. "Alright."

Taking her hand in his own, warmth spread through him. Their leisurely strolls together made him feel almost as if they were a normal couple.

The late afternoon sun struggled to filter in through a

gray slate of cloud cover. To most people, the day appeared gloomy. But for them, it meant they could go outside without getting drained by the light. They left the Angel of the Sea and ambled down one of the side streets leading toward the Victorian district.

"I notice you're not as scared to leave the Angel anymore," he said. "You're willing to go further and further each time we go out now."

She gripped his hand tighter and smiled at him. "I guess I just feel safe with you."

In that instant, his eyes connected with hers and his heart filled with so much love he thought it might burst under the power of it.

"Sarah, I know we met under the weirdest of circumstances," he began. "But I want you to know that whatever happens to us, I—"

He never finished his sentence, sensing them before he even saw them. A cold, nauseous feeling raced through his ghostly form like cryo-freeze. Above their heads, a maelstrom of black shadows revolved and swirled, writhing as one. Choked with fear for her, he said tensely, "Sarah, go back to the Angel."

"No," she replied, her whole body quaking. "I *won't* leave you."

The twisting mass began to descend, stretching out tendrils of dark, evil energy toward them. There wasn't much time. "You *have* to get out of here, Sarah. Now!"

Finally obeying his command, she pivoted to go, just as Matt materialized directly in her path.

Putrefied flesh hung from his face, as if his very soul were decaying. *He's becoming one of them. The transformation must be almost complete.*

Matt's mouth twisted into a sick smile, revealing disintegrated and blackened teeth. Taking a sudden swipe, he tried to rake Sarah with his razor-like claws.

She jumped backward and let out a terrified scream. With a sweep of his arm, Michael pushed her out of the way. Her eyes met his for a mere instant before she took to the sky, flying toward the Angel of the Sea. The dark horde above them wavered and stretched toward her for a second, but then let her go unharmed.

Relief flooded through him and he now trained his eyes like daggers on Matt. *This freak's gonna pay for threatening her.* Anger roiled within him, becoming a tempest. Still, he stalled for time, drawing in energy from his surroundings. "Man, you look even *worse* than the last time I saw you. You should take better care of yourself."

The half-demon gave a strangled laugh. "Everything will be fine once I capture you."

"And why would you want to do that?"

Something about the question appeared to rattle him. "I'm sorry," he said, his voice wavering. "I...I don't have a choice."

Michael searched his hideous, rotting face. "What do you *mean* you don't have a choice?"

"You're marked...and they want you," Matt stammered. "So...I *have* to collect you."

"Why? What does it matter to you?" he demanded. What was it he saw in Matt's eyes? Anger, yes. But also...*fear?* There was one way to find out.

Michael focused intensely on his adversary's mind.

Immediately, Matt's painful emotions enveloped him. Fear. Guilt. Regret. Glimpses of his memories flashed before his eyes. Matt staggering over to a car. Fumbling with his keys and arguing with someone behind him. A girl...a beautiful young girl...

"Enough!" Matt shouted, his face suddenly contorting with rage. "Get out of my head!"

"*Wait*," Michael pleaded, "maybe I can *help* you."

"You *can't* help me! *No one* can help me!" Matt screamed, as he raised his hands to strike.

Before he had the chance, Michael struck first, sending a beam of pure light and energy surging toward the demon. He didn't wait to see if he hit his mark.

My only chance is to orb and get out of here. "Catch me if you can," he taunted him playfully.

In the next moment, Michael was a small ball of light streaking through space.

CHAPTER TWENTY-THREE

VISIT

A SPLIT SECOND later, Michael arrived at his gravesite in the cemetery. The grass on top of his plot had grown in, all thick, healthy and green. *How nice*, he thought sourly. *Well, at least he couldn't follow me here.*

From behind him, a familiar voice hissed, "Don't be so *sure* of that."

He spun around and now stood face to face with the awful demon. Again, he tried to stall long enough to gather some energy, saying, "I thought cemeteries were like churches…you know…consecrated ground and all that."

"You thought *wrong*," Matt snarled, as he sent a blast of energy speeding in his direction.

Leaping to his right, Michael narrowly missed getting hit. The dangerous bolt rocketed past him and struck a grave marker, scorching the surface of the headstone.

Anger pulsed through his whole being now and he raised his hands to defend himself. A strong beam of powerful energy burst out of him, racing towards his adversary. It was a great shot.

Except…it missed. The demon moved with inhuman speed, ducking the blow and firing off another bolt of evil energy.

The blast hit him square in the chest. Pain radiated outward to his limbs. Still on his feet, as his vision blurred, he saw Tom materialize right behind Matt and send a stream of energy directly into his back.

He should've felt vindicated, but with his last bit of consciousness, he struggled to understand what he was seeing *behind Tom*.

Dad?

A fraction of a second later, blinded by a tremendous flash of light, Michael dissipated completely, as the world around him faded to black.

· · ·

Sometime later, he regained consciousness and found himself lying on the grass in the backyard behind his house. Weak, confused and disoriented, he looked up to see who was there. Instead of his father standing over him, it was Tom.

"Michael, you can't be *careless* with your soul." Tom extended a hand to help him up. "Demons are very dangerous. If they can't recruit you they will, for all intent and purposes, destroy you. Do you know that expression, a fate worse than death?"

"Yeah," he replied, getting up slowly. "I guess so."

"That's what happens when a demon hits you too many times. Your energy will eventually reconstitute, but you'll forget who you were and lose all your memories…forever."

"You can't be *serious*?" Michael said, but even as he did, the expression on Tom's face told him he was perfectly serious. "How many times do they have to hit you for that to happen?"

"It varies, sometimes five or six hits can do it, other times…it can be as little as three." Tom looked at him the way his coach used to when he caught him showboating on the basketball court instead of getting the assist from his teammates. "Why did you take on that demon by yourself? You *should* have summoned me."

Michael wrinkled his eyebrows together. "Wait a minute…that's *right*. I *didn't* call you this time. So, how did you know to come?"

"I came looking for you and happened to be in the right place at the right time, I guess," Tom replied vaguely.

His mind was still foggy, but he wasn't buying the coincidence. Yet again, Tom was being evasive. Unfortunately, he was too dazed to care that much.

Rubbing his head to try and clear his thoughts, Michael suddenly remembered. "I saw my dad! He was here!"

Tom furrowed his brow. "Really?"

"Yes," he said, frowning in confusion, "didn't you see him?"

"No, Michael…I'm sorry, but I didn't."

"You must have," he insisted. "He was right behind you. Why would he have left?"

Tom shrugged his shoulders lightly. "I can't say."

Without even waiting for Tom to follow him, Michael flew inside his house and desperately searched every room, floor to floor. No one, alive or dead, was home—the house was empty. After several minutes, it became obvious—his dad was nowhere to be found. As he walked back outside to join Tom, his mind tumbled in every direction. He wasn't sure what troubled him more. The fact that he'd seen his dad or, that his dad had left without saying anything.

Until that moment, he'd never even considered the possibility his father might be a ghost. He'd taken it for granted if there was a place to move on to, then that's where his father was. *After all, my father had been a good man.* Now, he was forced to consider the alternative. *What if my dad is actually still around and somehow stuck, just like me? Or worse, maybe my fears are correct and there really is nowhere to move on to?*

He crumpled onto the porch steps and hung his head in his hands. His leg started to bounce from pent up frustration. Out of habit, he placed his hands on his knees to steady them and calm himself. "I'm sure I saw him."

Tom came over slowly and sat beside him. "Maybe you did."

A few minutes later, the initial shock and confusion wore off. The thought of being reunited with his father cheered him a little and he blurted out, "Hey, do you think I can summon my dad, the same way I summon you?"

"I guess you could try," Tom said. "You know how to do it. Think very hard about your memory of him and call him with your mind."

Michael stood up and closed his eyes so he could concentrate. A deluge of memories rushed at him. In his mind, his father was right in front of him with that crooked smile he loved so much. *Dad? Eric Andrews? Are you there?*

Nothing. No response.

Next, he tried it out loud, "Dad? Eric Andrews? Can you hear me?"

After a few minutes, when nothing happened, he opened his eyes and asked impatiently, "What's wrong? Why isn't it working?"

"Tough to say." Tom shook his head as if at a loss. "I don't know."

"Look, if my dad's stuck somewhere like me, I've got to find him." He grabbed Tom's arm in desperation and pleaded, "How will I find him again?"

"I *don't* know."

"What about the cemetery?" Michael suggested, hopeful. "Do you think he could be there?"

"No, I don't think so," Tom said. "You saw the cemetery. The dead don't like to hang out there. It's too painful a reminder that they're dead. Besides, very little of their trace energy from life is actually there anyway."

Michael slammed his hand on the wooden stair, which caused it to creak loudly. "Then *where*?"

Tom sighed. "I have no idea, but the most likely place to find him would be along his energy path, basically all the places he frequented in life."

Michael thought for a moment. Besides their home, his father had spent the most time at his work. "I suppose he might be at his office in Jersey City."

"Have you been there before?"

"Yeah, plenty of times."

"Then you can memory travel there. But, I better come with you," Tom cautioned. "I don't want you fighting off any more demons by yourself."

"That's fine," he replied, secretly grateful for the assistance. Truthfully, he didn't want to run into any more trouble by himself either.

Michael concentrated on the memory of his father's office and Tom grabbed hold of his arm to draft along.

Next moment, they were standing in the foyer of a small manufacturing plant. "My father's office was on the second floor." He ran up the cement stairs, taking two at a time.

Tom didn't follow. He took a shortcut and floated through the ceiling above.

They now stood in an outdated office suite with three large wooden desks. Several metal filing cabinets and a copier sat lined up against the wall.

"His office was in here." Michael pointed to a door on the right. "The business was sold after my dad died, but everything looks about the same." As he sat behind the desk in his father's old chair, a crushing sadness swallowed him.

Tom cocked his head to the side. "What's wrong?"

"This business meant everything to him," he said in barely a whisper, running his hands over the armrests, while his father's words echoed in his head. "My dad used to joke that he was gonna grow old and die in this chair." He bit the inside of his cheek to steady his emotions. "He used to say one day we'd probably find him, still holding the accounts receivable report in his cold, dead hands." He gave a short, cynical laugh.

"None of us knew how or when we would die," Tom said gently. "Your father didn't leave you on purpose—it was just his time."

"Why? *Why* did it have to be his time?" he shouted,

swiping his hand through a stack of papers and sending them flying. "And for that matter, why couldn't *I* have had more time, *huh?* Why does it all have to be so *god-damned* unfair?"

Tom turned his back to him. "Michael, I'm getting tired of your whining and complaining," he chastised. "You were certainly no Charlie Brown."

"What the hell does *that* mean?" he yelled, leaping out of the chair.

Spinning around to face him, Tom gave him a hard look. "It means you had everything going for you. No one ever yanked the football out from under you."

"How can you *say* that?" he asked indignantly. "What about when my dad died? What about *that?*"

"Life happens, Michael, you have to get over it."

"*Get over it?* Are you *serious?*"

"Yes…no one owes you anything because you lost your father," Tom replied firmly. "You weren't entitled to a perfect life simply because you suffered one tragedy. No one gets a perfect life. In fact, lots of people suffer throughout their entire lives."

Michael gave a disgusted grunt. "Yeah, that's another thing. If God, or the Creator, *or whatever*, really is all around us," he said, motioning with his arms, "then tell me this, why is there so much damn suffering in this world?"

Tom focused his eyes on him intently and sighed for a moment. "I don't know Michael, maybe it's just necessary."

"*Necessary?* How can you believe all the horrible things that happen in the world are *necessary?*" he ranted, banging his ghostly hand down on the desk with a loud thud. "Is it absolutely necessary that a little kid should get a disease and die? Or worse yet, get abducted and murdered by a rapist? Or, what about a tornado that destroys a whole town in the middle of the night? Or, a baby who's born into a life of impoverished hell in some god-forsaken part of the world? I could give you a dozen examples of senseless shit that happens every day." He pointed at Tom and yelled, "For Christ's sake, you witnessed 9/11! How do you explain things like that, *huh*?"

"First of all, watch your language." Tom answered sternly. "Second, I believe everything happens for a reason."

Michael stared at him dumbfounded. He wanted to believe as strongly as this man obviously still did, but after all he'd been through, it was difficult to say the least. *How can he see it all so clearly, when he's still stuck like me?*

Not completely convinced Tom had answered his question, he retorted, "Well, I hope you're right. I sure as hell hope you're right."

"I am, Michael, you'll see," Tom said in a reassuring way. "You'll see."

He sat back down, this time on top of the desk. "I just don't understand," he said sourly. "I thought for sure my dad would be here. Why isn't he here?"

"Was this a happy place for him?"

"Of course," he mumbled halfheartedly, "my dad loved it here. When my grandfather retired, my dad took over running the business. He enjoyed the work and I think he was proud of all he'd managed to accomplish. When he wasn't home, he was usually here...slaving away, trying to keep this place going."

Tom stood silently in thought for a moment and then said, "Michael, it may be very difficult to find your father by searching for him. Think about it, he could be almost anywhere. If he's found a friend in the spirit world, he could draft to places off his energy trail, same as you."

Tom's point made no sense whatsoever. "Are you saying I shouldn't bother to look for him?"

"No," Tom replied, "I'm merely suggesting maybe there's a better way of going about this. Halloween is coming up in a couple weeks."

Michael floated around to the front of the desk. "*So,* what's that got to do with anything?"

"I know a place we can go on Halloween where we might be able to find someone who can contact your father."

"What do you mean…like a medium or something?"

"Yes, this one's quite powerful and she's usually in Salem for Halloween."

"Salem, Massachusetts?"

Tom nodded.

"That's perfect," he said anxiously. "My aunt Susan lives close to Salem, so maybe I can see if my dad's there."

"It's possible I guess," Tom said. "A number of spirits hang out there for Halloween. It's one hell of a Dead Man's Party," he added lightly.

Michael was about to ask him exactly what he meant, when Tom got that familiar look on his face again.

"I've got to go. I'll meet you on the beach right after sunset on Halloween," Tom said, as he quickly faded out.

Am I really going to able to contact my dad?

CHAPTER TWENTY-FOUR

SALEM

MICHAEL COULDN'T GO back to Sarah right away. He needed time to think. After Tom left, he paced the floors of his father's building. *Everything is just so complicated now. I don't know where my father is, or why he's stuck. Hell, I still have no idea why I'm stuck. Worst of all, the demons were able to find me and I put Sarah in danger* twice.

Several hours later, he'd come to at least one firm conclusion.

Terrified he might lead demons to Sarah, he summoned her to the beach instead of going to the Angel of the Sea.

Standing near the water's edge, he called out her name, "Sarah McConnell."

Materializing up ahead, she ran to his arms the moment she saw him, burying her face in his shoulder and sobbing.

She finally managed to choke out six words. "I thought they had gotten you."

Taking her face in his hands, he gently brushed away her spectral tears and kissed her fiercely. "I told you I'd be back," he reminded her as he stroked her hair.

She glanced up at him with those beautiful, yet fearful eyes. "Why didn't you come back to the Angel?"

"I was afraid if the demons could track me twice, then

they might be able to do it again...and I didn't want to lead them there." He looked away from her scrutinizing gaze. "I thought it would be safer to summon you here instead."

"Oh, *that's* what happened," she said. "All I knew was I suddenly felt compelled to come to this spot."

"That's how summoning works." He let out an exasperated sigh. "Now, if only I could get it to work with my dad."

Sarah puckered her face, looking completely confused. "Your dad?"

"Yeah..." he answered, in hushed disappointment.

As they walked along the beach, he told her all about what happened with Matt and also his father's mysterious appearance.

"I just don't understand why he would have left without saying anything, or why I can't summon him, like I do with Tom or you." He lowered his voice till he was barely audible. "I don't even know why he's still *here*. All I know is that I have to find him. Maybe he'll know why I'm stuck, or what I should do."

Sarah let go of his hand and turned to face him. Seeing the anguish in his eyes, this time it was she who reached up, softly touching his cheeks. "It's going to be okay." She laced her fingers in back of his neck. "I'm sure you'll find him."

He smiled, but only a little. Putting his hands on her waist, his eyes ticked across her face, as if trying to commit her features to memory. Then, he whispered, "I love you," and kissed her with all the desperation of a man about to be shipped off to war.

When they finally pulled apart, he couldn't hide the dark

cloud of intense sadness that hung in his eyes. Too heartsick to look at her, he stared gloomily at the sand.

Seeing the pained expression on his face, she started to say, "We're getting better at not having our energies slip—"

He cut her off. "It's not that," he said, his voice thick with tension.

"Then what is it?" She scanned his face, as if she might find the answers hidden there. "Are you angry with me?"

"No, of *course* not." He wrapped his arms around her even more. "I'm angry at myself for letting this happen."

With fear in her eyes, she asked quietly, "For letting *what* happen?"

"For falling in love with you," he said reluctantly. *And for putting you in danger.*

In barely a whisper she asked, "Do you want to leave?"

"*No*, I don't want to go anywhere," he said, pulling her tightly to him. "And neither do *you*. Sarah, don't you *see*...that's the whole problem." He searched her eyes, hoping she would understand what he was trying to say. This was going to be one of the hardest things he ever had to do, but he forced himself to continue. "I think the Elders might be right. We can't do this." He shook his head in dismay. "I don't know for sure if there is somewhere to move on to...but if there is...then I *don't* want to be the one to *keep* you here."

She stepped away from him and jammed her hand on her hip. Judging by the stubborn look on her face, she thought she could talk him out of this. "What if there's *nowhere* else in this universe I'd rather be?"

He took her by the shoulders and shook her lightly.

"Don't *say* that. Moving on is the *most* important thing. You *don't* want to be stuck here forever."

Closing the distance between them, she said emphatically, "If it means being stuck with you, then I don't mind."

"That's just *it*," he said, growing impatient. The words were like tacks in his throat but he had to say them. "At least I'm *trying* to figure out why I'm stuck, or where there is to go. You're content to sit at the Angel of the Sea never *knowing*."

She turned away from his gaze. "I told you," she whispered. "I already know why I'm stuck. God thinks it was a suicide."

"I don't believe that, Sarah, and neither do *you*. You hide behind that excuse because you're too *scared* to leave the Angel. You're too afraid to find out the *truth!*"

"But, I'm getting *better* about leaving the Angel...because I feel *safe* with you." Her eyes glistened with tears, but she reached up to gently lay a hand on his chest.

The warmth of her touch radiated straight into his phantom heart. He groaned and took two steps back. She wasn't taking him seriously. "You're *not* safe with me. Every minute I'm with you, I put you in more danger. What if I lead the demons to you again? We got away from them this time, but we might not be so lucky the *next* time," he said, pleading for her to see reason. "What if they mark *you*, because of *me*? I *can't* let that *happen*."

She shook her head in protest. "That's not going to happen—"

"You're right," he interrupted, "because I'm not going to *let* it."

Pushing away from her, he said, "Sarah, I want you to stay at the Angel of the Sea. Until I figure out which end is up, I'm not going to put you in danger anymore." His jaw hardened as he steeled his resolve. "Don't try to summon me," he said, forcing the words out quickly so he wouldn't stumble. "I won't come."

As he turned his back on her and faded, it took every bit of his strength not to turn around, especially when she started to cry.

·   ·   ·

Even the trees mark the passage of time. The lush green leaves of summer give way to the fiery orange, cherry-red and golden colors of fall. For Michael, time was at a painful standstill and like Dorian Gray, even aging would've been better than this.

He missed his family, but it was too painful to go home and see them. He missed his friends and wondered if they were enjoying their first semester at college. And if he was honest with himself, some tiny part of his soul still missed Melissa, too.

Mostly though, he longed for Sarah. Every day he wrestled with himself about going back to the Angel of the Sea. A few times, he almost failed, the painful void in his soul almost winning out. But in the end, he didn't dare go for fear he would put her in danger again.

Almost cruelly, the next two weeks passed like the

MARLO BERLINER

movement of a glacier, slow and imperceptible, while he waited at his grandmother's beach house—alone.

Each day he honed his skills, moving objects, turning lights and appliances on and off. Practicing was as natural for him as walking. It was the same as basketball—skill and drill. *Maybe haunting is just spirits doing exactly what I'm doing—improving their abilities.*

Finally, Halloween night arrived and as planned, he met Tom on the beach in North Carolina.

"What have you been up to?" Tom called out.

"Just chillaxin'," he responded coolly.

Tom offered his outstretched arm. "Are you ready to go to Salem?"

"Yeah, but hang on," he said confidently, as he extended his own arm. "I know the way. *I'm* driving."

In a split second, they were standing on Derby Street near the wharf. The Friendship, a 171 foot long replica of a tallship with triple masts, stood anchored nearby in Salem Harbor.

"This was the part of Salem I remembered most," Michael said sheepishly.

"That was pretty good memory traveling," Tom complimented with a wink. "But, I think we should walk further into town."

Making their way down Derby Street, they passed the New England Pirate Museum and then the Wax Museum of Witches and Seafarers, both of which he'd visited as a youngster. The lines stretched out the door.

"I've never been here on Halloween," he said. "We always came up to see my Aunt Susan during the summer. My dad said it was too damned cold up here the rest of the year." *Knowing Dad, he probably wanted to avoid the crowds.*

Dressed in Halloween costumes, people of all ages shuffled through the jam-packed streets. The old-fashioned walking mall was lined with quaint shops full of touristy souvenirs and trinkets reflecting the city's infamous connection to the witchcraft trials of 1692. Vendors on the street sold clothes, jewelry, and food, trying to make the most of the supernatural holiday. The only dissenters—the few protestors walking around with signs asking everyone to 'Repent of Ye Wicked Ways'.

On this night, Salem had become a virtual necropolis. Besides the living, the place teemed with ghosts from nearly every period of time. Some held conversations in small groups. Others danced on the street corner to music only they could hear. Several drifted casually by, paying them no attention at all. The only ghost that acknowledged him was a pretty young woman in eighteenth century dress, who smiled and batted her eye lashes seductively.

"You know," he said to Tom, "I remember all the creepy stories my Aunt used to tell us about Salem, but I never thought I'd be wandering around here as a ghost myself."

"I understand," Tom said sympathetically. "It takes a little getting used to."

Bizarre. Up ahead, the ghost of Marilyn Monroe walked beside a very deceased Kurt Cobain. With his arm around her waist, he was arguing intensely in her ear.

Unbelievable. Death sure makes some strange friends. Pausing in mid-step, he turned to Tom. "Why are all these spirits here?"

"It's Halloween," Tom said brightly. "It's our night—The Feast of the Dead, Ancestor Night, The Festival of Darkness. It's the one night in all the year when we're fully acknowledged by the living. On Halloween, the ghost community comes together in a few cities around the country and around the world. Salem, New Orleans, San Francisco, and London are all hot spots."

Presently, they reached the Salem Witch Museum, a creepy, stone Romanesque building, which ironically resembled a church and faced Salem Common. The line to get in snaked around the block.

"This is a popular place tonight," Michael quipped.

"I think we should try the Burying Point," Tom suggested.

From having visited his aunt so many times, Michael already knew The Burying Point was the oldest cemetery in the city of Salem and also one of the oldest in the country. The antiquated, crumbling headstones dated back to as early as 1637. An area of the cemetery was designated as a memorial to the unfortunate victims of the horrifying hysteria known as the Salem Witch Trials. The history was infamous—many of the accused were hanged, some died from sickness in jail, and a few were tortured, meeting their death by even nastier means.

Gliding through the cemetery entrance, Michael stopped short. Open-mouthed and wide-eyed he stared, as the spectres of two beautiful dragons came into view, soaring just above the tree line beyond the cemetery walls. Moonlight glinted off their skin, the most magnificent shade of deep, iridescent blue he'd ever seen. Spreading their wings wide, the two dragons rose majestically into the black velvet sky, locked in an aerial 'pas de deux'.

"Are those really *dragon* ghosts?" he asked in disbelief.

"Of course," Tom replied simply. "Don't you trust your own eyes?"

"I guess so," he said, still unsure, "but I thought dragons were only mythical creatures."

Tom grinned. "You mean like ghosts?"

"Yeah—" he started to say, before he realized he'd been setup. He shot Tom a look that said, "I can't believe you just did that."

"Why are you so surprised to see dragons?" Tom asked rhetorically. "Don't you know your bible? Daniel, St. Margaret, St. George, they all slew dragons."

Eyes still fixed on the mysterious creatures, Michael replied, "Wow. Could you *imagine* the hits if we could get this on YouTube?"

Tom shook his head slightly. "Poor dragons, they were misunderstood creatures. Like people, some were bad, but many were good. It's a shame they had to die out. Not surprising though, they never really numbered that many to begin with."

As they floated past the rows of crumbling, faded tombstones, Michael spied several of the living also hanging out in the cemetery tonight. Up ahead sitting on a wooden bench, he spotted a woman in her mid-forties wearing a witch's costume, pointed hat and all. She was murmuring to the thin night air, an ancient tome held deftly in her fingertips, a crusty talisman hanging from her neck. Her lips moved slowly, reciting something—an incantation, a prayer, a curse?

Michael stared at her a moment or two, then raised his eyebrows and asked mockingly, "What's she *doing*?"

"She's trying to cast a spell from the Book of Shadows," Tom explained. "It's similar to a grimoire used by magicians. For witches or those who practice Wicca, Halloween is the most important of the four Greater Sabbats, or the Witches Sabbath. It's also known as the Samhain, the Last or Blood Harvest."

Michael grinned with amusement. "So, she's *a witch?*"

"No, this one's a wannabe," Tom said. "She's one of those people that think it's fun to dabble in Wicca. Most of them practice it quietly behind closed doors for fear of ridicule. This one's out of the broom closet. See the medallion around her neck," he said, pointing. "She's the high priestess of her coven."

"So, *why* are they hanging in the cemetery with all the dead witches?"

"They feel a certain solidarity with the victims of the Witch Trials."

"You know, I grew up with a healthy fear of the occult," Michael said, not really content to be there.

"Most of these people are harmless," Tom commented casually. "They—"

"*Most?*" he interrupted.

"Yes," Tom continued, "they seek the attention and power they can get from these practices. Still, they should be careful. There is the power men *can* seek and then there is the power men *should* seek."

"I'm in agreement on that," he said. "The occult was not the can of worms I ever wanted to open. In school, I steered clear of the fringe element, like the Goths."

"You shouldn't be so judgmental of others, though." Tom peered down his nose at him. "What people look like on the *outside* is sometimes *not* who they are on the inside."

Michael crossed his arms, ready to make a clever comeback, but someone caught his attention. A young woman with fiery red hair, dressed in a long black cloak sat cross-legged on the grass just inside the stone wall. Like the other woman, she was also murmuring to herself with her eyes closed and she appeared to be in some kind of trance. She had a safety pin through her eyebrow and another through her lower lip.

"Oh, *yeah?* Perfect example right here," he mumbled, shaking his head disapprovingly. "I will never understand why people are into physical graffiti."

"What's that?" asked Tom.

"Physical graffiti," Michael repeated. "Tattoos and body piercing, stuff like that. I've never really felt the need to stick a safety pin through my face," he said, pointing up near his eye. "I mean, honestly, can your eyebrow actually fall off?"

Tom laughed heartily. "I don't think so. I'd have to agree with you there. A nose-ring infection never sounded like much fun to me either."

Michael twisted up his face in confusion and jerked his thumb at the redhead. "What's this one doing?"

Tom listened for a moment. "She's trying to contact the dead."

Without thinking, Michael quipped, "What a *freak*."

"First off, you're being judgmental again," Tom

cautioned. "And second, be careful what you say. You never know who might be able to hear you."

"Wait a minute, I thought you said the living couldn't hear us unless we project sounds we want them to hear," he reminded him.

"*Most* of the living can't," Tom corrected.

"Most? You mean some can?"

"Yes, a few, but true mediums are very rare. Most are frauds, but there are some who can contact spirits on this side. They can summon them the same way you summon me. Or, sometimes they can sense spirits that are around them."

Out of nowhere, the redheaded woman with the piercings suddenly looked up at them and said, "I can hear every word you're saying, you know."

Michael took two quick steps back, startled. "Can you *see* us?" he asked the girl.

"No, and please *don't* try to manifest. It's already cold enough out here tonight," she replied testily, pulling her cloak further closed.

Wanting to be polite and give introductions, he started to say, "I'm Michael Andrews, and this is—"

"Tom Wright," she finished for him with a confident air. "I knew it was you."

"Exceptional as always, Mariah," Tom complimented in a friendly way. "How have you been?"

"Just peachy," Mariah replied in a dry, sarcastic tone. "I'm trapped in a friggin' episode of the Twilight Zone, same as ever."

Tom laughed and a sardonic grin crossed the girl's face.

"Mariah, my friend here has a favor to ask you," Tom said, as he nodded to Michael, indicating he should speak for himself.

"Uh, I'm having trouble summoning my father from this side. So we were wondering if you could try to summon him from your side."

"I'll need to know your father's name and you'll have to put your hand in mine, so I can identify his energy from your memories," the strange girl replied succinctly, like a doctor dictating a routine prescription.

"His name was...uh, *is* Eric Andrews," Michael corrected himself, placing his hand in Mariah's open palm.

She shut her eyes and began slowly rocking back and forth. After several minutes, she said out loud in a nasally voice, "Paging Eric Andrews. Come in, over."

"*Mariah*," Tom said, reproachful.

"I'm only kidding," she said apologizing. "Just trying to lighten the mood and let the guy down easy." Addressing Michael directly she said, "I'm really sorry, but I'm not getting anything. Either your father can't communicate, or won't. He may have even moved on. I can't tell."

The disappointment stung. He truly thought he had a chance of seeing his father again and this failure pierced his heart like a blade. *All that waiting, for nothing.*

"I'm sorry," Tom said to him with great sincerity.

Michael turned toward Mariah and said feebly, "Thanks for trying."

She looked in the general direction of his voice and said, "You're welcome, Michael. Best of luck to you."

• • •

Michael hadn't been paying attention at all to where they were walking. He hadn't said much either since leaving the cemetery. Once again, it was as if he were falling into an endless abyss of despair. His mind felt numb, frozen.

Now, he realized they had somehow entered the deep, tangled woods surrounding Salem, something straight out of 'The Blair Witch Project'. The place matched his dark mood perfectly.

"I guess that's it then. I got my answer," he said in disgust, "there *is* no heaven."

"What makes you say that?"

"Because if there was a heaven, then that's where my father would be."

Tom was silent, as a veil of disappointment drew across his face.

Michael saw the look on his friend's face. "But I guess I still hope I'm wrong, because if there really is no heaven, then where the hell *is* my father? Why won't he come to me?"

"I don't—," Tom cut his answer short as his face went slack. "Michael, get behind me!" he suddenly commanded.

The alarm in his friend's voice took Michael completely by surprise. "*Why?* What's the matter?" he asked, searching Tom's face for answers.

"Remember when you were little and your mother and father told you there was no reason to be afraid of the dark?"

"Yes," Michael replied, fear rising in him, like the hackles on a dog.

"Your parents meant well, but they were very wrong," Tom said. "There really are things that go bump in the night."

"What the hell does that mean?" *Now, what am I up against?*

"Um, not to alarm you or anything, but there's a circle of vampires closing in around us."

"*Vampires*...you're joking, right?" But, even as his sarcasm slipped out, he realized from the expression on Tom's face that he was most definitely not joking.

"But how the hell can *they* hurt us? We're already *dead!*" Michael blurted out, his ghostly eyes popping wide open.

"Yes, but they aren't exactly like Bram Stoker or Anne Rice would have you believe. They're not going to bite you, although they do enjoy sarcophagy of the living."

His voice rose in fear. "What the hell is *sarcophagy?*"

"Feasting on the flesh," Tom answered, "but that's not what you need to worry about. Vampires are neither dead nor alive, they're somewhere in between, which actually makes them even stronger than a normal demon. And like all demons, their job is to claim souls both living and dead for the devil. Unfortunately, the difference is vampires possess a tremendous amount of evil energy, far more than your average demon."

Michael squeezed his eyes shut for a second in dismay. Then, an ironic grin crossed his face. "So, you're saying they're like *uber*-demons?"

"Precisely," Tom said, his words laced with anxiety. "And we've walked right into a pack of them."

"Well...*serendipity*. Why can't we just orb and get the hell out of here?"

"It's too late for that. They're too close and we're surrounded. We wouldn't be able to get away and orbing would leave us too vulnerable to capture."

Michael couldn't ignore a disturbing thought that now crept up on him. *Had Tom led him here?* It seemed all too convenient that they had come this way, only to be confronted by demons. He tamped out the thought, convincing himself it was ridiculous. "Then what do we do now?" he asked, sounding braver than he felt.

Beside him, Tom tensed, drawing in energy. "We stand our ground and we fight. Now listen to me, if attacked by vampires they'll try to make you give your soul willingly over to the devil. Whatever you do, never look them in the eyes for even a few seconds. That's when their power over you is strongest and you'll be most vulnerable."

As Tom said this, a host of men and women emerged from the dark woods, forming a ring around the two of them. Eight in all, they were dressed in elaborate Goth robes of black, deep purple and red. Tom was right, though…except for their fancy cloaks, these were not the seductive, handsome creatures portrayed in books and movies. In fact, they seemed barely human at all. They were hideous monsters, sneering, hissing and displaying their claw-like fingernails and frightful fangs in order to intimidate them. And it was definitely working. *Where's Van Helsing when you need him?*

He gave a sideways glance at Tom and whispered, "You mean these aren't just some teenagers playing Vampire Masquerade?"

"Sorry, but, no," Tom said. "Stand your ground Michael,

and remember what I told you about their eyes."

For the moment, he had no intention of leaving Tom's side. Seized by the steely grasp of terror, he could scarcely move anyway. The evil energy of the circle of vampires was getting ever closer, tightening around them. Intellect told him to turn and run, but instinct told him he wouldn't get very far if he tried. Nervous, uncontrolled energy coursed through him. His leg started to quiver and he placed a hand on the top of his thigh, forcing it to stop. *This is no time to get antsy. Whatever we're facing, I have to be brave.*

Directly across from him, Matt materialized in the center of the circle. It was hard to believe, but he had grown even more hideous since the last time. His yellowed eyes had now sunken deep into his skull. He resembled the walking dead.

The transformation is almost complete. "*You* again?" Michael said in disgust. "What's the matter? You couldn't handle me by yourself, so you brought more *friends* this time?"

Matt's only response was an ice-cold stare.

One of the vampires stepped forward to stand directly in front of Tom.

"*Vassago*, how nice to see you," Tom said coolly, averting his eyes and directing his gaze to the left of the vampire instead.

"Don't *toy* with me, Protector, you're outnumbered. Hand over the tyro, or my friends and I will destroy you both."

"Come, come, Vassago, you'll have no power here, now be gone, before someone drops a house on *you*," Tom retorted with a masterful grin on his face.

Michael glanced sideways at Tom. *Is he actually enjoying this?*

"Very well," Vassago replied confidently, with a smile of his own, "have it your way Protector." At once, the ring of vampires closed in on them. "Get the *boy!*" Vassago hissed and in a flash, the creatures attacked.

Four of the vampires lunged at him, two from behind and two from in front. Simultaneously, the three closest to Tom flew in his direction, too.

Without even realizing what he was doing, Michael raised his hands and a surge of energy shot forward, blasting two of the vampires backward. They let out a strangled snarl and crumpled to the ground, clutching their chests. Glancing next to him, he saw Tom had managed to hit two of them as well.

Michael whirled around to face the other two, but he was too late. Like before, a paralyzing pain shot through him draining all of his strength, as two vampires took hold of him. He looked to his friend for help, but Matt struck Tom with a powerful blow that sent him flying backward and into the bushes. As Vassago now advanced on him, Michael struggled to free his energy from their grasp, but it was no use.

Two male vampires held him, while a female vampire grabbed his face and forced it upward. "You *will* look at our master," she purred menacingly in his ear.

He tried all he could to not look the vampire in the face, but he was growing weaker by the second and couldn't resist. Vassago was face to face with him now and he locked eyes with him.

All at once the pain stopped, and a wave of relief engulfed him. "See Michael, is that so bad?" Vassago said to him telepathically. "Doesn't this feel better," he soothed. "You don't have to fight me. I'm going to give you a choice—I can either turn you or destroy you. It could all be over *very* quickly. All you have to do is stop resisting."

Matt now spoke up. "Lucifer can give you great power and immortality, all you have to do is declare your allegiance to him."

Michael forced the words from his mouth. "No...*never*," he growled.

"Why not? Don't you want to see your father again?" Vassago asked in a sing-song voice.

What the hell does he know about my father?

In answer to his thought, Vassago said in a cloying voice, "Ahhh, I know a great deal, Michael. Did you know Tom is *keeping* you from your father?"

He glared at the demon, saying nothing.

"Judging by your silence," Vassago continued, sounding amused, "I take it he *hasn't* then. But that's not the only secret he's keeping from you."

"You're a *liar*," Michael snarled.

Matt and a few of the other demons chuckled. "Oh, sometimes I am," Vassago said with a crooked grin, "but I can assure you, this time I'm telling the truth."

"*Screw* off!" he managed to shout.

Vassago's expression changed to one of fury and he unleashed the full force of his power on Michael's aura by placing his hands on his arms.

Pain shot everywhere, as if his body were riddled with

bullets. Growing weaker and more confused by the second, he struggled in vain to break free. Dizzy and disoriented, he began to lose possession of his mind.

I can't fight him, he's too strong. He's just too strong. Wouldn't it be easier to give in? It's easier this way. I won't be lost anymore. The pain is gone now. It's over now. It can all be over now…

From behind him, came the crack of breaking branches. With a swift, rushing sound Tom exploded out from behind the bushes and sent a blast that knocked Vassago and the other vampires off their feet. Swiveling to face Matt, Tom raised his arms again…

The last thing Michael saw was his father standing beside Tom. Then, a blinding flash of light. And then, nothing.

CHAPTER TWENTY-FIVE

MISTAKE

SOMETIME LATER, MICHAEL regained consciousness and opened his eyes. He was lying on the grass in his own backyard, his eyes fixed on Orion's Belt. Sitting up beside his dad's favorite tree, he dragged a hand over his face and drew in a ragged ghostly breath. His head throbbed unmercifully. *Great. A phantom hangover.*

Tom extended an arm and helped him up.

"Not bad, not bad at all," his friend praised.

"What do you *mean*? That *creature*...that *thing*, almost *powned* me." He shuddered. "That was *too* close, too damned close."

"Yes, but you used your power and fought off two of them successfully," Tom replied, sounding oddly triumphant. "We were really outnumbered for a minute there, and if you hadn't helped out, that might've ended badly. You did just fine."

"Thanks," he said begrudgingly, not very proud of his sorry-ass effort. Remembering the encounter, a curious question popped into his head. "How did you know Vassago was his name?"

After a long pause, Tom said, "If you're going to play in the neighborhood, you better know who the bullies are."

Michael was silent for a moment, as he considered Tom's sketchy answer. "Well, what was it that Vassago called me...a *tyro*, or something like that?"

"Yes." Tom answered, without elaborating.

"What does that *mean?*" he pressed.

"Um...it means young one," his friend said vaguely.

Again, all he was getting was Tom's clever avoidance. *I'll have to get my hands on a dictionary sometime soon.*

A few seconds later, his mind finally unscrambled and he remembered everything that had happened. "I saw my father again," he said, dismal.

To his tremendous surprise, Tom answered "I know."

He stared at him in blank confusion. "*Well*, did he *say* anything?"

"No, he didn't. After I took care of Matt and the vampires, I turned around and he was already gone."

"Why does he keep showing up like that and then leaving me?" He threw his arms up in frustration. "It doesn't make any *sense*."

"I'm sure your father must have his reasons," Tom replied in a low voice.

"You just don't *get* it," he said completely exasperated. "I didn't want him to be a ghost. He was supposed to be in heaven. It was important for me to get to heaven, because I assumed that's where my father was. Now, I don't know what to think. Maybe that demon was right. Maybe there is no heaven. Maybe there really is nowhere to move on to."

The expression on Tom's face was one of understanding, and pity. "Hang in there," he said kindly. "You'll find the answers soon."

Speaking of answers. "Uh…yeah, that reminds me. I have to ask you about something," he said slowly, narrowing his eyes on his mentor. "Did you hear Vassago claim you were somehow *keeping* me from my father?"

Tom stared at him hard before answering. "Yes, I heard that," he said in a tight voice. "Demons *lie*, Michael. You should never trust anything they say."

He searched Tom's face.

Before he could decide if this was the whole truth or not, his friend said gruffly, "I've got to go now, but call me if you need me."

This time, it was Michael who faded out quickly, before Tom even had a chance to say goodbye.

. . .

In the hazy fog of morning, a gull circled and swooped down to land on the sea. Four weeks had passed since Halloween. He longed for Sarah. Missing her was so painful that many times, he almost went back. Ultimately, he stayed at his grandmother's beach house, venturing out only for walks on the beach or along the bay, late at night or early in the morning.

On this particular day, he left his grandmother's beach house right before dawn. He preferred to be near the ocean. Since the birth of humanity, the one place on earth that seemed timeless and unchanged was the seashore. It wouldn't be difficult to imagine that a million years from now, the ocean's magnificent waves would still be crashing into these sands, as powerfully and continuously as ever. *An immortal force.*

Tired of not seeing people, he decided to walk down by the docks for a while to watch the boats.

Several fishermen were getting a jump on the day's catch and preparing to set sail.

Michael strolled passed one of the large party boats and a man's voice called out frantically, "It's him! It's his ghost!"

For a second, he was sure they were talking about him, but then he followed the man's shaking finger. The ghost of an old fisherman hovered inches above the quarterdeck.

At first scowling at the startled fishermen below on the dock, the spirit now caught sight of him.

Michael returned his gaze and waited on the dock.

As the ghost walked down to the lower deck and then off the boat, one of the other fishermen yelled, "He's gone!" Immediately, the fishermen started cursing about not being able to get their cell phones out fast enough to snap a picture. They talked wildly about their good fortune at having seen the ghost and how his apparition was a good omen for the day's fishing endeavors.

The ghostly old fisherman now stood in front of him. His white-bearded face, with its deep creases, had a kindly, yet careworn appearance. Everything about him looked as if it had been scrubbed raw by the salty sea air, except his eyes. They sparkled with a friendly excitement, as he extended a callused hand. "Captain Virgil Summers," he said warmly.

Taking the man's rough palm Michael introduced himself and without hesitating quickly asked him, "How do you do that? How do you make the living see you?"

The old ghost evaluated him with a wary eye before

answering. "It took me quite a while and a lot of practice."

"Would you teach me?" he asked, hopeful. He would have liked to ask Tom, but he knew his mentor would probably disapprove and not give him a straight answer.

The old salty dog rubbed his chin, looking skeptical. "I'm not sure if I'd know how to teach someone else."

"Please, can you *try*? I'd really like to be able to do it."

"Yeah, you think so now. Let me tell you, it's not all it's cracked up to be. The only reason I do it once in a while around here is to remind these dopey bastards to be careful out at sea," he said, "so they don't end up like me."

He hated to beg, but this was important. "*Please*," he pleaded, getting right up in the man's face.

"Alright, alright," the old man said, giving in. He thought for a second. "You know how we project what we want other ghosts to see us like?"

"Yes," he responded with a nod.

"It's actually the same thing," he said. "Except, getting through to the conscious mind of a living person is more difficult because they're so blocked. Tell me, have you been able to read the thoughts of the living yet?"

He nodded again.

"Okay, good," the man said. "That means you've managed to penetrate a living person's mind before, so then this shouldn't be too hard for you. Manifesting can actually be done in a similar way. Except instead of using your energy to extract thoughts from a living person's mind, you simply *implant* your thoughts."

"So...I think of how I want them to see me and take control of their thoughts?"

"Exactly," the Captain said. "You provide them with the picture. They'll *see* you, because you've told their mind that they'll see you. That's why two living people can be in a room with a spirit, and one can see the ghost manifest while the other can't. Some minds are also more difficult to penetrate. But for the most part, you can control how many people see you. If there's a room full of people, you can make everyone see you, or only some of them see you. It's up to you how many minds you penetrate."

Michael didn't even try to contain his eagerness. "*Cool*, I wanna do it."

"Okay, but remember, it's going to take a lot of your energy," the man cautioned, "and I don't want to be responsible for whatever might happen."

"I understand," he said impatiently.

"Alright then." The old fisherman pointed to a shack on the pier a short distance away. "Let's go to the coffee shop."

Michael practiced on a large man sitting at the counter for almost an hour with no results. The guy was too interested in the stack of hot cakes and sausage on his plate than anything else. Finally, he turned to the Captain and said, "Unless I materialize as a plate of bacon, I don't have a chance in *hell* of getting through to this guy's mind."

"Maybe you should try somebody else." The Captain suggested. "How about that blonde over there near the window," he said, jerking his thumb in that direction.

"Okay," he agreed and glided over to a booth where two young women sat drinking coffee. Sizing up the blonde, he decided to try her mind first. It was incredibly easy to penetrate. The girls were waiting here and catching up on gossip, while their boyfriends were out fishing.

Listening to the two of them prattle on was beginning to drive him crazy. Almost about to give up, he started to see something reflected in the window. He had managed to conjure a weak, misty image of himself.

For a split second, the blonde glanced up at his transparent form. Her mouth fell wide open as her cup slipped from her hand, spilling coffee all over the table.

Within seconds, Michael lost concentration and faded from the girl's sight.

"What's the matter with you?" her friend asked in alarm.

The blonde's face had drained of all color and her hands trembled like a victim of Parkinson's. "I...I thought I saw a man standing right next to you and then he...he just disappeared."

The girl's friend looked at her like she couldn't possibly be serious, as she began wiping up the spill with some napkins. "*Geez*, Beth, you really have been working long hours. That's enough coffee for you."

The old fisherman grinned at him, pleased. "That was *good*, I think she saw you."

Slightly disappointed, Michael asked, "How come I was so blurry, though?"

"Like I said, it takes a lot of energy. The more energy you manage to pull from your surroundings, the clearer you'll appear. It's difficult though. That's why most apparitions appear as no more than pale smoke, like you did a minute ago. You can even seem solid though, if you harness enough energy. But, it doesn't last very long. It works best if you're in a place where your energy trail is very strong, like where you lived, for instance. Also, the more charged the atmosphere is around you, the better chance you have of a good manifestation."

"Charged how?"

"On days when the air is full of excess energy due to a solar flare or a good thunderstorm, you'll have a surplus of energy to tap into," the man explained in an authoritative way. "Lightening ionizes the air and makes it easier to manifest. And the moon also affects us. The geomagnetic fields on the earth are strongest during the days around the new and full moon cycles. The jump in geomagnetic activity helps us manifest."

He stared at the Captain in utter amazement. "How in the *hell* do you know all that?"

"I had a little chat with Einstein a while back," the Captain replied in a matter of fact tone.

Michael lifted an eyebrow. *Unbelievable. I'm not sure if he's serious or not, but I wouldn't be a bit surprised.* "Thanks for teaching me," he said, "I really appreciate it."

"No problem kid, just don't go doin' anything stupid," the Captain said, shaking his hand once more.

"I won't."

I know exactly what I want to do and it isn't stupid. Tonight, I'm going to let my mother and brother know I'm still here.

• • •

Hours later, Michael stood on the sidewalk in front of his house. He was about to ascend the porch stairs when a commotion erupted across the street.

He spun around. Despite the full moon, the driveway was pitch-black, but he could hear angry voices. Voices he recognized. Kevin's car sat parked in front of Jamie's house.

What's he doing there? He wondered, as he crossed the street to see what was going on.

"Leave me alone Kevin," Jamie was saying, an anxious edge to her voice. "My parents will be home any minute."

"No they won't," Kevin answered in a smug tone. "I ran into them at the Mall a little while ago. They said they were getting you a belated sweet sixteen present." Pulling her against him, he whispered in her ear, "You are sweet, you know that Jamie."

She pushed away from him again. "Kevin, I told you I'm *not* interested."

"Come on, Jamie," he said his words sickeningly sugar-coated. "You know we'd have a good time."

"Yeah, I'm *sure*," she replied sarcastically. "I'm still not interested."

Kevin's face hardened and his nostrils flared. "*Well* then," he growled, "maybe I'll have to *convince* you." Grabbing Jamie's wrists, he slammed her up against the back porch steps and thrust his knee between her legs.

Michael lunged at Kevin, but passed right through him. He wanted to tear him apart, but he was helpless.

"Ow! You're hurting me!" Jamie exclaimed, panic rising in her voice.

"Be quiet," Kevin barked. Covering her mouth with his own, he kissed her hard, even though she didn't kiss him back.

This is escalating. He had barely a minute or two to stop this and he knew what he had to do. If anything, hopefully it would distract the bastard long enough for Jamie to run. Gathering his strength, he prepared to manifest.

Only he didn't have to. Seconds later, headlights flooded the driveway. Jamie's parents had come home.

Kevin quickly released his grip on Jamie and immediately changed his demeanor.

"I'll talk to you later Jamie," he said politely. "I gotta run." Walking swiftly down the driveway to his car, he faked a friendly wave back in Jamie's direction and said a quick hello to her parents before ducking into his car.

"What's going on?" her mother said curiously. "Wasn't that Kevin Manfreda?

"Yeah, it was," Jamie said. She gave her parents a tight-lipped smile, twitching her foot nervously from side to side.

"Why did he leave so fast?" her mother asked, clearly picking something up on her mom radar.

Jamie lightly bit her lip and hesitated. Her eyes darted back and forth between her mother and her father, lingering on him the most. She obviously wanted to tell her parents but she must've been afraid of how much to reveal. Her father was always yelling at her for the short skirts she wore and saying how she was "asking for it". He would probably place the blame squarely on her shoulders.

"I told him to go home…I didn't want to talk to him anymore," Jamie said, glancing away. "He's a *jerk*."

Jamie's mother scrutinized her daughter's face. "If he bothers you sweetheart, you let us know, okay?" Her mother must have known from experience not to press too hard for information from a teenager.

"I will Mom," Jamie replied in earnest.

That was the last thing Michael heard as he flew off to catch up with Kevin's car.

Once inside, he sat in the passenger seat glaring at him. Had he been alive, he probably would've killed him. "You were going to rape her, *you son of a bitch*." For the briefest of moments he considered manifesting, in the hopes it might scare the asshole to death. Luckily, Kevin's cell phone rang, derailing his train of thought.

"Hey, Melissa, what's up?"

Michael sat bolt upright and his ghostly body tensed. *Melissa? Is she home for Thanksgiving break?*

Kevin listened for a few minutes before saying, "Yeah, alright, I'll be right over."

Michael couldn't hold back. "You *son* of a *bitch!* I swear to *God* you so much as lay a *finger* on her and I *will* kill you!"

What if I did kill him? I could manifest right now and he'd probably wreck the car. If that didn't work, he might be able to turn the steering wheel and force his car out of control. Images of Kevin hurting Melissa filled his mind and he shook with uncontrollable fury. Could he concentrate enough to pull it off though?

After a short battle with his conscience, he reined in his anger and came to his senses. *I could never take the life of another human being, no matter how much of a piece of shit he is.* The only thing he could do was to warn Melissa and somehow let her know she was in danger. Instantly, he orbed and flew out ahead of the car at top speed.

When he arrived at Melissa's house, she was sitting up in bed reading a book. As he watched her, he thought of how much she meant to him, even now. His soul ached from deep within. He couldn't let Kevin hurt her. It would be unthinkable. *I have to do something.*

For several moments he stood there, concentrating and gathering all the energy from the surroundings. Maybe the full moon would help. Finally ready, he slowly and deliberately released the energy, using it to project himself into Melissa's thoughts. It took at least a minute, but just as he was beginning to think it wasn't working, she glanced up at him and her face went pasty white.

So many things happened so fast, they blurred into one. Recognition and then raw fear seized Melissa and she leapt from the bed, running past his ghostly form and out of the bedroom. She let out a scream, as she looked back to see if he was still behind her. But she was too close to the top of the stairs.

Michael flew forward in panic, grasping for her hand, but it passed right through his. Pure terror fractured through him.

"No! Melissa!"

She tumbled backward down the steep staircase, her head hitting the wall hard and her body banging against almost every step.

Her fall lasted for nothing less than an eternity. Finally, she landed in a crumbled heap at the bottom and lay there…deathly still.

Oh my God, what've I done?

The sound of running footsteps roused him from his petrified shock. Next thing he knew, Melissa's mother was kneeling beside her daughter's lifeless body. Her nursing training took over and she quickly found a pulse. Melissa's breathing was shallow, her chest barely moving. Karen snatched the cordless phone from its cradle and dialed 911.

Thank God she's alive. Filled with self-loathing for his awful mistake, he crossed his arms over his head and squeezed his eyes tight shut. *It's my fault. This is all my fault. What the hell was I thinking?*

Within ten minutes, the ambulance arrived. The paramedics carefully lifted Melissa onto a gurney and loaded her into the waiting ambulance. Karen dialed her husband's cell phone as they rode to Princeton Hospital.

Unbeknownst to them, Michael sat right beside them, his eyes pinned to Melissa's unconscious face. He had to make sure she was going to be alright.

They rounded the corner of Tanglewood and Pine. Peering out of the tiny window in the back of the ambulance, he froze. He'd spotted something up ahead. Something sickening. Kevin's red car was parked out in front of a house he recognized. He'd been there once before for a party. The house was Melissa Birch's, a slutty junior from his school. In rapid-fire succession his mind put the pieces together. Kevin had been talking to a *different* Melissa—*it was only a booty call.*

Great...now, I feel like a complete *ass.*

• • •

Karen stayed right at her daughter's side in the emergency room.

Michael stood by too, reading Karen's mind and experiencing her pain. Frustrated because the staff wouldn't let her do anything, she understood nonetheless. Being a nurse meant she knew exactly what needed to be done, but she was so upset she had to admit she didn't trust herself right now. Besides, every member of the ER staff who knew her had come to help. Thankfully, they quickly determined Melissa's only injuries were a broken arm, a few bruised ribs and a concussion. Within an hour, they addressed her wounds, admitted her for observation and moved her to a private room.

As Michael walked through the closed door, he saw Melissa lying in the bed and instantly hated himself. *How could I have been so stupid?*

She had a large, bulky brace around her neck, with her arm in a soft cast, and her chest heavily bandaged around her ribcage. She'd drifted in and out of consciousness during the last hour. The doctor had ordered that she be given a mild pain medication intravenously and at the moment, she was still asleep.

Karen sat in a chair across from Melissa's bed, watching her daughter intently.

Again, he scanned Karen's thoughts, which at that moment were a jumble of emotions and memories. Her mind was far back in the archives, recalling Melissa's first scraped knee and the tears that had fallen down her round little face. For eighteen years she'd kept her daughter safe from harm. This past year, when Melissa had started driving had terrified her. Especially, after what happened to Michael. *But, a fall, in their own home?* She never expected this. *Why had she screamed anyway?* It all made no sense whatsoever.

For only a second, Karen's mind jumped to the thought of having almost lost her daughter and her mind connected this to Mary's loss. She remembered taking her daughter's picture with him before the prom. Michael felt the emotion as the fond, but bittersweet memory flitted through Karen's mind. It hit him like a sucker punch straight in the gut.

Would she feel that way if she knew what I'd done…and that all of this was my fault? More than anything, he wished he could tell them both how sorry he was. *It could've been so much worse. And if it had been, I would never have been able to forgive myself.* At that moment, he vowed never to manifest in front of the living again.

Turning to leave, he heard Melissa awaken.

"Mom?" she whispered, her voice weak.

"Yes, honey, I'm here," her mother breathed.

Her voice barely audible, Melissa said, "Mom, where am I?"

"You're in Princeton Hospital, sweetheart," her mother answered calmly. "You fell down the stairs. You broke your arm and you have a concussion, but you're going to be okay."

When she didn't answer, Michael scanned Melissa's thoughts, wondering what she was thinking.

A beat passed as she tried to recall what had happened right before her fall. She remembered her fear and screaming, but she couldn't remember what it was that had frightened her so. Then it hit her.

"Mom…," she mumbled, "I saw Michael."

At that, her mother froze. And, so did he.

"*What?*" Karen asked incredulous.

"I saw Michael." Her words came slowly as she fought off the effects of the medication. "He was standing… right in my room. I…I think he wanted to tell me something."

Her mother tilted her head, her expression one of anguish and confusion. "You saw him *here?*"

"No, Mom, in my bedroom at home." As Melissa woke up more fully now, her head cleared, and she wanted her mother to understand. "That's why I ran for the stairs. I got scared when I saw him."

As a nurse, Karen had heard of strange things happening to people in traumatic situations. Even so, she found it difficult to wrap her mind around her daughter's words. For a moment, she sat perfectly still, debating what to say next to her obviously delusional daughter. *Could she have hit her head that hard?*

"Sweetheart, you must've imagined him," she said carefully.

Melissa raised herself off the bed a few inches. "*No, Mom*, I didn't imagine him," she shouted fiercely. "He was really there, *I saw him*! Why do you think I ran?"

"I don't know sweetheart," Karen said trying to calm her down, "maybe you saw a shadow, or something."

"It wasn't a *shadow*, Mom!" Melissa retorted, obviously growing angry that her mother didn't believe her. "I saw his whole face and his whole body. He looked right at me for God's sake!"

Great, I finally manage a perfect manifestation and almost kill someone I care about. Way to go, dipshit.

"Alright, calm down sweetheart, lie back down. I believe

you," her mother lied, afraid to further upset her daughter. "We'll talk more about it later. You need to get some rest."

• • •

The beach in the Outerbanks was deserted, except for a lone surf caster standing by the shoreline. Angry, gray clouds roiled in the sky, blocking out the sun. A late afternoon storm was brewing. It fit his mood perfectly.

Walking along the beach with his mentor again, Michael told Tom about the incident with Jamie and Melissa's fall.

"We should do something about Kevin before he *does* hurt someone," Michael said.

Tom gave him a sidelong glance. "And how do you suppose we go about doing that?"

"I have no idea," he admitted. "I just wish Jamie would tell her parents. I know she's gonna feel horrible if Kevin does anything to anyone else."

"I agree with you," Tom replied, "but that's her choice and she'll have to live with the consequences of that choice."

"Speaking of consequences...manifesting was an *epic* mistake...a *disaster*," he lamented. His eyes roamed the sand at his feet, not willing to look Tom in the face. "I never meant to hurt Melissa. I can't believe I was so *stupid*. She could've been *killed*."

"You were only doing what you thought you had to," Tom said, obviously trying to make him feel better. "But I must say, I warned you manifesting might scare the living to death."

"Thanks," he said sarcastically, "the I-told-you-so really helps."

"No problem." Tom grinned. "That's what friends are for." He started to walk away and then added, "You made a mistake, Michael. Let it *go*. Remember what I told you about regret."

Regret. The word pulsed in his mind, going off like an alarm clock. Suddenly, he was overcome by a tectonic shift in emotions.

Tom turned back around slowly. "Something *else* on your mind, Michael?"

He gazed out over the churning ocean. "Yeah, I think I made an even *bigger* mistake. One I'm going to regret *forever*, if I don't fix it."

Tom dragged a hand slowly over his face in exasperation. "Look, I know what you're thinking of doing and I have to advise *against* it. You broke one rule by manifesting. You're *lucky* you haven't been reprimanded yet. The council may *not* tolerate it if you break another rule." He shook his finger at him. "Now, I can't tell you what to do, but—"

"Good, then *don't*," Michael responded, resolute in his decision. "I've made up my mind. I almost lost one person I care for. I'm not going to lose the one I'm in love with. If I've learned anything so far, it's that you have to appreciate what you have, while you *still have it*."

"But, what about the demons? What about putting Sarah in danger?" Tom shot back.

"*What about it*," he nearly shouted, his patience almost gone. "I'm *not* going to live in fear. I don't *know* if Matt and the demons will catch up with me again. All I *do* know… is

I'm going to be with Sarah while I still can."

He didn't wait for Tom's response. Becoming a tiny ball of light, he sped northward up the coast.

CHAPTER TWENTY-SIX

FOREVER

ARRIVING AT THE Angel of the Sea before sunset, Michael stood on the pavement staring up at the balcony. His mind slid back to that first night and his first mesmerizing glimpse of Sarah up above on the porch. While he were alive, if anyone would've ever said to him that he would one day believe in love at first sight, he probably would've knocked them out just for being a moron. Now, not only did he believe in that kind of miracle, but he was also convinced of something else. *True love is an immortal force.*

Above him, Sarah floated onto the porch and stopped abruptly.

Their eyes locked.

Heaven help me. I love her with every bit of my soul. How could I have been such an idiot? What if I've lost her?

Michael said the only thing he could think of, "Take a walk on the beach with me?"

The next second she was there, next to him. Tentatively, he reached out to give her his hand.

But she didn't take it and he awkwardly let his arm fall to his side. His ghostly heart fractured within his chest and a pain like frostbite invaded his limbs. *I have lost her.*

They walked in hollow silence all the way to the beach,

with the setting sun painting ribbons of orange, purple and butterscotch over the horizon.

Unable to take Sarah's condemning silence a minute longer, he whipped around to face her. "*Please*, Sarah, you're *killing* me. This is worse than dying all over again. I'm *so sorry* for leaving you," he said in a mad rush, the words pouring from his mouth almost involuntarily. "I must've been out of my mind. Everything was just so *damned* confusing." He raked a hand through his hair, trying to rein in his emotions and find the right words. "I was afraid of putting you in danger and not being able to *protect* you. Then, my dad suddenly showed up and left without even *talking* to me. Nothing made any *sense*."

Looking down at her feet she asked in barely a whisper, "And now?"

"Now the only thing that makes sense to me is I *love* you with all my soul. I feel a little closer to heaven when I'm with you...and that can't be wrong. It just can't." Desperately searching her eyes for forgiveness, he thrust his arms out—aching to touch her, trying to reach her, wanting to pull her back. "We may only have ten minutes, ten days, or ten years, but I don't *care*. All I know is that I want to spend the time I've got with *you*. Can you forgive me?"

She smiled and the universe fell into perfect alignment again. "I forgave you the minute I saw you... I love you," she whispered, as she drew closer to him.

He picked up on the electricity flowing between them as the distance dwindled, but he was still holding back, trying to be responsible. "I love you too, Sarah, but I...I don't know what will happen...if we..."

She touched his fingertips with hers and slowly their hands entwined. Instantly, a surge of energy pulsed through his hands as if he'd touched high voltage wires. Yet, it felt good. Really good. All rational thought left him as he gasped out her name, "Sarah."

He wanted her. He needed her. Like a powerful electromagnet, he pulled her close, wrapping one arm around her waist while the other roamed across her back. As soon as his lips melted with hers, the kiss sent a fire through his soul. His hands moved over her, wanting to touch every inch of her.

Instantly, Sarah surrendered to him, her kisses hungry and desperate. She needed him and wanted him just as much, if not more. She pressed herself harder against him, carnal hunger overwhelming all reason.

His tongue traced hers and the smoldering warmth of her aura felt electric against his skin. As if their ghostly bodies were causing some kind of friction, rings of radiant light and energy enveloped them both. The boundary between their energies was barely there at all now—he felt it slipping, slipping, slipping...

The joining...we're joining. The thought roared in his mind becoming a tempest, *I can't let this happen.* With a monumental effort, he used all of his strength to pull away.

For a second, he could've sworn he was out of breath. He flopped on the beach recovering, his entire spirit body tingly and on fire. The feeling was wonderful; he hoped it would linger.

After a few minutes, he turned to Sarah and their eyes met. She was trying to regain her composure too, so he spoke first. "I think we almost...*joined?*"

"Yes, I think so," she replied with a wicked little grin on her face. Her gaze dropped to the sand and she said in a bashful voice, "It's the first time I ever…uh…almost…was it your first time too?"

"No," he answered, wanting to be honest with her, and yet still searching her eyes for a reaction.

She smiled, reassuring him. "It's okay. I could sort of tell you knew what you were doing."

His mouth curved into an impish grin and he cupped her hands in his own. "Sarah, I love you more than anything, and I want you like you cannot *imagine.* But, I don't want to hurt you or anything. So…this is the *one* thing I won't do until I'm sure of what will happen."

Her eyes were full of love and understanding. "Alright," she agreed. "We probably should play it safe." She was thoughtful for a moment, and then her mouth turned up in a half-smile. "Was it almost the same as if we'd been alive?"

"Better," he said, smiling back. Taking her hand, he lifted her off the beach. In all his life he'd never felt so alive, as he did at that moment.

Together they walked holding hands and watching the sun set. His heart swelling with happiness, he felt the most hopeful and sure of anything since his untimely death. If this was so wrong and he was going to hell for falling in love, then he wanted to go with Sarah.

• • •

Michael rolled on his side to face Sarah, who lounged on the bare floor a couple feet away. Deep in thought, he rested his head on his arm and glanced at the clouds outside.

The late afternoon sun cast a dim glow on the antique furniture covered in white sheets, strewn about the attic—the inn's leftovers and castoffs. *Like us.* Specks of dust drifted lazily through the air, twinkling in the dappled light streaming through the windows. *I wonder if that's what I look like as an orb.*

Refocusing his attention back to their conversation, he said, "So…what have we learned so far?"

Sarah rolled over and propped her head up on her arm, pondering for a moment. "Well, some spirits have trapped themselves by their regret, guilt or loss of hope. Like Al Capone and the rest of the ghosts at Eastern State."

"Exactly," he nodded.

She chewed her lip, thinking some more. "And since the alien can't get back to his planet…maybe that's why he can't find closure and can't move on," she hypothesized.

"Could be," he said. He rubbed his chin, while churning through memories of the last few months. "Some spirits are still here by *choice*…like Babe Ruth and the Captain."

She scooted closer to him. "It seems that way."

Cocking his head to the side, he squinted at the ceiling, lost in thought. "And it's definitely not a function of time, because there are ghosts that have been here a short time and some that have lingered for much longer," he said. "Like the ones from the 1800s."

"Right," she agreed.

"You know, I'm starting to believe what Tom said is true. The reason for being stuck as a ghost *is* different for everyone." He paused while a phantom stab hit his chest. "I only wish I knew why my dad is stuck."

"And us…," she added in a murmur.

He bobbed his head slowly without taking his eyes off her. A malignant mass of doubt shifted uneasily in his gut. *I may as well just come out with it.*

"Honestly…I still wonder if maybe there is no place to go after we die," he admitted, his words barely above a whisper. "Maybe our energy simply fades away at different rates."

He hadn't wanted to say it. He didn't want to destroy her hope. But he couldn't deny it either.

In her eyes, he saw the doubts that haunted him reflected there. "I hope that's not true," she said haltingly.

After a long pause, he said, "Me, too."

He hadn't noticed it before, but he did now. While they had been talking, they had been inching closer and closer to each other—two magnets drawn together by a force of nature. Sarah now lay right beside him, her warmth touching his ghostly skin.

He was just beginning to enjoy the heat from her aura spreading through him when her body suddenly went rigid. She let out a fearful scream and jumped into his arms, trembling and shaking from head to toe.

Clutching her tightly, his eyes darted around the room searching for the danger. That's when he saw it—a huge black spider crawling right through her leg and out the other side.

A quasi-obnoxious laugh sprang from his mouth before he could stop it. "Ummm, I *don't* think he can hurt you."

"I guess…," she said, as she shivered in his arms, "but

I've always *hated* spiders. There used to be bloody large ones in the barn back home. Big, hairy…*nasty* things."

"It's okay," he said, moving his hands in slow circles over her back to soothe her. "Here, maybe this'll take your mind off of him." He placed his mouth on hers in a gentle kiss. "I'm sorry for laughing at you. I actually think it's rather *cute* that you're still afraid of spiders."

They exchanged a smile. "Do you want me to zap him for you?" he offered, raising his hand toward the spider.

She quickly pushed his arm down. "*No*, you can't *kill* him. He might have a family. Maybe even a wife and kids." In a meaningful way she said, "Let him *live*."

The compassion in her emerald green eyes nearly melted him to the floor boards. He stroked the softness of her cheek and traced his thumb across her lips. "You're incredible, you know that? That's exactly why I love you."

He pressed his lips to hers and it was as if he had kissed a light socket. A jolt of pure energy shot through him, searing his soul. She kissed him back harder and he tensed his muscles trying not to lose control. He had never felt anything so intense and yet so incredibly wonderful at the same time. Her lips—soft, hot and wanton—begged for more.

He encircled her even more tightly, molding his body to hers.

She responded by rising up to meet him and trying to roll him onto his back.

"*Careful* now." He pushed her back down gently, but firmly. "It's harder for me to control myself if you do that."

Her eyes twinkled and her mouth curved into a wicked smile.

He let out a half-moan, half-growl, and shook his head lightly. "You red-headed temptress...you're *gonna* be the death of me."

She started to chuckle but he caught her mouth with his own, kissing her intensely. With one hand behind her head, he moved his free hand over her breast. She trembled with pleasure.

He eased on top of her.

Bodies intertwined, electricity buzzed everywhere they touched. Friction. Heat. *Bliss.*

Then...fear.

Slipping...we're slipping again...

With near-monumental effort, they pulled away from one another. Michael flopped onto his back, his limbs still tingly and warm.

After regaining his composure, he rose to his feet. "Come on." He pulled her off the floor and planted a tiny, tender kiss on her forehead. "We better take a walk."

"Or a cold shower," she said, laughing behind a devilish grin.

• • •

With winter approaching, the days were getting shorter now, gray and gloomy. Crisp, dead leaves swirled near the gutter at his feet, driven by a frosty wind—*the perfect kind of day for two ghosts to go for a meandering walk.*

For a brief moment, the weather jogged his memory—*basketball season is in full swing by now.* Annoyed with himself, he shoved the thought from his mind. *That was the past. Sarah is my present. And my future.*

Just in case she had read his quiet thoughts, he clenched Sarah's hand more tightly. "You know, I think I might ask Tom what he knows about the joining after all. He might—"

The loud honking of a car interrupted him and a commotion up ahead caught his attention.

Several cars were pulling into the parking lot of the large white church on the corner. Guests shuffled through the large front doors, as two silver limousines came to a stop near the curb directly in front of the church.

He read the sign in front out loud, "Nuptials today, 5 P M—Michael Morris and Sarah Jackson. Hey, they both have our first names," he said to her. "Let's have a little fun and play along. What do you say, you wanna marry me?"

Sarah knew he was only kidding, so she took a mere second to answer, "Sure, why not?" *After all, a mock wedding's better than no wedding at all.*

"Alright, cool...let's do it," he said with an impish grin. Taking her by the hand, he led her up the stone steps and into the foyer of the church.

A few guests straggled in, one of which, was a hunched over elderly woman. Wearing a flowery dress and a fancy hat, she looked about as frail as rice paper. As one of the ushers took her arm to guide her to her seat, Michael called out, "Aunt Pauline, my, don't you look lovely." Sarah started laughing, so he added, "What a pretty shade of pink, it goes perfectly with your blue hair."

"Oh, stop," she chuckled, "you're awful."

After a few minutes, the ushers had seated all of the guests. From the choir loft above, someone began to play the organ. Michael and Sarah stepped aside as the wedding party walked slowly by, arm in arm with their partners.

"They'll never wear *those* dresses again," he commented, grimacing at the hideous lime green color of the girl's gowns. She laughed again and slapped him on his backside.

The groom now proceeded down the aisle with his mother on his arm. He kissed her and led her to her seat, taking his place at the front of the altar.

"That's my cue," Michael said, kissing Sarah's hand before he let go of it. Making remarks and waving at several of the guests, he raced up the aisle, "Uncle Frank, so good to see you. Cousin Ruthie, I see you got that wart removed, how nice. Uncle Tony, they let you out of prison for the wedding? That's great!"

He was still waving and goofing around at the front of the church when the music suddenly changed to the "Wedding March". Walking ever so slowly, the bride entered the church with her father on her arm. Sarah glided close behind them. When they reached the altar, the father kissed the bride, and sat down in a pew. As the living bride took her groom's hand, Michael held out his hand for Sarah.

In the instant their palms connected, everything changed. Sarah was no longer wearing the sundress she had been, but a floor-length, champagne-colored gown instead.

Sarah caught the astonished look on his face. "I wore this to a cotillion once."

"It's beautiful," he breathed, his voice stuck in his throat. "I guess I should be dressed for the occasion too," and with that, he conjured up the memory of the tux he'd been wearing at the prom. His leg wiggled slightly and he locked his knee. *What are we doing? Are we still just pretending?*

She smiled so warmly at him, for a second he honestly thought he might disintegrate on the spot. Was he ready for forever? How long would they have anyway—a day, a year, a hundred years?

For several minutes, he listened to the faraway voices reading the passages from scripture. "Love is patient, love is kind…" these words mixed in between his own thoughts.

Love is everything. I know I love her. I may never fall in love like this again. I may never have another chance to get married. Why shouldn't I do this? At that exact moment they read each other's mind, and realized they'd had the same thought. *Are we doing this for real?*

Before he knew what was happening, it was time for the vows and what had started as a joke was quickly turning into the real deal. Looking lovingly into Sarah's eyes, he repeated each vow after the groom, pausing only once to smirk at the "till death do us part" line. At last, with a deep conviction in his soul, he made the traditional vow. "I do."

Next, it was Sarah's turn and with a clear and committed voice she repeated those same vows and gave herself to him completely saying, "I do."

Turning to the congregation, the priest joyfully announced those time honored words, "I now pronounce you husband and wife. You may kiss the bride."

Michael slipped a strong arm around Sarah's waist and kissed her with all the passion burning in his soul.

Pulling away from her lips, he took her hands and entwined them with his own. Standing face to face and searching her eyes for commitment, he said, "I love you."

"I love you, too." She smiled happily as a shock of electricity passed between them.

In that instant, they both knew the truth. They had meant their vows with all their souls and were now bound to each other, for all eternity.

• • •

The wedding party and a flow of guests exited through the back of the church, so he and Sarah ducked out a side door near the altar.

Laughing like any other happy newlywed couple, they started to walk back to the Angel of the Sea.

Just then, Michael stiffened. An unpleasant wave of energy coursed through him, putting his whole being on alert. He stopped short.

Damn it, they've found me.

"What's wrong?" she asked, picking up on his emotions.

"The demons are back," he said, his jaw tense. "I don't know how many, but I can tell they're close." Fear gripped his insides like a vice. *Sarah's in danger again.*

She gave him a worried glance. Trying to sound brave, she said unconvincingly, "I'll help you."

"*No*...Sarah, it's too dangerous. I want you to go back to the Angel," he ordered, pulling her close and kissing her quickly. "I'll come back as soon as I can. Sorry about this," he said with a tiny smile, as he reluctantly let her go. "Looks like the honeymoon will have to wait."

Terrified for him, Sarah still managed a faint smile of her own. "It's okay," she said. "We've got plenty of time." A second later, she faded quickly.

With Sarah safely away, he wanted to find the demons and make sure she hadn't been followed. The evil energy was somewhere nearby, so he followed his instincts. Quickly, he charged around to the front of the church, where the strongest vibes came from. Sure enough, a hideous demon with hairy limbs and long razor teeth, almost wolf-like, stood right below the steps of the church scanning the crowd of wedding guests.

Michael froze in mid-step, almost barreling right into him.

The demon whirled around and an evil smirk crossed his mangled face. "I thought you'd never come out of there," he cackled, advancing on him. "You almost had me fooled. I figured you would come out through the front."

The transformation was so unbelievable he almost didn't recognize the demon he was now facing. Only the eyes gave him away. *It's Matt. He must be nearly a full demon now.* Drawing in energy, he readied for the fight, but he needed to stall for time.

"Gee, I'd say it's good to see you, too, but I'd be *lying*," he mocked. "Have you gotten a good *look* at yourself lately? You've *really* gone all to hell."

At the mention of hell, naked terror crossed Matt's disfigured face, before dissolving into pure rage. "Funny, that's *exactly* where I intend to send *you*," he snarled. Thrusting his hands forward, he prepared to strike.

But he didn't.

As Michael stood ready to defend himself, Sarah suddenly materialized right next to him.

Oh. My. God.

Panicked, his eyes jumped from her to Matt and back again. "What are you *doing?*" Seized by fear and frustration, his voice hitched up two octaves. "I *told* you to go back!"

"I couldn't leave you!" she blurted out.

"Awww, how *touching*," Matt said, raising his arms once more to deliver a blow.

There was no time to think. Trying to distract him long enough for them to get away, Michael sent a huge, powerful blast rocketing toward his adversary. He didn't even glance back to see if he hit his mark. Snatching Sarah's hand, he shut his eyes and memory-traveled to the first place that popped into his mind.

CHAPTER TWENTY-SEVEN

FIGHT

MATERIALIZING INSIDE HIS high school cafeteria, Michael whipped his head around looking for any sign they had been followed.

A split second later, he got his answer, as a green lightning bolt of energy crashed through a nearby window exploding the glass. Millions of shards rained down on the linoleum floor tinkling like tiny bells. Luckily, the shot missed them both.

Grabbing Sarah's arm, Michael yanked her toward the exit that lead to the classrooms. He charged through the doors, ready to break into flight. Instead, he jammed on the brakes, paralyzed by fear.

Nightmare sounds filled the hallway. An all-consuming knot of black shapes twisted and constricted at the far end.

Michael and Sarah swiftly back-pedaled into the cafeteria, startled by the horrid forms.

But that was nothing compared to what was waiting for them outside.

Through the windows, he now saw black shadows gathering on the other side of the school parking lot. Behind them, a distortion had formed in the evening darkness—a warped fissure that seemed to go on forever, its mouth gaping wide. With each passing minute, the ominous black hole grew larger, as more and more demonic minions slithered their way out.

We're surrounded.

He turned to Sarah, gripping her hand tightly and trying to come up with a game plan.

So far, I've got nothing.

"Why don't we just orb?" She pointed to the ceiling, suggesting they should go up and out through the roof.

"We *can't*," he huffed with frustration.

"Why not?" She trembled.

"Because...the last time we were surrounded, Tom said not to. He said it would somehow make us more vulnerable to capture."

"How?"

"I don't *know*," he said in exasperation. He let go of her palm and raked his hand through his hair. "Tom never got the chance to explain and I never thought to ask. Maybe it's because...if they come after you, you can't fight them off if you're in that form?"

Opening and closing his fists over and over, he began stalking around the room like caged prey, searching for something...*anything*...

Sounding rattled, she asked, "Then, why don't we just memory-travel somewhere else?"

"It's no *use*. They would just follow us again." He balled his fists at his sides and steadied his quivering leg, issuing a final cease and desist. "We have no choice...we have to fight."

The implications settled on her face, her expression

turning from distress to courage. "I'll do whatever you tell me to," she said.

"Okay. Come on then, I have an idea."

With Sarah in tow, he turned on his heel and made a beeline for the rear of the cafeteria's kitchen.

Gliding swiftly through the walls, he explained to her, "I sometimes had to bring the basketball equipment to a storage closet back here. I think I remember seeing a breaker panel in one of these rooms."

"In here!" he exclaimed, rushing over to a door marked, 'UTILITY'. Ghosting into the room, they found four gray, metal boxes that ran from the ceiling to the floor, housing the electrical service for the building. Each box displayed a sign that read, 'DANGER—HIGH VOLTAGE'.

"Okay, here's the plan," he said. "You and I are gonna suck up all the energy we can stand. I don't know if it'll be enough to hold them off, but it's the only idea I've got. Oh...and one more thing." He closed his eyes, using all of his concentration to summon Tom.

But nothing happened.

Sarah read his thoughts. "Why isn't he coming?"

"I don't know," he said, the disappointment sinking in slowly, "but I think...we might be on our own."

Turning to face the electrical panel, he thrust his hands inside the metal doors. Electricity began to stream throughout his body. "Now you do the same," he said to her.

Cautiously, Sarah slipped her hands through the cover, placing her fingers directly on the wires within. Judging by the wide-eyed look on her face, it was working for her, too.

After a few minutes, his limbs started to vibrate

uncomfortably from the intense energy. Hers were now shaking, too. "*Stop*," he told her in earnest, "it's getting to be too much."

She pulled her hands away from the box. "Now what?"

He cupped her chin and gave her a quick peck on the lips. He was anything but calm, but he wanted to reassure her. Straightening his spine, he stood up to his full height and locked eyes with her. "Let's go," he said with determination, "but stay close to me."

Side by side, they charged back into the cafeteria, ready for anything.

Only to be greeted by Matt's cold, malicious glare.

Michael ducked in front to shield Sarah, who let out a frightened squeak as her body shuddered.

Matt now stood between them and the doors leading to the hallway. With his appearance, the menacing whispers on the other side had grown into wild, primal shrieks. The demonic shades were close, probably just on the other side of the metal door.

If I hit him now, they'll pounce. I have to find a way to get Sarah out of here first.

Matt said nothing, his dark eyes boring into Michael's. Slowly, he turned his head to peer out the window.

Michael followed his gaze.

Oh, shit.

Their little problem had grown. It was only early evening, but the far end of the parking lot had been plunged into absolute darkness. Tendrils of inky black mist oozed out in every direction. The horde of demon souls slid across the asphalt like an approaching storm, stretching and pulling the black hole along with them. As the damned souls drew closer, row after row of the domed lights in the parking lot burst in a shower of glass and sparks.

Matt turned his head and looked at him as if to say, now-what-are-you-going-to-do?

Unflinching, Michael returned his icy stare. He jerked his thumb towards the window. "More *friends* of yours?"

"Yes, I called them," Matt said, his words devoid of emotion. "They're coming for you."

For a spare second, Michael thought of giving himself up to save Sarah. Unfortunately, he forgot to block his mind and she heard him.

"No, you can't!" she shrieked, jumping between them.

"Sarah!" Michael clawed at the air, reaching to yank her back, but it was too late.

In one swift motion, Matt threw a snakelike coil of energy around Sarah, ensnaring her.

She screamed, but only once. Her phantom eyes rolled back in her head. "Michael...," she gasped, "it *hurts*..."

That unfathomable pain. His mind reeled—to see her in agony was too much. His anger frothed over, out of control. *I'm going to* annihilate *him.* He drew his hands up to attack...but he didn't move fast enough.

Matt had anticipated his retaliation. Before Michael could release the blast, Matt flung a twisted coil around his arms.

Pain like ice-fire radiated outward from the bonds and his legs buckled, dropping him to his knees in front of the demon.

Only one thought clanged like a gong in his mind—he had to use his stored up energy fast, before he grew too weak. With herculean effort, he forced the electricity against the coil. His arms shook and the bonds began to stretch.

Seeing what he was doing, Matt spewed a spinning ball of green light from the ends of his fingertips. It now hovered only inches from Sarah's head. "*Ah, ah, ah*...I wouldn't *do* that if I were you," he cautioned. "If you so much as *move*, I'll let this energy obliterate *all* her memories, including those of *you...forever.*"

"Let her go! It's *me* they want...now let her go!"

"It's not that simple," Matt replied in a monotone.

Damn it! He's holding all the cards now. Wait a minute, though...why is he hesitating? If he's completely evil, why doesn't he just do it then?

As Matt read his thoughts, for one precious second his grim expression wavered only a fraction.

But it was enough for him to read Matt's poker face and sense his vulnerability.

"You don't *want* to hurt her...and you don't really want to turn me over to them either. I can *feel* it," he said at the realization. "There's still some good inside you."

Matt gave his head a slight shake, obviously still fighting the turmoil in his soul. "You don't *understand*. They *whisper* to me...in my *head*." He clamped his hands down over his ears, his face scrunched up in pain. "They say if I do this, I won't *have to go*. They'll leave me here to collect more marked souls. I'll never have to endure the tortures of *hell*."

Drawing on all his remaining strength, Michael cried out, "They're *lying* to you! Demons *lie*. They're only *using* you." As the words left his mouth, something else occurred to him.

"The real question is...why are you letting them? What makes you think you're going to hell?"

Trapped in a torture device, with the demons closing in and Sarah in pain, Michael didn't have time to wait for an answer. Concentrating hard on Matt's mind, he forced his way into his thoughts and memories.

Out of focus scenes flashed rapidly before his eyes—Matt slipping into the driver's seat. Swaying back and forth, struggling to put the key in the ignition. Clumsily turning on the car. Slurring his words at the girl sitting next to him. The girl with the striking face.

But who was she?

A second later, Matt expelled him from his mind, but not before Michael had seen enough. It was her eyes that gave it away.

"She wasn't your girlfriend," he said, quickly putting the pieces together. "She was your *sister*."

Matt's face twisted in anguish. "*Yes*," he choked out. "I made her get in the car with me that night. I was so drunk I couldn't even stand up, but I was so...*arrogant*." His yellowed, bloodshot eyes welled with tears. "She trusted me...and I killed her," he mumbled, his words trailing off.

"*Listen* to me," Michael implored. His eyes darted to Sarah—she was still squirming. He stole a quick glance outside—the horrible blackness had almost reached the windows. Focusing once more, he used Tom's own words, "Enough regret can crush *any* man, living or dead. I'm sure deep down you're a *good* person."

"*No!*" Matt spat back at him. "I'm *evil!*"

"*No*, you're *not*!" he yelled. "You made a *mistake*, but

you're *not* evil. You'll be making an even bigger mistake if you do this. Turning me over to the demons, hurting Sarah...it won't *change* anything. It won't bring your sister *back*."

Suddenly, someone whispered in his own head. Even though the words were low and strained, he recognized his father's voice immediately. *The sister...the sister is the key.*

"But, it's my fault she's gone," Matt said, choked with grief.

Gone...and I had thought my father was gone, too. An idea ignited like an ember in his mind. "Wait a minute," Michael said, trying to think through the pain that threatened to overwhelm his senses, "maybe she *isn't* gone. Have you tried summoning her?"

"No," Matt retorted, his voice laced with mistrust. "What is this *nonsense?* I don't even know what you *mean*."

That's it. He knew it. That's what his father had meant. "Call her name with your mind," Michael said hurriedly. "Ask her to come to you."

"That's not going to *work*," Matt shouted angrily. "You're trying to *trick* me!" He raised his hands again readying to strike Sarah.

"No, I'm not! Just *do* it!" he screamed fiercely. "What have you got to *lose?*"

Still looking distrustful, Matt squinted, concentrating hard on calling his sister. *Emily? Emily, can you hear me?*

A beat passed, before a young girl materialized in front of Matt. The moment he saw her, his face, his hands, his whole body instantly returned to normal. The fangs, claws, the ragged skin, all vanished. Even his eyes softened to a natural, warm brown color.

The sister's eyes, at first filled with terror, went wide with recognition and she threw her arms around her brother. Spectral tears flowed down her cheeks. "I couldn't find you," she sobbed.

"I took up with the wrong crowd, I guess," Matt responded. "I'm so sorry."

All at once, the coils of evil energy fell away from Michael's arms and Sarah's, too.

She gasped, dragging in a phantom breath.

Michael flew to her side, taking her in his arms in a tight embrace. She clung to him, her arms ice cold where the bonds had been. He rubbed them, hoping to warm them up. Then, he looked out at the parking lot.

We're not outta this yet.

"Um...I hate to break up this happy, little reunion," he said, gesturing toward the window, "but we still have a little problem."

Before he had even put his arm down, Tom suddenly materialized on his left side.

"It's about time you decided to show!" Michael blurted out.

"Sorry," Tom apologized, "I got a bit held up. If you haven't noticed, the building is surrounded."

Michael scowled for a milli-second. "Well, I'll have to introduce you later," he said with a touch of sarcasm. "Right now, what the *hell* do we do about *them?*"

Tom swept his gaze from the hallway doors to the parking lot outside, where the greatest threat was drifting ever closer. "I honestly have no idea," he said flatly. "I've never seen this many demons gathered before."

"Great." *How do we get out of this one?* What was it his father had always said? *To win any game, you have to play to your strengths.*

"Alright, we *got* this," Michael said excitedly. He looked around at all of them. "Everyone at least a *little* familiar with basketball?"

All four of them formed a circle around him, nodding in unison.

"Okay, then, here's the plan—*zone defense.*"

They barely had time to choose which approaching mass of trouble each of them was going to defend against.

"Tom, Matt, and Emily, you take the ones from the hallway! Sarah and I will take the ones coming from the lot!"

Just as he finished, the demons on the other side of the double doors burst through, tumbling into the cafeteria like a black tsunami. They spilled into the room, moving toward Tom's small group.

A split-second later, the horde of demons outside smashed into the building beginning their assault.

Every window burst at once in a deafening explosion of glass and metal.

Suddenly, everyone, everything broke into fluid motion. Violent, bluish flames spread out in front of the demons, rippling across every surface. Tables splintered. Chairs overturned. Fluorescent lights rained down.

Any second now, and the demons would be on top of them.

"Tom, grab their arms, use all of your energy as one!" Michael shouted over the din.

He joined his own hands with Sarah, still thrumming from some of the electricity they had absorbed earlier, and directed a burst of energy toward the black mass spilling in from the parking lot.

Bright, radiant light burst forth from their hands—a shield of blinding brightness, stretching from the floor to ceiling in a huge parabola.

The gigantic shield of luminescence spun before them, rotating and rotating, faster and faster.

Michael shot a quick glance at Tom and the others. Their own shield had driven the demons back into the hallway.

"Move *forward…towards* them!" he yelled.

He and Sarah took a few cautious steps forward, closer to the writhing horde.

The demons shrank back, flowing out into the parking lot.

The black hole began convulsing.

This is it! Please dear God, if you're up there…

He pushed forward quickly, thrusting one last powerful jolt of energy at the shrinking black mass.

Twisting in on itself, the black hole swallowed up the darkness, as the demonic minions retreated into its depths.

Through the twilight, Michael could once more see the trees on the other side of the parking lot.

Exhausted and drained of energy, he and Sarah collapsed to the floor.

Out of the corner of his eye, he saw the others had done the same. The hallway was now empty, too.

It was finally over.

He started to rise to his feet when a loud shriek echoed from down the hall. Raising his hands again, he froze.

Monty and Jake rushed into the cafeteria, brooms in tow. Shoes crunching on the broken glass, they surveyed the destruction around the room. Their mouths fell open in complete disbelief.

Jake took another step and picked up the scorched fragment of a table top. "What the *hell* happened in here?"

"I don't think...I...wanna *know*," Monty stammered, arms and legs trembling. He let his broom fall to his side, smacking the floor.

One side-long glance at each other, and the two old janitors bolted from the building as fast as their legs could carry them. Monty was in the lead, with Jake still clutching his broom as he ran.

"That's it! I'm *outta* here!" Monty yelled back at him. "They can *keep* my damn pension. I quit!"

"Me, too!" Jake blurted, as he struggled to keep up.

Michael couldn't help it—he bent over double with his hands on his knees and laughed himself dizzy.

• • •

The group glided out the front of the building together, past the police and fire trucks that had arrived to investigate the blast. Officers and firefighters darted about, scratching their heads and speculating everything from gas explosion to a series of Molotov cocktails.

Michael cracked a lop-sided grin. *They have no earthly idea what happened here...which is probably a good thing.*

"Thank you," Matt said, sounding both grateful and remorseful at the same time.

He let him off the hook easily with a broad smile. "No problem, man, anytime."

All at once, Matt's expression changed from apologetic to deadly serious. "Listen, I think they're going to send others after you," he warned under his breath, evidently not wanting to frighten Sarah who stood a few paces away, chatting with Tom and Emily. "I don't know why, but for some reason, they *do* want you very badly."

"So I get the feeling," he replied heavily. A painful knot of uncertainty twisted in his gut, as he watched the firefighters clearing the debris. *We came awfully close to not getting out of there with our souls.*

Then, he straightened up and squared his shoulders. "Don't worry," he said with renewed strength and resolve, "I'll keep an eye out."

Matt reached out to shake his hand and he gripped it firmly in his own.

"I owe you everything," Matt said, glancing quickly at his sister and then back at him. "If you ever need my help, please don't hesitate to ask."

"You can count on it." After a pause, he added lightly, "Something tells me, I may need all the help I can get."

CHAPTER TWENTY-EIGHT

CHRISTMAS

AN EARLY WINTER snow had fallen in Cape May, draping all the gingerbread style houses in a white frosting. As Michael watched the crystalline snowflakes cascading down in perfectly random patterns, his thoughts drifted to his family. *It's almost Christmas. I should go home to see Mom and Chris.*

He'd avoided it long enough and he missed his family. Turning to Sarah, who was standing on the porch with him watching the snow, he started to say, "Sarah, I need to—"

"Go home," she interrupted in a lilting voice. "I understand and I can't blame you. If I wasn't so afraid of traveling on a ley line like you did, then I would go home to Ireland and see my family too."

"Do you want to draft home with me?" he asked, even though he was pretty sure he knew what her answer would be.

"Would you be mad if I said I'd rather stay here?"

"Of course not," he said, "I know it frightens you to go too far from The Angel."

"I've been here so long," she said faintly. "I feel safe here."

"It's okay, you don't have to explain," he said, kissing her softly on the forehead and then on the lips. "I love you."

"I love you, too," she said with a smile.

He dropped his mouth on hers and kissed her again, while listening to the wicked thoughts that prowled her mind.

"I'll be right back," he said, "hold that thought."

Closing his vision, he focused his mind on Fieldpoint Drive with all his might. Next thing he knew, he was standing in his front yard, looking up at his house. The car was missing from the driveway and no one appeared to be home. He frowned. No Christmas lights were hung on the house. *That's weird. Why didn't Chris put them up for Mom?*

He floated straight through the front door and stopped in his tracks. At first, he thought he was in the wrong house. *Everything sure looks wrong.*

The place was in complete disarray. The only hint of Christmas—a pathetic little tree in the corner, barely decorated and badly in need of water. It looked as if his mom hadn't cleaned or picked up anything in months—unopened mail on the coffee table, newspapers scattered on the floor, decaying food cemented to a plate on the sofa, shoes and clothes thrown all around. The grandfather clock hadn't been wound and was stuck at eight fifteen, as if someone had wanted time to simply stop.

He moved on to the kitchen and it was even worse. A sticky, brown liquid had been spilled on the floor and left to dry up. A broken glass lay on the counter next to a moldy pot of coffee. Filthy dishes and pots were strewn everywhere. *What a god-damned mess.* He certainly had never seen the house look like this while he was alive.

For a second, he quaked with fear. Maybe his mother had become ill or something while he'd been gone. Just then, his mother's car pulled into the driveway. Right away, he knew something was very wrong. His mother and Chris were still in the car, but they were arguing so loudly he could hear them from the kitchen. His mother had rarely ever yelled like that. *What the hell could they be fighting about?*

His mother came through the back door still angrily shouting. "I can't believe you've gotten suspended again!"

"That's great Mom, because I can't believe you still have a *job*!" Chris retorted, slamming his backpack on the table.

"Chris we're talking about you, not me! Why are you always fighting at school?"

"I'm not always fighting, will you just leave me alone!" he blurted out. "What's the difference anyway?"

"You know what, *you're right*," his mother shrieked, throwing her keys on the coffee table. "What *is* the difference? You're hardly in school anymore. When you're not suspended, you skip out anyway. Your grades have gone right down the toilet and you don't even care! I just don't know what I'm going to do with you." She gave him an exasperated look. "This *has* to stop. I *swear* you better shape up, or I'll—"

"You'll *what*, Mom? You'll do what...*nothing?*" Chris shot back, cutting her off. "Why don't you just *shut up* and have another drink," he bellowed, as he stormed up the stairs.

What the hell did Chris mean by that? A few moments later, when he followed his mother into the dining room, he got his answer. With an unsteady hand, she opened the liquor cabinet and took out a nearly empty bottle of whiskey. Except for holidays, he'd barely ever seen her touch alcohol.

His mother sat down at the table, poured herself a large glass and belted it back like a pro.

Incredulous, Michael took a good look at her now. She had aged so much in such a short time. With deep lines on her face and bags under her eyes, she looked like hell.

"What are you doing?" he whispered, almost unable to speak and knowing he would get no response. He'd never felt so angry with his mother before and his stomach roiled. He couldn't stand feeling like he was in the room with a stranger, so he went upstairs.

He passed through the door to Chris' bedroom. This room was as unrecognizable as everything else he had seen so far. Nothing looked the same. It was as if a different kid lived there now. His brother had taken down all his Yankees and Giants pennants. In their place, he'd hung Marilyn Manson posters, interspersed with pictures of scantily clad women in compromising positions.

Chris was rummaging in the bottom of his backpack for something. A minute later, he yanked out a small bag of pot.

Michael went stone cold stiff. He couldn't have been more shocked if his brother had pulled out a human head or a dead squirrel. "What the hell is *that?*" he shouted.

Oblivious to his question, Chris opened the closet and took down a large teddy bear that had been his favorite as a toddler. He opened the stitching on the back of the bear enough to shove the stash inside, tightened the threads again and returned the stuffed animal to the shelf.

Michael stood rooted to the spot, unable to move.

Chris passed within inches of him, as he walked across

the room to his cluttered desk. He picked up his cell phone, which was now screaming, "I bleed it out..."

"Nick, yeah man, what's up?"

"Really? Guess what. I got suspended for three days, can you believe it? Yeah. Merry fuckin' Christmas to me. Vacation's come early this year." He laughed. "I can't believe I won't have to look at McCormick's fucking face for three whole days."

"Yeah, I got some. Can you get out later?"

"Cool. How about Justin?"

"Awesome. I'll meet you at his house around 7:00."

"Yeah, no problem, I'm sure she'll be passed out by then," he said, an ironic smile creeping across his face.

"See ya later, man. Peace out."

Michael was livid. A tempest roared in his head. "Nick Rossi and Justin White! What the hell are you *thinking!* Are you out of your *mind?* They're the biggest *stoners* in town! This isn't who you *are!*" Pacing around the room, he ranted in a crazed fury. "What the *hell* do you think you're doing? Smoking pot, ditching school! You're acting like a *freakin'* loser!"

Unaware of his brother's presence, Chris had flopped on the bed and was quickly falling asleep.

"I can't believe this shit. I don't even *know* you anymore. I don't know either of you anymore," his voice dropped off out of futility. He searched around the room helplessly and his gaze fell upon two pictures taped to Chris' bedroom mirror. One was of his smiling father in a rowboat holding up a large trout. The three of them had gone on a fishing trip to Maine, one of many. The other was a picture of him surrounded by his teammates, holding up the championship trophy. So much had changed since those photos were taken. So much would never be the same.

Michael had never felt so undone, had never imagined it was possible. It was as if he was coming apart at the seams. Seeing his mother and brother like this was unbearable. He'd been through so much since the accident and this was the very last straw. Since the beginning, he'd tried to remain positive that some good might come out of his death. Now, his mind reeled with thoughts and emotions. *Is this where things are headed? Maybe I shouldn't have stayed away so long. Maybe I could've done something to help them. But what? I'm dead.* He felt so impotent, so useless.

One thing he knew for sure. He needed to talk to someone or he was going to go crazy. He wished he could tell Sarah, but he felt too ashamed, too guilty. *This is all my fault.* After a few minutes wrestling with what to do, he decided he would talk to Tom first.

Going outside to the backyard, he closed his eyes and summoned him from within his mind, willing his presence. "Tom, can you hear me?" he implored telepathically.

"Yes," his friend replied, materializing out of the night air.

Michael sat down at the patio table and Tom followed his lead.

As always, Tom showed genuine concern and spoke with calm reassurance. "What's going on?"

"Oh my God, it's so bad," Michael croaked, finding it difficult to choke back his emotions.

"What's so bad?"

"My mother and my brother, they're all messed up." He gestured at the house behind him. "I barely even recognize them. It's like they're not the same people."

"What exactly do you mean, *all messed up*?"

"What do I *mean*? Here, let me sum it all up for you," he said tersely. "The whole house is a wreck, my mother's drinking, and my brother's doing drugs!" Shaking his head back and forth in disgust, he muttered slowly, "This can't be happening. This just can't be happening. If I was alive, none of this would be happening." He paused and then shouted at the back door in frustration, "I hate them for letting this happen!"

"You don't *hate* them," Tom said reproachfully. "You don't mean that. You *know* you don't."

"Yes, *I do*. I don't *know* those two people," he shot back, motioning toward the house again. "My mother was always so strong and my brother was a good kid. What the hell happened to them?"

"I'll tell you what happened to them…grief."

"Bullshit!" he snapped. "That's no excuse. Lots of people have terrible things happen to them and they don't act like this."

"That's true, but give your mother a break. She took a one-two punch straight to the heart—first your father, and then you. Even the strongest person might have trouble recovering from that. You have to understand. Death is the toughest part of life for the human spirit to endure. Don't be so hard on her, Michael. She's not made of stone."

"Oh *yeah*, well she *used* to be," he said, hanging his head.

"No, you only thought she was. Your mother probably

had unresolved grief from your father's death and then losing you on top of that pushed her over the edge. The sudden death of a child is one of the hardest experiences for a person to go through. It simply goes against the natural order of life," Tom said. "It was easier for your mother to embrace Jack Daniels to try to numb the pain and comfort herself. I should know...I was good friends with him too, remember?"

Michael picked his head up slightly to look at Tom, but said nothing.

"And as far as your brother," Tom continued, "your mother was so mired in her own grief that she couldn't reach out to Chris to support and comfort him. Even if she had, teens grieve differently than adults. They often look for help from their friends and engage in more impulsive behaviors, like drug or alcohol use. Problem is he probably thinks the drugs can't hurt him. He thinks he's invincible, just like you and your father."

Jumping to his feet, he shouted indignantly, *"What?* I don't think I'm *invincible!"*

"*Oh*, no? *How* many times did you try to take on those demons all by yourself without my help?"

"Alright, *look*, I'm in a *bad* mood as it is. I'm not getting into this with you again," he said, trying to maintain his cool. "Stop changing the subject. This is partly *your* fault, too. You told me I had to accept my fate and part with my past life, so I stopped going home and look what happened!"

"Michael, you couldn't have done *anything* to prevent this."

He gripped his temples with both hands and huffed out a

ragged breath. "Maybe *not*, but tell me what you think I can do to help them."

"Nothing." Tom shook his head slowly. "Your mother and brother are going to make their own choices in life. There's nothing you can do as a spirit. You have to accept that. I told you before, it's best not to interfere with the affairs of the living."

"So, you want me to do *nothing?* You expect me to just stand by and watch as they both kill themselves!" he roared.

"There's no need to shout," Tom admonished him. "I know it's difficult, but if you even tried to interfere, you could wind up making things worse. Have you already forgotten what happened with Melissa?"

Ouch, that stung.

"Come on Michael, think about it," Tom said calmly. "Realistically, what could you do for them anyway?"

As much as he hated to admit it, Tom was probably right. Being dead left him with no way to help his family. Still, standing by and watching them self-destruct was going to crush him.

He sat back down on the porch step and was silent for a long time. Finally, he looked up at Tom and in a low voice declared, "I guess you were right after all. I *did* lead a sheltered life. We buried my father and to be honest with you, it's the only truly difficult thing I've ever had to deal with. I'm not cut out for this," he said, covering his face with his hands. "I'm going to *snap*."

"You're *not* going to snap," Tom reassured him. "You're stronger than you think. It's just time to man-up, that's all."

A moment later, Tom got that mysterious look on his face

again. "I'm sorry but I have to go." He placed his hand on Michael's shoulder, gave it a squeeze, and stood up. "I'll be back as soon as I can."

Michael had been planning this for a while now. He finally wanted answers about where Tom kept running off to and why. *Why all the secrecy? Is he hiding something? Why does he always keep me in the dark?*

As Tom turned to walk away and disappear like he had so many times before, Michael swiftly flew towards him, grabbing his shirt lightly from behind.

If Tom felt him drafting along, he did not let on.

CHAPTER TWENTY-NINE

D.C.

WITHIN SECONDS, THEY landed on the steps of the Lincoln Memorial in Washington, D.C. The Washington Monument stood tall in the distance beyond the reflecting pool, casting a warm glow on the surrounding trees and mall. As soon as Tom turned around and saw him, his expression was cross.

"You shouldn't have done that," Tom said, his voice as hard as nails. "If I'd wanted you to come with me, I would've *invited* you. You should *not* be here."

Sounding purposefully like a defiant teen, he shot back, "Why not?"

"Because I *said* so," Tom responded in a mock-parental tone. "You should go back." Before Michael could fashion a reply, his friend was gone, vanished into the still night air.

He stood there perplexed, balling his fists. Whirling around toward Lincoln's statue, he shouted furiously at the president's wise and stoic countenance. "Who the *hell* does he think he is? What a *jerk!* And after all we've been through, too." He let out one last yell and gestured indignantly. "I've had it up to *here* with his secrecy!"

Now, with the tirade out of his system, he floated down the steps toward the National Mall.

As he walked passed the World War II Memorial, his

mind flashed to the last time he'd been here in D.C. His Boy Scout troop had toured the Capitol building, Washington Monument, U.S. Mint, and several of the museums. He'd been disappointed though, because his scout master couldn't get tickets to visit the White House. The gates near the south lawn had been as close as he had been able to get. He was here tonight though, wasn't he? *I don't have to go back right this minute if I don't want to. Why should I? I've always wanted to see the White House. Here's my chance. I don't have to listen to him. I'll just take a quick tour before I go back to The Angel of the Sea.*

He remembered the way and took a left onto 17th St. right before the Washington Monument. Except for the occasional taxi or limousine, the streets were mostly deserted. Minutes later, he had crossed The Ellipse and was once again standing in front of the tall gates facing the south façade of the White House.

Gazing up at the magnificent, gleaming-white building before him, he couldn't help but swell with a deep sense of pride. Dead or alive, he would always be an American and always love his country.

Being a ghost allows a person unfathomable freedom. He walked right through the high black gates and casually strolled across the south lawn, invisible to every form of protection surrounding the White House. *All the guards, motion sensors, and surveillance equipment in the world are useless against a ghost.*

After pausing to admire the large white columns and the enormity of the mansion up close, he stepped across the threshold onto the ground floor unimpeded. The two guards standing on either side of the door were oblivious to his presence. He now stood in a circular room decorated like an elegant formal parlor. Off to one side, a flocked holiday tree glittered with blue and silver ornaments.

Leaving the Diplomatic Reception Room, he drifted into the room on his right. Dimly lit cases on each wall displayed collections of fancy tableware. *Must be the China Room.*

Again, he floated through the wall to his right. Similar to the China Room, this room held an extensive display of gilded silver. A plaque on the wall read, *The Vermeil Room.* He took a second to look at the portraits of recent First Ladies, but not terribly interested, he moved on.

As he glided across the hall, he came to a rather austere library. He wondered if anyone ever really read the books in here anymore, or if the ancient looking tomes would simply disintegrate if removed from the shelves. *I bet this place smells as old as it looks.*

Exiting the library, he ascended the stairs to the State Floor above, floating right past a guard stationed at the base of the staircase. He was now on the east side of the Cross Hall, one of the two colonnades that connect the East and West Wings of the White House. As he placed his ghostly feet upon the plush, crimson carpet which ran the length of the Cross Hall, he felt like a king. *No wonder the power goes to their heads.*

He turned now to his left and discovered the East Room. *Man, this room is ginormous. It's like a grand ballroom.* From the elaborately decorated ceiling, glistening glass chandeliers hung above a polished marble floor. The only pieces of furniture—a concert grand piano in the corner and another elaborately decorated Christmas tree.

As he made his way around the State floor, from the Green Room, to the Blue Room and finally to the Red Room, he was impressed by the grandeur and opulence of the rooms. Each one was magnificently appointed with fine antique furniture and artwork, sparkling chandeliers, Italian white marble mantels and decorative flower arrangements. Traditional swag and jabot draperies, made of luxurious fabrics adorned each window. With each room decorated for the holidays, this only added to their extravagance. *This place is more like a palace than a house.*

Coming out of the Red Room and back into the Cross Hall, he passed all the Presidential portraits hanging along the walls. *This place is filled with a sense of history, power and prestige. I wonder if each of the Presidents could feel it while they lived here.*

He treaded ghostly footsteps across the gleaming marble floor of the Entrance Hall, his attention now drawn to the Grand Staircase. Covered in the same vivid red carpet as the Cross Hall, the Grand Staircase, with its ornate balusters covered in festive swags of white pine garland, led the way to the second floor. Having only encountered a few stone-faced guards, he was rather enjoying his private tour of the White House.

On the second floor, he entered the famous Lincoln Bedroom; a room he'd heard about at one time or another. The Lincoln Bed, a nearly eight foot by six foot rosewood bed with an enormous headboard of intricate woodwork sat against the far wall. Fringed and tasseled drapes of velvet surrounded the bed and an ornamental crown-shaped hood of gold hung on the wall above the headboard. The valances on the windows were gilded as well. *This room's fit for royalty.*

Next, he entered the Yellow Oval Room, stopping dead in his tracks as his jaw dropped.

He was no longer alone.

Staring out of the window in deep contemplation, with his hands clasped behind his back, stood a tall slender man in a long, black evening coat and stovetop hat. Still dressed as if he were about to attend the theatre, the ghost of Abraham Lincoln now stood only a few feet away.

Without turning around, Mr. Lincoln said, "Come in, William."

Confused as hell, Michael had no idea what to say. *Who's William?*

Mr. Lincoln turned from the window and gazed at him wide-eyed for a long moment. Finally he spoke, "You are not my William." Extending his palm, he said in a deep, yet friendly voice, "Young man, my name is Abraham Lincoln. I am pleased to make your acquaintance."

He took Mr. Lincoln's strong, warm palm into his own and stared at his face in awe. "Michael Andrews. It's a pleasure to meet you too, sir...uh...I mean, Mr. President." *Oh my God, I can't believe it. I'm talking to Abraham Lincoln.*

Lincoln waved a long arm about the room in a wide arc explaining, "This used to be my private library and study. I still enjoy the view here from time to time. Tell me, have you seen my William about?"

"No, sir...I don't think I have," he answered tentatively. "Actually, I'm not sure who William is..."

"William is my third son," Lincoln informed him. "He

died at the age of eleven from a fever. I have all these years been attempting, with no degree of success, to convince young Master William to depart from this world, so great is his fear of the unknown."

The idea of a child being stuck in the afterlife was incredibly sad and his insides nearly ached from thinking about it. "I'm very sorry to hear that."

"There is no greater joy than one's children," Lincoln replied, a light-hearted smile crossing his face. "Do not let the plight of my son trouble you, young man. With patience and perseverance I shall achieve my purposes where Master William is concerned."

The man seemed so confident. Perhaps Lincoln knew the answer to the one question burning in his mind? He couldn't hold back. "Mr. Lincoln, you want your son to depart with you, but...where does a spirit *go* when they leave this world?"

The famous president arched a thick brow and looked at him questioningly. "Don't *you* know?"

Michael cast his eyes on the floor, uncertain how to answer. Doubt still festered in his soul. There was no denying it.

"Might I inquire the reason for your look of consternation?" Lincoln asked.

His thoughts must have betrayed the blackness in his mind. Slightly embarrassed, he changed the subject. "I just can't believe I'm actually here in the White House, talking with one of the greatest presidents this country has ever had."

"Thank you, young man," Lincoln said in a humble tone,

as he paced in silence near the window for a moment and then turned to him. "Were you at all aware that I almost did not live to become President?"

"No sir," he said in shock. "I didn't know that."

"It is quite true," Lincoln explained. "En route to my inauguration in Washington, I received compelling evidence of an assassination plot by Southern secessionists bent on perdition of the Union. In order to elude the perpetrators, I was disguised as an invalid and in utmost secrecy placed onto a special train bound for Philadelphia, several hours ahead of schedule."

Wow, they never tell you this stuff in the history books.

"Arriving late at night at one train station," Lincoln continued, "I was spirited in a closed cab across the city to the Wilmington & Baltimore depot where, unnoticed by spies, I was placed in the rear car of a train bound for Baltimore. At 3:30 the next morning, the rear car was uncoupled from the rest of the train and pulled by a team of horses to Camden Street Station, where it was coupled to the Baltimore & Ohio train bound for Washington. Thankfully, the true identity of the 'invalid' in the last car was never discovered and by 6:00 the following morning I had, by the will of God, arrived in Washington for my inauguration."

"That's quite a story, Mr. President."

"Yes, especially when one considers that some four years hence I would be shot to death at the theatre."

He cringed at the trite tone Lincoln used to describe his own assassination.

Seeing the look on his face, Lincoln said, "Do not be troubled, Michael. I firmly believe my death to have been in accordance with the will of God. Therefore I shall not question its necessity. Man is not equipped with the intellect to understand the managings of the Almighty."

"It just…surprises me that you're not…*angry*."

"Would it also surprise you to learn that I bear the administrator of my death, Mr. John Wilkes Booth, no ill will?"

Thinking of the truck driver responsible for his own death, Michael replied, "Yes, to be honest with you, sir… it *would* surprise me."

"Young man, I value honesty in discourse," Lincoln said with appreciation. He paced with his hands clasped behind his back. "The reason I do not harbor any resentment towards Mr. Booth is that God uses many human instrumentalities to affect His purposes. In that righteous purpose, Mr. Booth was simply chosen to be the actor."

He'd always heard what a great man Abraham Lincoln had been, but now to hear him speak in person was absolutely incredible. With great respect and admiration, he said in a low voice, "You did so much for our country, Mr. Lincoln." He sighed heavily and continued, "Even if I could forgive the man that caused my death, that's one of the things about my death that bothers me the most. I left no legacy, no mark on this world. I accomplished nothing special…nothing even remotely significant." *I never got my shot.*

"I understand how you must feel," Lincoln said with great sympathy, "to be cut down so young with work unfinished. You and I have that in common, Michael.

However, I think you will learn that it does not matter if you fulfill your destiny on one side of the veil or the other. We are all here for a purpose."

A question burned in Michael's mind. "Mr. Lincoln," he said, "Are you still here in the White House only because of your son?"

The famous president smiled wryly. "Your keen intellect presents itself, young man. That is only part of the reason." Pacing the floor once again, Lincoln said, "I have decided that while it is in my power, I shall watch over the men responsible for the preservation of the sacred Union of these United States. As long as there remain forces acting against her and working toward her destruction, I shall remain here to act as a beacon and a reminder to those whose commission it is to protect her."

"But how do you actually *do* that Mr. President?" he asked, perplexed.

Lincoln peered deep into his eyes for a long minute, as if reading his soul. "I'm probably not the one who should tell you this…but you remind me of my own son and you seem to be equally as lost." He placed a firm hand on his shoulder and said, "Michael, five types of souls walk this earth—Messengers, Navigators, Protectors, Seers, and Warriors. I am a Protector."

Michael remembered what Vassago had called Tom in the woods. *A Protector.* He would definitely have a few more questions to ask Tom next time he saw him, but for now he wanted to learn all he could from Lincoln. "I don't understand, Mr. President. What can you do to protect our country?"

"Oh, I manifest in front of someone here in the White House," Mr. Lincoln said, "and over time they have learned my appearances are meant to serve as dire warnings of trouble on the horizon."

Michael scrunched up his face trying to understand. "Isn't that against the rules?"

Lincoln held up his thumb and forefinger about a centimeter apart, and gave a sly wink. "Only in the smallest margin."

"But, sir…how do you *know* what's going to happen?"

With a clever glint in his eye, Lincoln replied, "It's my job to know."

Boy, he's as good at avoiding a real answer as Tom is. "I *understand* that," he pressed, "but who *tells* you?"

"Michael…I think you *know* the answer to that."

He was quiet for a moment while Lincoln's words sunk in. He wanted to believe, truly he did. But he still had so many questions. He barely knew where to begin. *Could I really be stuck in the afterlife because I have a job to do?* He hadn't even considered this possibility.

"But…how will I know what kind of soul I am?"

"One will come to you who can tell you, but only when you are ready," Mr. Lincoln said reaching out to clasp his hand and shake it again. "I truly hope you find your way, young man."

He didn't want their conversation to end, but obviously Mr. Lincoln had said all he was going to say. So, he reluctantly replied, "Thank you, Mr. President…and good luck helping your son."

"Ahh, Michael, I do not believe in *luck*. After all…I was

shot in box number *seven*." Smiling, he tipped his stovetop hat and slowly faded from sight.

• • •

Well, I guess it's on to the West Wing. Making his way in that direction, he mulled over everything Lincoln had told him. He had a ton of questions for Tom that was for damned sure.

The activity in the White House seemed to be picking up. Gazing out the window, Michael saw the sun already up over the Potomac and glanced at a clock. *Eight-thirty?* As usual, he was surprised to see that time had moved forward at some improbable pace. *I've been here all those hours? It certainly doesn't feel like it's been that long.*

As he neared the Oval Office, he suddenly heard an incredibly loud bang in the distance and the walls shook. Vases and chandeliers rattled all over the place. *What the hell was that?*

Seconds later, secret service men scrambled about, giving orders into headsets. His eyes went wide as basketballs, as several of them hustled the President out of his office and down a stairwell. A White House staffer came out of a nearby room, grabbed one of the secret service agents by the arm, asking in alarm, "What's going on?"

The man listened to his headset for a moment. "A bomb went off near the White House Visitors Center. We've been told to leave the White House as a precaution." A split-second later, right on cue, an announcement echoed throughout the building, repeating every few minutes. "Code

Black. Evacuate the building and move to a secure location immediately."

Michael flew outside, ducking inside the back of a capitol police cruiser as it left the White House grounds. The car drove two blocks and turned a corner.

As the police arrived on the chaotic scene, the dead and dying were everywhere. Next to the twisted remains of a motorcycle, the charred skeleton of a Metro bus lay flipped on its side. The hijacked bus had slammed into the front wall of the White House Visitors Center and ripped a gaping hole.

Passers-by were pulling out the wounded and the dead, including a young girl wearing a Girl Scout uniform. Capitol police swarmed on the scene. People rushed to cover the bodies of victims whose clothes had been burned off. One man staggered from the building, his face covered in blood.

Michael stopped short. Tom was standing right in the middle of the street with an incomprehensible expression of indifference on his face.

What's he doing here? Just then, Michael was seized by a terrible thought. *Did Tom have something to do with all this?*

Watching the horrible scene before him, the skies suddenly took on a brilliant, luminescent glow. A long, shining column of light descended, reminding him of an elevator shaft. He tried to take a step but couldn't move at all. His arms and legs wouldn't obey him. Unable to go any closer to the light, Michael stood paralyzed, eyes transfixed on the extraordinary phenomena.

Dozens of souls rose up into the air as if the light were pulling them in with a tractor beam. All of them had the most peculiar, completely blissful expression on their faces, as they rose higher and higher into the sky. They drifted straight into the kaleidoscopic splendor, becoming a part of it. Near as he could tell, this lasted for what must've been at least five minutes of earthly time.

Mesmerized by the dazzling light, even amid the sounds of sirens, shouts and screams, Michael thought he could hear a soft hum that sounded like music far off in the distance. *Am I hallucinating this whole thing?*

Of course, no one but he and Tom were at all aware of the magnificent sight unfolding before them. Like standing at a distance from a roaring campfire, the light radiated with a tranquil peace and glowing warmth. After all these months of questioning, his doubt melted away.

Slowly, the light began to ascend and fade, as no more souls rose up. Desperately, he wished the light wouldn't leave. It had been so close. So incredibly close.

Gathering the courage to speak, Michael said the only thing he could think of, "That was unbelievable."

"I know," Tom replied in a slow, almost reverent tone, as he turned to walk away. He didn't seem nearly as shocked at what they had seen.

All of a sudden, the truth hit Michael like a sharp, cold slap to the face.

"You've seen this before, *haven't* you? The day you died...you saw them all go."

In solemn confirmation, Tom repeated, "I saw them all go."

He stared at him for a moment, stunned. "Why didn't you ever *tell* me?"

Tom hesitated, glancing away and then back at his face.

317

"It's something you needed to see for yourself. And even if I'd told you, would it have changed anything?"

Michael searched his soul for the truth. Tom was right. It probably wouldn't have changed a single thing he had done so far.

• • •

As Michael walked along the beach next to Tom, he turned over in his mind all that had happened to him since his death. He still had so many questions. One answer he now knew for sure though, there was definitely a place to go after mortal life. On the other hand, one big question remained. Why couldn't he move on?

"I can't believe the light was so close and they stopped me from going. It's not fair," he said with an angry edge to his voice.

"What *do you think*?" Tom retorted sharply. "You're the *only* one who's ever had that happen? How do you think I felt as I watched a *multitude* of angels gather to escort all those poor souls on 9/11, except for me? I was prevented from going, same as you, without *any* explanation or *any* acknowledgement at all. But, let me tell you this," he said with deep conviction, "that was the most beautiful sight I'd ever seen and it filled me with hope. I knew they would come and get me when it was my time to go. I knew there must be some reason, some purpose, for my being left behind."

"Yeah, well…I wish I knew my purpose, my reason, for still being here," he said feeling very discouraged.

"Ohhh be patient Michael, in time you'll know."

"How much time…twenty years, fifty, a hundred?" he asked somewhat testily. "You seem to have all the answers, how long before I can go on?"

Tom turned fully to him now, his eyes unreadable. "Michael, let me ask you something," he said slowly. "If it means leaving Sarah, are you sure you still want to go?"

Michael was thunderstruck as the painful realization smacked his consciousness. *I don't think I can answer that.*

Tom's expression turned sympathetic. "Listen, I don't know all the answers either," he said. "That's why I'm still here. Ancaro imparo."

"Now *you're* talking in mumble-speak," Michael replied. "What the hell does ancaro imparo mean?"

Tom grinned. "In Italian it means, I'm still learning. Do you know who uttered those most humble words?"

Sensing another tidbit of adult wisdom coming his way, whether he wanted it or not, he waved his hand dismissively, "No, I don't have a clue."

"Michelangelo…after he'd already painted the Sistine Chapel, created the Pieta, the David and St. Peter's Cathedral in Rome. *Remarkable*, wouldn't you say?"

Michael shook his head. "Look, I understand it may take a while. I mean, some of these people have been stuck for so long. But, I don't feel like I'm getting *anywhere* or learning *anything*. I feel like I'm just wandering around *lost*."

In a reassuring way Tom nudged him lightly on the shoulder. "Ahhh Michael, don't you remember what Tolkien wrote? Not all who wander are lost."

Michael smirked. *Good old Tom, always quick with the*

clever comebacks. Enough playing around, it was time to wheedle some answers out of him. "So, when were you going to tell me you were a Protector?"

Tom turned to stare at him, his eyes sharp, his expression enigmatic. Finally he said, "I suppose...right about now."

AUTHOR'S NOTES

The Angel of the Sea is an award-winning bed and breakfast in Cape May, NJ. This spectacular inn has been featured on several television programs and in magazines throughout the world. Most notably, it was chosen by Oprah Winfrey as one of the "Best Vacations in the World" and included in her television talk show. The Angel of the Sea is one of the most recognized Victorian structures in the United States. Legend has it that in the late 1960's, a girl did fall to her death at the Angel of the Sea and did at one time, haunt the inn. The story of the girl has been included in several non-fiction books about ghosts in Cape May. Sarah's character in THE GHOST CHRONICLES was inspired by this legend. You can learn more about the Angel of the Sea by visiting: http://www.angelofthesea.com/

ACKNOWLEDGMENTS

So many people helped make this book possible that I'm terrified I'm going to leave someone out of these acknowledgments. So if I do end up forgetting someone, please reach out to me so I can make it up to you. First, much love and thanks go to my family: my husband, Chris, my sons, Michael and Andrew, and to my Mom, Dad, sister and brother for their unwavering support and faith in me. To my dear friend Beth-Ann Kerber, who first heard my crazy idea to write a book and didn't tell me I was crazy. To all my writing friends, but especially to Brynn Chapman, Dan Krippene, Natalie Zaman, Charlotte Bennardo, KT Hanna, Jami Nord, Veronica Blade, Katia Raina, Laurel Wanrow and Robin Haseltine for reading, critiquing and/or generally sharing your expertise. To all of my early beta-readers (whom I hope I didn't leave out it in the list above), but especially to my friends, Andy Morris, Laura Lee Morris, and Ellen Armstrong for their keen insights and fierce loyalty. To Mary Kennedy, who years ago shared her wisdom and the best piece of writing advice ever—in order to make it in this business you need to have a fire in your belly. To my fabulous cover designer, S. P. McConnell, for his incredible talent and patience. To Carol Van Den Hende, for lending her opinions and additional expertise on my cover. To all the fantastic writing organizations and groups that have brought me so much knowledge and camaraderie over the years, New Jersey Romance Writers, Romance Writers of America, YA-RWA, NJ-Society of Children's

Book Writers and Illustrators, TeenLitAuthors, WritingGIAM, and WritingYoungAdult. And last but certainly not least, to Ronald and Theresa Stanton, owners of The Angel of the Sea, for their friendship and for allowing me to use the name and image of their 'beautiful angel'.

ABOUT THE AUTHOR

Formerly an accounting manager for a Fortune 500 company, Marlo is currently an intern with a literary agency based in New York City, as well as, an editor at Chimera Editing. Marlo writes young adult, women's fiction, and short stories. She is currently working on her third novel.

When she's not writing or editing, Marlo loves reading, relaxing at the beach, watching movies, and rooting for the Penn State Nittany Lions. After having spent some wonderful time in Pittsburgh and Houston, she's now back in her home state of New Jersey where she resides with her husband and two sons. This is her first novel.

You can connect with her online at www.marloberliner.com or on Twitter @MarloBerliner.

You've finished! Before you go...

- Please visit my website http://marloberliner.com and be sure to sign up for my newsletter so you can receive advance notice of the next installment of THE GHOST CHRONICLES and other upcoming releases.
- Rate/Review this book on your favorite retailer's site and Goodreads. Reviews are like candy for authors.
- Tweet, or share on Facebook, that you finished this book.
- Read some of my other stories for free on Wattpad.

MORE BY THIS AUTHOR:

SECRETS BENEATH—coming soon!

THE GHOST CHRONICLES, Book Two—coming soon!